Game

Justine Elyot

mischief

Mischief
An imprint of HarperCollins*Publishers*
77–85 Fulham Palace Road,
Hammersmith, London W6 8JB

www.mischiefbooks.com

A Paperback Original 2013

First published in Great Britain in ebook format by
HarperCollins*Publishers* 2012

A catalogue record for this book is
available from the British Library

ISBN-13: 978 0 00 753329 9

Automatically produced by Atomik ePublisher from Easypress

Chapter One

In the forest, it's reached that point of perfect darkness. The tree branches no longer provide a visible tracery against the gathering gloom, just a sighing canopy above my head and I have to reach out to avoid stepping into a bramble bush or hitting a trunk. Much as I want to stop moving, to crawl into my bivouac and wrap myself in my blankets, I know I can't. The steady dry crunch of distant leaves tells me I am being followed.

I hear it now and then, sometimes coming from my left, sometimes my right, or my rear or ahead, never in the same place twice. I know I can't elude the stalker because my own feet, tiptoed as they are, inevitably disturb the brushwood forest floor. Tiny snaps and crackles accompany every hesitant step. North, south, east or west? It doesn't matter. He, she or it will be on my tail.

I crouch against a tree and everything goes quiet. I concentrate on training my eyes and ears to pick up every single piece of information that they can, but all they process is that mournful branch chorus and a faraway neighing from one of the many wild ponies in the forest. That, and a load of looming dark shapes that don't help me one little bit.

Once I can no longer hold my breath, I creep forwards, my sense of direction pulling me in a north-easterly direction, further into the depths. There is a sudden, sharp crack of twigs and a heat, a human male smell that cuts through the piny forest scent, and I am lost. Taken.

Of course, I put up a fight, but he is much taller and stronger than I am, spare-framed but steely. My stupid dress doesn't help either. If only I'd had time to organise my escape from the palace I'd have sourced buckskins and stout boots, but circumstances were sprung on me and I had to flee in what I stood in. Stained, torn satin slippers don't pack much of a kick.

Although there is nobody to hear us, his hand clamps straight away over my mouth.

'Easy,' he says, and his voice is incongruously soft and gentle. 'You know you can't fight me. Hold still and I won't hurt you.'

He is right. I might as well preserve my energy.

I let him pin my wrists together behind my back and nudge me, hand still covering my lower face, forwards to some unspecified location.

When I hear the sound of a zip, I have to bite my cheeks to squash down the smile. Of course, it would have been too much to expect him to construct an authentic woodsman's hut out of branches and tree roots and whatnot just for the sake of one night's entertainment, but a tent will have to substitute. At least it'll be much more comfortable. Less risk of creepy-crawlies in the nooks and crannies.

With his hands on my shoulders, he pushes me down to my knees on the pile of sleeping bags and attends to tying my wrists together above my head.

'That's a good girl, Princess, nice and quietly,' he says,

approving of my compliance. 'Now lie down and I'll get you something to drink. You must be thirsty and hungry – you didn't stop to grab any provisions, by all accounts.'

I let him manoeuvre me into a supine position, arms arched over my head. He brings a hip flask to my lips and water trickles around my mouth and, occasionally, into it. Yes, I hadn't realised it, but I am thirsty, my throat parched by panic and exertion. I probably couldn't have screamed much even if I'd been allowed to.

The air mattress shifts as he lengthens out beside me, propped on one elbow. I can make out the shape of a face looking down at me in the dark. Suddenly there is light and I squint and turn away from it for a moment, but he steers the back of my head round to face him.

There he is, my captor, pale and intent, full lips curling in pleasurable triumph.

How dare he smile at me?

'When my father hears about this,' I tell him, 'he'll have your head on a pike.'

He puts a long finger on my lips and shakes his head, tutting, still smirking.

'Princess, your father is paying me for this.'

I try to toss my head, but his finger remains at its station, sealing my mouth.

'He won't suffer the dishonour of having to tell the Dark Prince that the deal is off. Do you really think your father would just sit back and let you ruin his historic accord? He is going to have you delivered to the Dark Prince whether you like it or not – but first, I'm taking you back to the palace.'

'You're a bounty hunter?' I manage to drive the words past his gate-keeping digit.

'I prefer "personnel retrieval operative" myself,' he says.

3

'How about "mercenary scumbag"?' I try to bite his finger but, quick as a whip, he silences me with an alternative method, one that involves the hard pressure of lips against lips.

This low-down piece of peasant flotsam thinks he can kiss a princess of the blood royal! It is not to be borne.

But my struggles lead only to capitulation and heaving of the bosom, because this low-down piece of peasant flotsam kisses like no man I have ever known. His lips are skilled, his tongue firm in its probing. Against my will, against every noble instinct I possess, I yield to the pleasure it brings.

Or rather, I forget my role and slide, so easily, so sweetly, into my lover's kiss, pushing my tongue against his, tasting and scouring him, greedier than ever for him.

But this isn't the game. The game is about resistance, about dubious consent that turns, eventually, to desire.

So I try to shake him off, working against the craving in the pit of my stomach, the blossoming in my crotch.

'You're passionate,' he says. 'Feisty, yes, but what a little firecracker you'd be in my bed. I'd like to take you, but the Dark Prince ...'

'Fuck the Dark Prince and fuck you, peasant. How dare you kiss me!'

His hand smacks down on my hip and he yanks me around on to my side. 'It seemed the best way to shut you up,' he hisses into my ear. 'Besides –' he pulls back, makes sure he has my full attention '– I have licence to do more than that.'

A warning flare shoots from solar plexus to groin.

'What do you mean?'

'Lie back down, Princess. I'm going to clean you up. And don't argue – I'll gag you if you swear at me again. Consider your rank and station, for heaven's sake.'

I nearly laugh out loud at his tone of schoolmasterly disappointment. He's got so good at this lately, not that he was ever bad.

'That's exactly what I am doing,' I grumble, watching him retrieve a bottle of soapy water from a backpack and pour it into a mess tin. 'That's why I object to your … familiarity.'

'The familiarity's only going to get more … familiar,' he warns me. He's looking in the backpack again. This time he draws out an odd thing, a small round sponge attached to the end of a wooden handle. 'I'm instructed to clean you up.'

'What?' I try to lift my spine, but the best I can manage is a tilt of the neck.

He dips the sponge in the soapy water. I hope to goodness it's warm.

'Don't say you don't need it,' he says teasingly. 'You're tattered and torn to pieces and covered in bits of leaf and thorn. Here.'

My dress is low-cut and he begins by dabbing the sponge over my collarbone then along the square-necked edges of my décolletage. The water is not completely cold, but I shiver all the same as the suds slide along my skin, sinking in while the tiny bubbles burst.

'Forgive me, Princess,' he says gruffly, and then he unlaces my bodice so that the sponge can glide underneath the material, wetting my breasts, circling my nipples until they are hard, soaked little bullets dimpling the damp cloth.

'Surely I'm not dirty there,' I protest, but it's a gasp, almost a yelp, and I can see my chest rise and fall in front of me, faster and faster with each breath.

His voice is almost a whisper. 'Oh yes you are.' He sucks air through gritted teeth. A steam cloud of lust takes its form in the space between us.

He removes the sponge from my bodice and runs a palm over the peaked mounds, his face down low, his breath warming the goose-pimpled flesh.

'Mmm,' he says. 'Now spread your legs for me, Princess. I'm going to lift your skirts.'

'Oh,' I whimper, the resistance draining fast. 'Why? Why must you …?' But I spread them and raise my knees as well.

'Because the Dark Prince wants you clean there, runaway Princess. Among other things.'

He pushes up the layers of skirts until they lie heavy on my stomach. Underneath, no knickers. Apparently they were a Victorian innovation. I'm not sure what time period we're in, but it's a draughty one.

I watch with thrilled dread as my captor loads his sponge with soapy water once more then carries it, dripping on to my breasts and stomach, down to my split thighs, drenching them so that rivers of liquid run down to my open sex.

Not that it needs to be any wetter.

'Oh fuck,' I say, having lost control of my voluntary reactions at the first brush of sponge on clit.

'Nice and clean,' he croons, sweeping it between my pussy lips and over my pulsing vagina, letting soapy suds impart their mild sting to the crack of my arse. He increases the pressure when the sponge returns to my clitoris, pushing it against the swollen bead, rotating it very slowly until I arch my back and voice an inarticulate plea.

Before I can come, he removes it. I feel its loss, my entire lower body seeming to collapse in on itself in an effort to suck it back.

The tips of his fingers flutter and waft around my cunt.
Use them.

'The King suspects,' he whispers, never quite letting them

6

close enough to touch while I moan and strain towards them, 'you may have conspired with a lover. He has asked me to gain proof of your virginity.'

'Oh God.' My hips tremble.

'Lie very still, Princess. Don't move a muscle.'

One finger sheaths itself and my cunt seems to sigh with relief.

'Mmm,' he says, adding another, then another, until I am stretched and feeling the invasion. His thumb lands on my clit, lightly, tenderly, but enough to bring every nerve ending to rapt attention.

'Hmm, still intact,' he lies. 'I've done the King's bidding. Shall we prepare for the journey back to the palace?'

'Oh.' I want to cry with the pitch of my need. He is holding me on that edge, skimming it so expertly, keeping me in piteous thrall. 'No. Please.'

'No? Wilful spoilt princess is lying on her back with her legs spread and a peasant's fingers up inside her and she doesn't want him to stop? Is that right?'

'Yes. Yes.'

'She wants him to make her come?'

'God, yes.'

'Then she'd better tell him so, because humble serfs need royal permission to finger the royal cunt, don't they? Not to mention fiddling with the royal clit.'

'Jesus, Lloyd ...'

'Nuh uh.' His fingers slide halfway out and I clamp my thighs, trying to catch them. He smacks the accessible part of my bum and tuts at me. 'None of that, missy. We're finishing this in character. Come on. Do as you're told.'

'Please, peasant, make me come. Please, please, now, please.'

He presses down; the fingers reinsert themselves.

I come, thrashing and snarling, twisting into his hand.

'How about that?' He sounds so smug I'd slap him if I weren't both bound and sapped by the force of my orgasm. 'Princesses come just the same as wenches. You're just a wench underneath it all, aren't you?'

'Insolent,' I pant, but I can't finish the thought. I don't have it in me.

'That's me.' He stretches himself out at my side, watching me so hard that I have to turn my face away. 'Oh, are you shy now? Now you've begged me to finger you. Bit late for that.' He chuckles. 'What a pisser about the Dark Prince and his insistence on you being virgo intacta. I'd love to show you how a man can make you feel.' His fingers are gentle on my waist, running up and down its slopes until I can't turn my back on him any more.

My eyes meet his.

'What would the Dark Prince do if I were no longer a virgin?'

My captor doesn't understand me at first, frowning in vague bemusement.

'I mean,' I expand, 'would he still want me for his bride?'

'He would shame you before the populace and send you home.'

'Send me home. And the marriage would be dissolved?'

'Most certainly it would. And your father would vow to kill the man who had touched you first. So if you're thinking …'

'I would lie. Tell some story of a band of brigands in the forest.'

'Who would be sought. Then some innocent man would be arrested and killed. Your father wouldn't rest until he had somebody to hold accountable.'

8

'You're right.' I sigh, bite my lip. 'I shall say I forced the man to do it.'

He laughs. 'Who would believe that?'

'My father knows me. He knows I'll do anything to avoid this match. He would believe it. I would simply refuse to name my deflowerer.'

He strokes my forehead with a thumb. 'You put yourself in terrible danger, Princess, if you do this. The Dark Prince isn't a man many would cross.'

'I'd rather risk it than face the certainty of having to spend the rest of my life with that brute.' I drop my voice to a whisper. 'Do it for me. Take my maidenhead for me.'

'Gods, Princess, I ... it's not ...' He struggles.

I watch the weighing-up process through his shrewd blue eyes. I see it all – doubts, temptations, fears, rationalisations, temptations again, settling finally into outright lust.

I seize my moment. 'Take me.' I let my spine arch and my leg rub against his. 'Let my first time be with a man who knows how to pleasure.'

'Princess ...'

'Let your cock sink into my tight sweet embrace and ...' The florid language isn't coming so easily now. I want him too much. My imagination is failing, hamstrung by my need to be shagged, good and proper, with my wrists tied and my pretend hymen breached. 'Look, just fuck me, all right? Just give me what I need.'

With a growl, he almost tears off his shirt then rolls himself over me, palms flat by my ears, his milky freckled chest hovering over my straining breasts. He dips his head and takes the bodice between his teeth, wrenching it down over the small portion of my chest that remains concealed. He buries his face between my breasts, consuming and devouring, suckling the nipples and biting the soft flesh.

'I'll give you what you need all right. Get ready.'

He rears up on his knees, yanking his belt through its loops, snarling down at me. My body sings with triumph at the light in his eyes, the hard gleam that shows he has gone past the point of caring about anything but sex. I have him.

He frees his cock then takes my buttocks in his hands and yanks my thighs wide, lifting me towards him.

My tethered hands want to grab the back of his head and pull him down on top of me, but they can't. I know what's coming, but I want to have it quicker, harder, more urgently than is even possible. I manage to hook my knees around his hips, drawing the tip of that fat feast of a cock into me.

'You know this might hurt, yes?'

'I don't care. I hope it does. I want to feel it. I want something to remember you by.'

'Here it comes then.'

He crouches over me and pushes in, slowly at first, oh, too slowly. I try to remember that I am meant to be virginal, but I am so eager I just can't wait.

'Do it,' I gasp.

'Hot little bitch, what do they teach you at the palace? Oh God.' He pushes through and I rejoice in the blunt force of it. 'Oh fuck. They teach you how to use your cunt, I think. Jesus, you're tight, so wet.'

'Oh, you feel good; you're so big. You fill me right up. This is what the peasant girls get. Why can't I get it too?'

'You're getting it now.' He thrusts, deeply and steadily, in and out, dropping lascivious kisses that leave teeth marks on my neck. 'Oh yes, you're getting it. You're feeling that, aren't you?'

'Oh.' I can't say much more. 'Yes.' The air mattress rolls

and waves madly underneath me. I hammer my heels on the tight cheeks of his arse.

'Remember this, Princess.' He seats a brutal thrust, buried so deep inside me that I feel impaled. 'It'll be the fuck of your life. Your princes and courtiers won't know what a princess really needs.'

I have time for one luxurious moan before he speeds up, jackhammering like a red-headed blur, pounding me to my second orgasm.

His face in the torchlight contorts in a sort of pain. I feel the tension, then the ecstatic release beneath his skin as he pours himself into me, roaring.

His stalwart strength drains from him and he flops on top of me, groaning and shivering. I kiss the top of his head and think how lucky I am not to be that princess really. For one thing, what if she got pregnant? Imagine the king's face. Whatever kind of face he had.

No, I much prefer being a twenty-first century woman with a lover whose filthy-mindedness matches my own. I never thought I'd take to relationships, but this one actually seems to have some mileage in it.

Lloyd stirs and rustles among the sleeping bags, then unties my wrists. 'Did that work for you?' he asks with a yawn.

'You know it did.'

'I know how you love a forced seduction.'

'And you don't?'

He chuckles guiltily. 'Bang to rights.'

'In fact, I'm considering a sequel. I want to know what happens when she turns up at the Dark Prince's lair now. I'm imagining lots of pointy towers and turrets on the side of a crag. She'd turn up and the Dark Prince would subject her to a virginity test.'

'Surely he'd just go ballistic and run her through with his mighty sword?'

'Well, yeah, running through with your mighty sword is always good, but my Dark Prince isn't as dark as all that. He's miffed, of course, but he's still interested in the dowry the Princess brings, so he decides to go through with the wedding.'

'Really? You think he would?'

'He wants that alliance. But the wedding night would be pretty fierce. Quite a BDSM scene, I think. Some punishment, maybe a bit of bondage. And anal sex. He wants to take *a* virginity, even if it isn't the traditional kind.'

Lloyd exhales heavily. 'Don't turn me on again, Sophie. I seriously think you've broken my cock, what with all that shagging al fresco on the forest floor earlier.'

'Aww.' I reach down and fondle the poor little semi-tumescent soldier. 'I won't make you fuck me again,' I promise. 'Not tonight. But that scene has to be played sometime soon.'

'Oh yes. I'm not arguing about that.'

He removes my hand from his cock and puts an arm around me, drawing me against him so that we make one big bundle of satiated sleepiness.

'Soph,' he says, just before I nod off.

'Hmm?'

'Do you think we'll ever get into a rut?'

I am amused. 'Our relationship is one long rut, isn't it?'

'You know what I mean, Oscar Wilde. Do you think you'll ever get bored with this?'

'What, with a metric tonne of quality sex? I don't think so.'

'It's just … I can't help wondering why you carry on paying rent on that flat when my suite at the hotel is big enough for –'

Ah. This again.

'Lloyd. I said I'd think about it. I'm still thinking.'

'Your thought processes are seriously slow. You said that six months ago. You can't fob me off forever.'

'I won't.'

'I know you, Sophie Martin.' He turns, props himself on an elbow and puts a finger to my protesting lips. 'You will.'

He's right. But I don't understand the big deal. We see each other all the time – we work together, for heaven's sake. We couldn't be any closer. Why do we need old-fashioned symbols of commitment to prove it? I'm a person who lives for the day, and the day is sunny right now. It makes no sense to change that.

I can't be bothered to argue though, so I mentally prepare myself for the nth recitation of Why Sophie Should Move In With Lloyd.

It doesn't happen. What he says instead is exponentially more interesting.

'You won't ever make the decision, Soph, so I'm going to help you.'

I try to say 'How?' but his finger prevents the framing of the word.

'I'm going to make it a game. If you lose, you move in with me. If you win, you don't.'

He removes the finger.

'I don't understand. What sort of game? Cluedo? Chess?'

'It doesn't have a name. It's a sex game, our favourite kind.'

'Oh, good.'

'The stakes are potentially high – for me at least. I'm going to set you a series of challenges. You don't have to take them, but if you turn them down you incur a fail. You might find a scene or a person that attracts you more than

Justine Elyot

I do – that's the risk I'm taking. But if you don't, and if you incur three fails, or decide to quit, you move in with me.'

'Hang on. So – you're going to send me off to have sex with various strangers or groups of strangers?'

'Yeah, basically.'

'And if I take them all on, I keep my flat?'

'That's right.'

'But if I chicken out or get fed up with all the shagging, I have to move in with you?'

'Are you up for it? Do you dare?'

Lloyd knows my weakness for a dare, the bastard. But it takes the pressure off me. All the tedious weighing up and sifting of pluses and minuses. Not to mention the fear. The fear is what really holds me back.

'Would you be involved in these challenges?'

'Sometimes, perhaps. Sometimes I'd just want your post-match report. You know I like hearing about your adventures. It turns me on.'

I smile, thinking back to the days when I used to sit at his cocktail bar and tell him all about the threesome I'd just enjoyed, or whatever I'd been doing. I did it to wind him up, but obviously it had had a bigger effect than that.

'You're sure you'd be OK with it? You wouldn't be jealous?'

'When have I ever been jealous?'

'Good point.' Then some other words tumble out, slipping past my careful emotion-filter like undisciplined fish. 'I wouldn't ever want to hurt you.'

He strokes my brow, smiling sadly. 'That's nice to know. That's the sweetest thing you've ever said to me. In fact, it might be the *only* sweet thing you've ever said to me.'

'Fuck off. I'm not that bad.'

14

'You are, my darling. You are very, very bad. That's why I like you.'

'OK. So, these challenges?'

'I shall deliver one a week in a sealed envelope to your pigeonhole at the hotel. You will send me a reply, telling me whether it's a go or not. Then, on your day off, you make it happen. I'll design the challenges so that some kind of proof of your success gets back to me, if I'm not there to watch or take part. It could be anything from, say, performing in a strip club –'

'Been there, done that.'

'I see I shall have to use my imagination. Hmm. Anyway, it could involve fetishes, groups, unusual situations. Or it could be something very simple. I'll have to give it some thought. Actually, I might do a bit of research now. Exactly what *haven't* you done, Soph?'

I puff my cheeks out. This is a tough question. 'Most of the stuff I haven't done is stuff I would never do.'

'Right. But there are different ways of doing the things you have done. I'll have to concentrate on those, I think. Multiple partners, S&M, sex in public, picking up strangers. All your favourites. Actually, fuck, you'll pass this test with flying colours and then I'm shafted. Leave it with me. I'm going to come up with something fiendish.'

'Oh, I'm sure you will. You've yet to disappoint on that score.'

'Thank you. Another compliment – twice in one day!'

'Don't get used to it.'

'As if I would. Now, about that Dark Prince ...'

* * *

The very next evening, after work, the Princess presents herself to His Royal Highness the Prince of Petite Mort. She is belligerent and feisty, thrusting out her chest as she stands before him.

'I demand an explanation,' says the Prince, who is rather dashing in leather trousers and a sword belt, though the sword is only the plastic toy kind. The riding crop in his hand, however, is real. 'Why did you run away to the forest?'

'Because I didn't want to marry a tyrant.'

'Tyrant, eh? I'll show you tyrant.' He whacks the crop against his thigh, making a delicious whippy sound that melts the Princess's resistance, not to mention her pussy. 'Thought you could dishonour your pledge, did you? No such luck, my tempestuous beauty.'

Smirk break. He does overegg it a bit sometimes.

'You won't be smiling for much longer. I'm going to continue with the marriage.'

'Oh, but –'

'And you will bend to my will. And my whip.'

'Yikes. But there's something I must tell you. It might change your mind. I am no longer a virgin.'

'Wha– but, you, what? No longer a virgin? How?'

'The usual method, I think.'

He cracks the whip again, then grabs me by the forearm and pulls me close, capturing my chin in a firm grip.

'Who? I'll have his head on a pike.'

'I don't know his name. Some peasant of the forest.'

'He violated you?'

'No, I wanted it. I begged him to deflower me.'

'A peasant!' The Dark Prince's roar could wake the slumberers of neighbouring lands. 'You gave your maidenhead to a peasant? Willingly?'

16

'Aye. Still want me for your bride?'

He yanks me over to the table and bends me over it, holding me down with a hand on my spine.

'You'll pay for your sluttish ways, my little whore princess. And yes, you will be my bride. I'm not giving up the chance to rule your father's lands because you can't keep your legs shut. Oh no. But you will learn not to repeat your loose behaviour, unless it's in my bed.'

God, he's good at this. My juices gush and I squeeze my trembling thighs together. My blood is up and rioting through my veins. *Do it*, I silently beg him, *whip me*.

The skirt comes up, petticoats and all, and I barely have time to screw my eyes shut before the first stroke whistles down, a bar of red heat lighting up my arse.

My lusty yell is only partly one of pain. I am wild with exhilaration. The rougher he plays, the crazier I get. I wonder what it would take to break me, and if he'll ever reach that point. The idea excites me even more.

He wields the crop with an expert hand, laying a succession of hard, fast strokes until I want to jump up and hop about, but his other hand on my back holds me in place so that all I can do is take it. Stroke after stroke, burn after burn, while he rants and raves about what a whore I am and how I will submit to him and him alone.

I don't know how many he gives me, but it must be near fifty at least when he lays the crop aside and runs a hand over my scorched and welted bottom.

'What did that teach you, Princess?' he pants, sounding quite exhausted.

'It taught me who my master is,' I sigh.

'Yes. That was my intention. So, I have conquered you?'

'Oh, you have. It's so sore, ouch.'

His hand glides over the burning skin and then dips lower, to the wet ridges of my pussy, alighting on my needy clit.

'You are in heat, Princess. The whipping has given you pleasure?'

'No,' I lie. 'Only pain and humiliation.'

'Then why are you so wet here? Are you truly a slut who wants cock all the time?'

'No, no.'

'You are.' He shoves two fingers up inside me. 'And this is where you took peasant cock. How was it? Was he a good size?'

'He was long and thick and he used it well.'

He smacks my bum hard and I whimper and twist my hips.

'I have decided that I will take your virginity, Princess.'

'What? But ...'

One wetted fingertip slips between my rear cheeks until it finds the tight pucker it seeks.

'There is more than one kind of virginity.'

'Oh God. Not there. Please, not there.'

'You should have thought of that when you welcomed peasant cock into your hungry cunt, Princess. I'm not going where some serf has been. I shall have to use an alternative. It won't get me many heirs, I suppose, but we'll cross that bridge when we come. To it.'

Cold lubricant drips onto the tiny aperture. My hot arse welcomes it, but I am still nervous and focused, as I always am when Lloyd takes me this way. Somehow, it seems like a much bigger and bolder step than mere cock-in-cunt sex. There's a momentous quality to it.

But he knows I can take it, and he knows exactly how rough he can be, and that's exactly how rough he is, shoving his cock firmly into my bottom until he is wedged tight and

18

I have squealed and squirmed through the difficult moment of full penetration.

'There we are, Princess,' he whispers. 'Your arse is stuffed with a royal cock. How does it compare with what that peasant gave you?'

'I feel owned, sir, and taken.'

'That's what you should feel. That's what you are.'

He edges back and I cringe, then he thrusts himself to the hilt again.

'Take it, my princess whore bride. Take my cock in your sore whipped arse and be grateful I wasn't harder on you.'

So I take it, gratefully and meekly, offering my most private and intimate place to the man who has mastered me.

He uses it firmly while I finger my clit, loving the way my stomach bumps against the table with each forceful sheathing, glorying in the slap-slap of his pelvis against my burning bum cheeks.

A good buggering always results in the kind of orgasm that makes me wonder if I'm actually dying and this one is no different. I am torn into pieces, floating about in space, while he finishes with a grunt and a spurt of warmth deep inside me.

I reach blindly for his hand. He clasps mine and holds it tight while we recover, sighing and trembling over the table.

'That learned ya, didn't it?' he says eventually, with a self-conscious chuckle.

'It was incredible ... just gets more incredible ... every time.' My wonderment is evident.

'It does, doesn't it? Makes you think.'

'No, that's what it doesn't do. It makes me feel.'

'You still want to go ahead with this challenge? Because we could just scrub it and you could move in tomorrow.'

For a split second I consider saying yes, OK, let's do that. Why can't I say yes? I thought saying no was the thing I couldn't do.

Chapter Two

He makes me wait two weeks for the first envelope.

Two weeks of cajolery and attempted entrapment into spilling the sex beans – but Lloyd is not to be drawn. Even when I stopped wanking him, right on the teetering tip of orgasm, and told him I wanted to milk him for information before I milked him for anything else. Even when he entered the office to find me posing on top of the desk in corset, suspenders and stockings, promising great things in exchange for a clue. Even when I locked myself into a chastity device and told him that the key would only appear on receipt of certain intelligence.

None of it worked.

He finished himself off. He swept me off the desk and sent me away to dress, with a smack to my arse. He ... well, he didn't have to do anything about the last one. I got bored of it after about ten minutes.

So now, two weeks after the deal was made, I am none the wiser about my first challenge.

I am completing some induction training for a group of new kitchen staff when my PA, Kathleen, trots up to me and tells me that 'Mr Ellison says there's an important note for you in your pigeonhole'.

I dismiss her, fling a bundle of leaflets and whatnot at the newbies and almost run out of Conference Room One towards the staffroom.

In the internet age, the pigeonholes are only used now for payslips and birthday cards, but they still cover one wall with boxy wooden monotony.

A couple of chambermaids are taking a tea break. They watch me march up to my mailbox and take out an A4 manila envelope. It's quite thick. Nothing is written on the front.

I nod at the maids and subdue my urge to rip the thing open there and then, taking it instead into the privacy of the office.

The office, this quiet and sane oasis amid the hotel's perma-bustle, always calms me. After a year, it's lost all the associations I used to have with the former manager, Chase, and the stupid fixation I had with him. Now it belongs to me and Lloyd. Especially since the day we christened the desk …

Sitting at it, I visualise us on top of it, me riding Lloyd energetically while the stationery tipped over and fell on the carpet. It makes me smile.

I am still smiling when I pick up the paperknife and make an elegant slit in the envelope. I tip it upside down on the desktop, watching its contents slide out.

One sheet of Luxe Noir writing paper, one vellum business card.

Dear Sophie

Don't ever tell me I'm not good to you. I've designed this first challenge around two of your favourite pursuits. One, of course, is sex. The other is photography. I don't know what's in your dark room these days, but one day I hope you'll do your fixing and developing in our shared place of residence.

A task with you behind the camera would be too easy, though. Where would be the challenge in that? No, what I'm asking you to do is swap places and become the model.

The lady whose business card you will find in here is a highly regarded photographer who specialises in human sexuality. Her 'thing' is to capture the face at the moment of orgasm. Nice, eh? I've booked you in for a session.

Call the number on the card when you get this letter and she'll give you your appointment time, and directions to the studio.

I think you'll agree that this is a gentle, easy opening challenge for you. Nothing to scare a seasoned campaigner. Best of luck – and, of course, the evidence will reach me in the form of the completed photo set.

I look forward to viewing it.

Love
Lloyd.

I put the note down, waiting for the sinking feeling to hit the pit of my stomach before inhaling.

Lloyd knows I hate having my photo taken.

Ridiculous, isn't it? It's not as if I'm shy. I've put out and opened up for so many men. I've worn outrageous outfits. I've demonstrated sex toys at live events. I've even danced in a peep-show booth. But there's something about the camera that scares me. It captures you, holds you in a moment, forces you to see yourself the way you are seen by others. I find that scrutiny very difficult to take. It reminds me to be self-conscious, something I rarely am. I don't need the reminder.

I have enough pictures of Lloyd to fill a gallery, but the only extant photographs of myself in the last two years are a head shot on the hotel website and a picture of my arse taken on his mobile phone.

He has set me up to fail.

'Damn you, Ellison,' I murmur, picking up the business card.

She is called Sasha Margetts. She has all the right letters after her name, but underneath it I read 'Boudoir and Erotic'. Is this where wannabe porn starlets go for their portfolio shots? I wonder. Will she have me licking suggestively on a lollipop while I shake my airbrushed booty? Or will it all be dead tasteful with soft lighting and feathers covering the rude bits? Only one way to find out …

I reach for the phone at least a dozen times before finally going through with the call. I contemplate ringing Lloyd first and haranguing him for picking such an odious task, but that would only give him some kind of perverse satisfaction, so I don't. I'm not going to fail this on the nursery slopes.

'Hello, Sasha Margetts.'

'Hi, my name's Sophie Martin.'

'Oh, yes, my afternoon booking! Is it still OK? Can you make it?'

'I think so. Not sure of the exact time though – I didn't make the booking myself.'

'Oh no, that's right. It was your agent, wasn't it? Lloyd?'

I have to take a very deep breath. My *agent*? 'S'right,' I manage.

'Well, I'll be ready for you at two. Do you know where we are?'

'Your card says Carrington Mews – I think that's quite near here. Sloane Square tube station?'

'Yes, that's the closest. We'll do the solo shots first.'

'We'll … solo shots?' I struggle to make sense of this. Does she mean that there will be another model in some of the photographs?

'Yes. You don't need to bring anything, by the way. I've a full wardrobe of costumes and props and I'll do make-up here. So, two o'clock then?'

'Yeah. Great.' I put the phone down, and then I can't prevent myself calling Lloyd. 'Lloyd!'

He chuckles down the phone at me. 'You got it then?'

'What the fuck does she mean? "We'll do the solo shots first"? What does that mean? What else did you tell her to do?'

'Wait and see.'

'I think, as my *agent*, you should keep me in the loop.'

'I think, as the orchestrator of the challenge, I should make this as hard for you as I can. Ah, why did I say that? "Hard for you." I think I am. Thinking about what's going to happen –'

'Which is?'

'As I said before –'

'Oh, don't bother.' I hang up.

I look at the clock. Eleven fifteen. Am I going to do this? Yes, I am. Failure is not an option.

I think about changing for the appointment, but in the end I turn up in the chichi Chelsea courtyard in the same char-coal-grey skirt suit I wore to work. At least Sasha Margetts will see that I am not some Botoxed bimbo but a bona fide businesswoman who doesn't get messed around.

Though I suspect I might get messed *up*.

The door is answered by a smiling woman in her forties, casually but expensively dressed, giving every impression of a model-turned-photographer. In fact, I think I vaguely recognise her.

'Yes, yes,' she laughs, responding to my quizzical frown. 'Sash Derby as was. That's me.'

'Oh God. It *is* you, isn't it? I remember those perfume adverts you did.'

We climb a staircase, quoting in unison the corny line she had had to speak.

'I know, dreadful, weren't they?' she says, ushering me into a vast white studio space, lined and surrounded with clothes racks and storage units. 'I much prefer what I do now. No more pouting and trying to look mysterious. Oh, sorry. I didn't mean ...'

'It's fine. I'm not really a model. I'm a hotelier.'

'Oh? But you want to break into the scene, your agent said.' She stands over by a small sink unit and waves a kettle at me. 'Tea? Coffee? Or sometimes my models need a tot of something stronger, just to dispel the nerves.'

'He said that, did he? Oh, tea's fine. White, no sugar.'

'Isn't it true?'

'Oh, if he says it is, I'm sure it is.' I'm skirting close to a fail, I think. I have to go with the flow. She has been given a story, and it's my job to stick to it. 'The hotel's great, but I'm looking for something on the side. Where I can express myself.'

'That's terrific. That's what we need to discuss. How do we best express you, your personality and your individuality, through the medium of my camera?'

Stumped, I look for inspiration amongst the portraits on the wall. Most are innocuous enough – beautiful girls in cashmere wraps or naked but for jewellery. Until you look at their faces. Rapt, caught in another world, another state of being. Their vulnerability is shocking and arousing.

'Seems to me,' I say, trying not to let my voice tremble, 'that I won't get much choice in that. One's face does what it does at that crucial moment.'

'Yes, you can't fake it.' Sash appears at my shoulder, inspecting her work along with me. 'It's a moment when you are nothing but yourself. The masks peeled off, the face metaphorically bare.'

'That's a strangely frightening thought.'

She puts her hand on my shoulder. I'm not tactile, outside the bedroom, and I flinch a little.

'You're not the first person to think so. Come on. Sit down and we'll talk about your needs.'

I take my tea and perch on her white leather sofa. 'Didn't Lloyd give you any idea of what was wanted?'

She laughs. 'Oh yes, he did. But I'm starting with you. You're the girl in the picture. What are you getting out of this?'

A win. I'm getting to win.

'I'm getting to represent myself as what I am.'

'Which is?'

'An insatiable whore.'

She is taken aback. For a moment, all she can do is stare at me.

'Sorry not to put it more delicately,' I say. 'I suppose people

27

generally say that they want to express their flowering sexuality or their empowering femininity or whatever. But I don't
dress it up. I'm not a flowery feminine sexually empowered
blah-de-blah. I'm an insatiable whore. That's what you'll see.
That's what you'll get.'

Sash sips at her tea.

'Oh,' she says. 'You sound a little bit angry. Are you sure
you want to do this?'

'I'm only angry because people don't like insatiable whores.
Well, they do really, but they won't admit it, so we get bad
press. It's not fair, is it?'

'I suppose not. So, when we pick props you want something fairly full-on? Aggressively sexual, almost?'

'Yeah.' I think of Lloyd looking at the photos, knowing
that I hate standing behind a camera. I want him to know
how I feel about it. 'Aggressively sexual. That hits my spot.'

'That's a powerful concept. We could build some strong
images around it. You're a woman in charge of your sexuality,
using it freely, without guilt. Actually, I can really work with
that.' Sasha's face lights up. 'This could be a wonderful set.
Come and pick some props.'

Sasha has every type of luxe fabric and body decoration
imaginable. I run my fingers through marabou and faux fur
and lace and ropes of pearls. In another box, she has her
kinky stuff. It looks tempting, but I'm not going to be tied
up or trussed for this shoot. I'm going to be free.

'I don't want props,' I decide. 'Maybe just that chair. Just
me, in the buff, on a chair. Keep it simple, yeah?'

'I think simplicity will be the key to this set. It's all about
you and your attitude. Are you ready? Do you want to take
off your clothes now?'

I distract her while I strip off my business suit by talking about the make and model of her camera. I want her to know that I know my stuff. I want her to know what she is dealing with.

By the time I'm down to my black bra and knickers, we have covered image processors and the respective merits of manual and automatic focus adjustment.

'Do you want some underwear shots first?' she asks politely.

'Nah.' I look her in the eye as I unhook my bra then ease down my panties. I maintain a smile that I hope isn't too forced. 'Let's start as we mean to go on.'

I fling up my arms to reveal everything, my breasts rising to optimum presentability as my hands stretch high.

'OK, OK, keep this pose, legs wide, arms up, looking straight at me. Lovely, perfect, that's great, Sophie.'

Light flashes, pow pow pow, while I face down the lens, my expression almost a scowl. Not a come hither, but a come and get it if you dare.

I move to the chair and sit, legs akimbo, imagining the photographs and how Lloyd will feel when he sees them. I glare, thrust out my chest, kick out my legs, cup my breasts, snarl, muss my hair, bend my knees and, finally, when Sash has melted away and become her camera, I put my hand flat on my crotch, between my pussy lips and throw back my head.

'Are you ready for this, Sophie?' Sash's voice is gentle and breathy. I wonder briefly if this turns her on. Is this her perversion?

'Ready to wank for the camera? Bring it on.'

She exhales, almost whistling, and lines herself up behind the viewfinder, hand on the button. Not the same button I have my hand on.

'Tell me what gets you off, Sophie. What do you think about when you touch yourself?'

'I think about how much I need it. How much I want a cock. How much I want to be bent over with something thick and hard pushing into me, pinning me down.'

'Lovely. Go on.' Pow pow pow. I draw languid circles around my clit.

'I think of all the men I've had. Men and women. All the tongues that have licked me, all the arms that have held me down, all the come I've swallowed, all the cocks I've had in my cunt and my arse, so many, loads of them, loads of loads, all shot in me.'

Pow pow pow. I breathe more deeply, dig more deeply, rubbing faster.

'Are you really insatiable?'

'God, yeah, ask anyone at the hotel. Ask Lloyd. He can do me four, five times a day but I'll still try for more. Before we got together I used to pick up strangers, just because I wanted to. They used to offer me money, think I must be a prostitute. When they found out I was just a slut, they thought all their Christmases had come at once. They came back, and they brought their friends, and my life was one long, hot gang-bang, cock after cock after cock ...'

'But now Lloyd's fucking you?'

'Yeah, but he likes to watch too. He gets off on me being this horny bitch who needs it all the time. That's why I'm here ... I think ... I can't remember ...'

'Stop thinking. Just work yourself, get yourself there.'

'He wants the world to know it. He wants everyone to know I'm a sex-mad whore with a cunt that's open all hours. Everyone will see this, everyone will look at my face and see it ... oh.'

That's it. It's done. I have been staring at the camera lens all the while, but now, after one stunned stretch of my eyes I have to screw them shut, have to hide from that implacable gaze while the impulses sweep and swoop through my nervous system and gush out through my clit.

'Oh Sophie,' whispers Sash, clicking her last and rushing over to take my hands and stroke them. 'That was perfect. That was astonishing. Are you all right?'

'Uh-huh. Gimme a minute.'

The doorbell rings.

'Ah, that'll be him.'

I stop lolling and sit bolt upright, thighs clamped shut, arms crossed over breasts. *Him?*

The solo shots are done, but there is more to come.

Sash slips away down the stairs. I hear her unbolt and open the door, but the voices are too faint to pick up. As the sound of feet hits the steps again, I grab a fur throw out of the prop box and wrap myself in it before the company arrives.

'Oh, don't cover up on my account.'

'Lloyd!'

I give him my fiercest glare, but he is unruffled, threading his way past the tripod and camera towards me.

'Who's looking after the hotel?'

'Kathleen's fine for a couple of hours. There's nothing exciting going on.'

'Famous last words.'

He touches the side of my face, just above my temple, but I draw away, angry with him about all kinds of things, only some of which I can identify.

'Chill,' he says. 'Smile. You're on candid camera.'

'A bit too bloody candid,' I grumble.

'I thought you'd be in your element.'

'Do you want to see what we've got so far?' invites Sophie, and he goes to join her as she fast-forwards through a few digital stills.

'Come and see, Sophie,' he says, but I don't want to look at them. 'Suit yourself,' he mutters.

I watch him from the corner of my eye. His lips are curled up at one side, as if something amuses him, but his eyes are intensely focused, almost anxious. 'I remember when you used to look at me like that,' he says.

'I *was* looking at you.'

'Back when I worked in the cocktail bar. You always had this look. Kind of "I want you, but I hate that I want you, so I'll pretend to myself that I don't." Remember?'

'No. Because I didn't want you. Not back then.'

'Yes, you did.'

His flat assertion needles me, and makes me question myself. Is he right? Did I want him without knowing it? What were the implications of that? Were my thoughts not to be trusted?

Sash switches off the viewer and claps her hands, dispelling the tension. 'So. Lloyd. You had some ideas for this section of the shoot, I believe.'

'Yeah. Soph, come over here.'

He sounds conciliatory, a little exasperated. He sits on the sofa and pats the space beside him. I wonder if he wants me to fail or succeed. Which would be the better outcome for him?

I sit next to him, but not on the side he indicates. Instead, his discarded jacket lies between us, a no-man's-land of light-grey pure wool.

'What are you going to make me do?'

'Oh goodness, I only photograph consenting subjects!' exclaims Sasha. 'There's no forcing involved.'

Lloyd turns so his face isn't visible to her and mouths the word 'Fail' with a raise of his eyebrows. I have to save this if I want to pass the test.

'It's OK,' I say. 'Lloyd and I ... we have this sparring kind of relationship. It's just our idea of fun.'

'I see,' says Sash, but I doubt she really does.

'We like to push each other's boundaries,' he adds. 'Challenge each other. That's what this is all about, really.'

'A challenge?'

'Exploring limits,' he says. 'Isn't it, Soph?'

'Something like that.'

'So, I told Sasha we could do some action shots.'

'By action you mean ...?'

'Sex.'

'Porn?'

'No!' trills Sasha. 'I don't do *porn*. I do *erotic and boudoir*. These will be sensual, non-explicit shots of your faces and upper bodies during the act of love.'

I nearly vomit. *The act of love.* With his customary presence of mind, Lloyd speaks hastily over my incipient snort.

'Of course, we understand that. Sophie's being cheeky.' He gives my wrist a little tap. 'Bad Sophie.'

The bastard has me hot again. Fuck him. How dare he?

I move a little closer to him, rumpling the jacket. He reaches an arm behind me, pressing a fingertip to the nape of my neck, a small but devastating connection. I start to believe that I can do this. My breathing deepens.

'So, I can fold out the couch for you to use,' suggests Sash. 'Or I can put cushions on the floor, or in the cupboard I have a sex chair, even a swing ...'

'A swing! Ooh, exciting! Can I see?'

'I was going to say I don't really recommend the swing. I have to be seriously on top of my game to get good shots from it. It's just so … swingy.'

'Well, the sex chair then? Lloyd?'

'Yeah, sex chair sounds interesting.'

'OK, I'll get it out. Can I get you two a drink while I set it up?'

'No,' says Lloyd. 'We'll just get warmed up.'

And, without warning, he tilts my head and swoops down to claim my lips. God knows what happens to his jacket, but we crush it between us, too caught up in arms and legs to care about its pristine creaselessness.

'So,' he questions me, between thrusts of tongue, 'did you come just now? For the camera?'

'Shut up. You know I did.'

'I wondered if you would.' Tongue goes back in, tongue draws back out. 'But you're so flushed. I love it when you're flushed.' More kissing. 'I can't wait to see the pictures.'

'Who says I'll show them to you?'

'Oh, they'll come to me first. I'm paying for them.' His leg wedges itself over mine, trapping me underneath it.

'I hate to think how much they'll cost.'

'Hmm, well, yeah, so do I.' He kisses me again, the longest, dirtiest snog so far. 'But I'm thinking of it as an investment.'

'Oh my!' Sash interrupts us from the centre of the floor. 'Please come and do that for my camera. You have such chemistry.'

I cast a bleary look over to the chair she has assembled. It's not what I imagined. For some reason I thought it would be a dungeon fixture with cuffs and stuff – in fact, it is a simple padded S-shape in expensive-looking zebra print leather. It's almost more a bed than a chair, good and wide and full of possibilities.

'So this is a sex chair?' Lloyd rises to his feet, freeing me from my limb bondage.

'There are various designs,' says Sash.

'I know. I haven't seen this type before though. It looks so comfortable.'

She laughs, patting the padded upholstery. 'It is. Come and see for yourself.'

She flits back to her camera, preparing for the highlight of the set. 'So then, Lloyd. Time for your striptease. Now, you're a male model, you need to bust out the moves.'

He mock-snarls at me and does that whip-cracking belt buckle thing that makes my knees weak. It lands on the floor in a curl of shiny leather, reminding me of all the times I've been struck with it.

Once the socks and tie are disposed of, he deals with the trousers, stepping out of them elegantly, then removing his pants so that he stands in only his long white work shirt, open at the collar, linked at the cuffs.

The inevitable fiddling with cuff links leads to the moment of revelation – the slow unbuttoning of the shirt, opening up on to a pale freckled chest, a stomach flatter than it used to be (must be all the sex) and then finally powerful thighs framing a cock in full-blooded erection.

It astonishes me that I used be indifferent to Lloyd. As he shrugs the shirt over his shoulders, I want nothing more than to pull him on top of me and shag him into the fifth dimension. It's not about his looks. It's about the looks he gives me. Nothing sends an arrow of devastating lust straight to my sex as fast as one crinkle of a Lloyd eye, one curl of a Lloyd lip.

The familiar alarms ring and buzz in my body. A man stands before me and he means to have me and there ain't nothin' I can do about it.

He waves a hand at the chair. 'Shall we?'

I bend over it. 'How do we do this? What's the best way?'

He sits himself in the shallow bend of the S and clasps his hands together behind his head, letting his legs rise up and then drop down over the seductive leather curves.

'This feels good to me,' he says. 'Hop on.'

His lazy, entitled posturing inflames me, as he knows it will. I leap on and straddle him, giving the side of his head a playful slap.

'So very fucking romantic, aren't you?' I chide. '*Hop on.* Charming.'

'Sorry, should I have invited you to step aboard the lurve ride?'

I kick my legs, which dangle either side of the chair, causing me to jolt and rock a little on his pelvis. He yelps and grabs my hips, stilling me.

'Play nicely now. Best behaviour for the lady.'

The tips of our noses touch. I pretend to bite him, snapping my teeth together. He forces a kiss, which I pretend to struggle against, enjoying as ever the combative nature of our relationship.

I emerge from the kiss panting and grinding my hips, violent joy coursing through my blood.

'Are you going to behave yourself?' he whispers. 'Hmm?' He gives my bottom a light smack.

'Never,' I reply.

His smile is broad and white. 'Say cheese.'

'I'll give you cheese.'

'Thanks. Got any crackers?'

'You're bloody crackers.'

He catches me again, lips on lips, his hand cupping my bottom, pulling me towards him. His cock butts my thigh. I reach down for it, curling fingers around its fat width. Soon it will be inside me. Do I have to wait long? I move it so that its tip sits between my labia, up and down, gathering juice, round and round my engorging clit.

He grabs my wrist and lifts my hand off his cock. 'Not so fast,' he whispers. 'Let's take our time. Let's build up slowly.'

'But you're already ...'

'I know. I don't care. Nice and slow. No rush.' He buries his face in my neck and kisses hard. I hold on to the back of his head, run a hand down his shoulder blades, feeling the muscles flex and move under the skin. His hands toy with my breasts, circling my nipples with practised fingers. His hard cock eases up and down my thigh. I try to crouch on to it, but he holds me above it, keeping me in a state of suspended readiness.

Flashes of light behind my eyes remind me that there is photography going on, but I am away from that world now, deep inside my other self.

'You're gorgeous, Sophie, you're so fucking gorgeous. You make me want you all the time. Oh God.'

He takes a long time licking one nipple then the other. I gyrate my pelvis, my mouth wide open, eyes glazed, loving the feel of his arms propping me up. One of his hands strays down my side, over the bump of my hip, then it flashes across a thigh and finds the target.

He releases my nipple from his mouth.

'You're wet,' he says.

'You're Captain fucking Obvious,' I hiss into his ear.

'Any more of your lip and I won't fuck you. How about that?'

'Don't you dare.'

'I know you wouldn't like that. Because you really are so …
very … wet.' He dabbles his fingers in the juices then pushes
them into my mouth, making me taste myself. 'There's a lot
more where that came from. Why are you so wet, Sophie?'

He removes his fingers, allowing me to speak.

'Want it,' I say, jerking my pelvis forwards, bending his
cock to my will.

'Want what?'

'Your cock.'

'Where?'

'In here.' I catch him in my slit. If only it could snap
shut like a Venus flytrap, keep him there to devour at my
leisure. I rock back and forth, rubbing his tip, preparing to
push down on it.

'How much do you want it?'

'So much, so much.'

'What would you do for it?'

'Anything.'

'I'll get that in writing.'

'Just put it in, for fuck's sake. Just fuck me. Now.'

He kisses me, chuckling into my mouth, dark and low. 'If
you insist. Act of Love commencing in three … two … one …'

He cups the undermost innermost part of my buttocks
and pulls them wide, opening me up to him, then slides
in slowly. I try to pack him all in at once, greedy for his
stretching, spreading girth, but he holds me in check,
making sure I feel each maddening inch as it glides past
my barriers.

The sex chair's great advantage is the way it aligns Lloyd's
pelvic bone with my clitoris. All I have to do is circle my hips
with minimal effort and I can have all the multiple orgasms

I want. I narrow my eyes and grin at Lloyd, who seems to have clocked on to my evil plan.

'Oh no you don't,' he murmurs, lifting my hips and urging me forwards, making me thrust. Better still, the two sensations combine, working my pussy into a fomentation of colliding pleasures.

'Ohh,' I sigh, almost overwhelmed. 'This is good. Really good. Let's get one.'

Lloyd has gone to a realm beyond speech, at last, and I work on the perfect rhythm, ending each forward thrust with a little circular rub of my clit against him, building myself up so sweetly.

Even better, I realise that a very slight adjustment of my feet so that they rise a little from the floor nudges Lloyd's cock right up to my G-spot. I anchor myself to his shoulders and push, push, push, three fast strokes bringing me to an orgasm that starts in my toes and engulfs my whole body like wildfire.

'Oh yes.' He finds his voice to mutter into my hair. 'That's what you need, darling, lots of that, more of that, yeah.'

While I am still bathing in the radiant waves of my climax, he flips me over and takes control of the coupling, powering into me while my eyes try to focus on his face above, blinking and rolling back, never quite coming back down until he reaches his own fierce conclusion. I have to keep my eyes open because his face when he comes is something I can never get enough of. If I could get a picture of it ... oh.

The camera flashes. He shakes his head, still in that heart-warming welter of post-orgasmic confusion, and stares at me. He looks so helpless, so stunned. *What just happened?* his eyes seem to ask. *Where am I?*

I reach up to cradle him, bringing his head down to my

chest. I shut my eyes and hold him, stroking his slick damp hair, feeling my heart bump into his cheek.

A line from a song by Marc Almond slips into my head. *Tenderness is a weakness ...* Is it?

I'm so comfortable, so at peace here on this strange piece of furniture that I could almost fall asleep.

But small scuffling movements from the corner remind me that we are not alone, and presumably this strikes Lloyd at the same time. He lifts his head, kisses me and looks over at Sasha. I look too, but she is obscured by the camera, discreetly 'not here'.

He looks back down at me. 'Amazing,' he says.

'As ever,' I say.

'Thanks.'

'I think I had a hand in it too!'

'More than a hand.' He smiles and looks back at Sasha. 'So was that OK?'

'Oh, don't ask me,' she says with a self-conscious giggle. 'I think that's between the two of you. But the camera loved it.'

'That's great,' he says.

'Do you want to go through to the shower? I'll put the kettle on.' She scuttles off to the sink, turning her back on us.

Lloyd rears up and pulls out of me. He runs a hand through his hair, shutting his eyes for a moment, re-orientating. 'Shower, then.' He picks up his clothes, frowns at the terrible state of his jacket and gives me an encouraging nod. 'Oh dear,' he says, clicking his tongue. 'Can't you stand? Poor afflicted thing.'

'Shut up. Of course I can stand.' I swing my legs over the side and give a fair impression of Bambi's first few upright seconds. Lloyd swoops forwards and helps me. 'So gallant, proper Sir Walter Raleigh, aren't you?'

From the kitchen corner, Sasha snorts. 'Are you two always like this?' she asks, without turning around.

I pick up my neatly folded clothes and hug them to my chest. 'Always.'

In the shower, Lloyd directs the water over my breasts and my sticky thighs.

'You didn't fail then,' he says, sounding disappointed.

'Did you think I would?'

'I need to up my game.'

The jets spray on to my breasts, tingling my nipples. Lloyd cups the underside of my breasts, holding them in place while he keeps the shower head no more than an inch above them.

'What's next?' I ask, flexing my toes, splashing them in the lovely warm water. 'Sex while parachuting from a plane? In a canoe going over a waterfall? In space?'

He puts the shower head back in its cradle, takes the bottle of gel cleanser, squirts it into his hand, lathers it up around my breasts and stomach and shoulders.

'Yeah,' he says, with an enigmatic look. 'You keep thinking along those lines, Soph.'

'What do you mean?'

He smothers me with bubbling foam and pulls me against him so our chests slip and slide together. Water rains into our mouths while we kiss, leaking into the cracks of lips, dripping off our noses, clogging up our eyelashes.

He turns me around and washes my back and bottom, very thoroughly, far more thoroughly than is quite necessary.

'I mean what I mean,' he says, letting the suds slip down the crack of my arse, parting the cheeks, massaging the slightly stinging soap inside.

'As Confucius would say. What's that supposed to mean?'

'It's supposed to mean what it's supposed to mean.'

I try to slap him, but it isn't easy when you're facing the wrong way and he has his hands on your bum. I manage an awkward collision of elbow (mine) and hip (his) and reap my inevitable reward.

'Ouch!' I always forget that a smack on a wet bottom is worth about three on a dry one.

'Impatient,' he reproves, keeping me close and tight with an arm around my ribs. Something semi-hard pushes into my right buttock, distracting me from the newly laid sting. 'All will be revealed in time.'

I lean my head back on his shoulder, looking up while he looks down.

'You know, I really hate you, Lloyd.'

He nuzzles his nose against my cheek and kisses the space beneath my ear.

'Mmm, I know you do. That's why you're always so wet for me.'

'That's because I'm in the shower.'

'Not all the other times. All the dozens of scores of hundreds of other times. All those times you've begged me, on your wide-open knees …'

'That's because I'm trying to kill you with sex. I'll do it one day.'

'Mmm, best assassination technique ever.'

His hands are low now, fingers moving down with the trickles of water, flowing and meeting at the delta of my sex. He holds me by my cunt and bites down into the softness of my neck.

I give in to it. My body knows no other way. I spread my feet further apart, granting him full access to my lips and clit and vagina, all so recently used by him.

The water provides an extra element of friction when he

starts the slow up-down rubbing of my clit with the side of his hand. It almost feels rough, refractory, needing extra force, which he gives.

Because I am facing away from him, I can see the way his arm crosses my body, watch the sinews move beneath the skin, slide my gaze down to his wrist, see the point where the fingers bend and disappear beneath me. Watching the intricate interplay of those muscles, knowing but not seeing what they are working on, is powerfully aphrodisiac. I can see what he is doing, and I can feel what he is doing at the same time.

But then he changes tack, puts his hands on my thighs and slides down behind me until he is on his knees. A tongue joins the lapping water at my pussy, a strong push brings it between my lips. I pivot at the hips and press my palms flat against the wall, holding myself up, keeping myself in position for more of this oral delight.

It's as if he drinks the warm water away, lapping it up, replacing it with his own luscious licking, cleaning me to make me dirty.

I drip into his mouth, rotating my hips, beginning to moan. He holds me fast, flicks that tongue faster, flicking the engorged bead of my clit over and over. My palms begin to slide. I fear I might fall, but he claps his hands on my hips, keeping me upright.

In the cage frame of his arms, my body slumps. My core burns and blooms, ribbons of sensation unfurling inside me, gushing out to join the combined waters of his tongue and the hot water pipe. I become a fountain.

My splashing self slips down to the tiled shower basin. I want to lie there while the droplets cover and bathe me. But Lloyd has other ideas.

Still on his knees, he clears his throat and looks forlornly down at his erection.

His hair plastered to his scalp, his eyelashes brimming with water-sparkles, his face clean and shining, he looks too completely fucking adorable. I can't resist him. I haul myself to my knees facing him and take his testicles in my hands, testing them for firmness and fullness. Lloyd has seemingly endless supplies of testosterone, as his cock testifies.

I suck him gently at first, then with increasing urgency, pinching the base of his shaft, squeezing his balls, getting my lips down lower and lower until he is deep in my throat. My cheeks are wet when his thick load of cream shoots into my mouth, but the shower isn't the only reason for that. There's a saline element to the damp patches, a stickiness.

When I lie back in his arms, letting the water engulf us both, I hope he hasn't noticed, but the way he traces a finger beneath the lower lid of both my eyes suggests he has.

Chapter Three

'Someday my prints will come,' I sing, checking through the mail while Lloyd pores over a spreadsheet at the desk. 'But not today.'

He glances over. 'No sign of the photos? She said it would be a couple of weeks.'

'It's been a couple of weeks.'

'Yeah, fourteen days exactly. Cut her some slack. She probably wants to hang on to them a bit longer for her own personal use.'

'Ugh, shut up. I don't want them used as masturbation aids. Unless it's by me.' I open a big A4 envelope. 'Cool, *Fashion Forward* wants to do a shoot in the restaurant and a couple of the penthouse suites. They've sent a contract.'

'Uh-huh. What's that one?'

He points to a less glamorous envelope, a thin brown one tossed aside to be dealt with once the post with posh watermarks has been opened.

'Dunno, looks like ... it isn't stamped.' I look sharply up at Lloyd. His face answers my question, a little bit tense, a little bit excited.

He feigns absorption in his spreadsheet, but I can tell he's

45

watching me from the corner of his eye. I slide a fingernail under the loosely gummed flap, watching him back.

A compliment slip flutters out, one of the hotel's own. On it, in Lloyd's handwriting:

Whip me, hurt me, any way you want me
As long as you want me, it's all right.

I hold it out to him. 'What's the meaning of this?'

'I booked one of the dungeons at Fetish Fantasy.'

'We've done that before. More than once.'

'Not this way. As the note implies, I don't want to be in charge this time.'

'You never are in charge.'

'I don't want to play at being in charge this time,' he amends. 'I want you to get your kinky boots on and practise flexing that whip hand.' He leans forwards in his chair, his pupils skittering from side to side, his lips wet. 'I want you to hurt me.'

He sounds like he means it. But …

'When have you ever been interested in pain?'

'I'm not. I'm dreading it, actually. I'm hoping you'll be more into the mental domination stuff.'

'I'm not really into *any* domination stuff,' I point out. 'I've only ever been on the receiving end.'

'Well, that's what makes it a challenge, isn't it? It's new, it's exciting, you get to wear loads of fucking sexy gear … you don't look convinced.'

I blink at him, trying to imagine what his face looks in pain. I don't want to imagine it, though. I really don't.

'Come on, Soph. You'd have killed for the chance to do me some serious damage not so long ago. Now's your chance to let it all out. Show me the red-in-tooth-and-claw Sophie, the take-no-prisoners Sophie, the woman who's always one hundred per cent in control.'

'That's why I like submission,' I grumble. 'It's a holiday from all that.'

'Well, have a busman's holiday then. Or am I sensing the delicate aroma of ...' He sniffs the air. 'Failure.'

'Fuck off. It'll be easy enough. Just ... I don't know. Nothing. It's fine. Let's do it.'

Lloyd claps his hands with apparent delight. 'Can't *wait* for you to walk all over me in your spike-heeled thigh-high boots,' he claims.

'I'm not sure I believe you. But neither can I.'

'Great. I've booked it for midnight. They suggest you get there half an hour beforehand to pick out your costume and select your instruments of torture and terror. I'll see you there.'

He launches himself out of the chair, kisses me passionately until I almost fall over, then waltzes off to take his lunch break.

I sit myself down in the chair he has vacated and stare at the computer screen, a sea of meaningless figures in rectangular boxes.

It strikes me now as more than a little odd that I've never done anything like this before. Call myself a hussy ... Yet somehow I've always managed to signal my desire to submit rather than dominate before the action has reached its crisis. Nobody has ever asked me to hurt them, though one man once wanted me to tie him up and tease him. That was easy enough, though, just a bit of fun.

This seems much more serious.

* * *

By eleven thirty I am in the giant fancy-dress wardrobe at Fetish Fantasy, being shown around by its proud mistress, Zuleika.

I have in mind something skintight and shiny, and she obliges by finding the perfect figure-hugging number in wet-look latex. Once she has talcum-powdered and trussed me into it, I peer at myself in the mirrored wall, searching for bulges of unforgiving flesh, but the rubber nips it all in, giving me a catwoman silhouette I think I might wear more often.

When I turn around and look over my shoulder at the generous swell of my bottom, I almost purr with satisfaction. Lloyd is going to *love* that.

But he's going to have to be content with looking at it.

Tonight, he gets nowhere near my arse.

'So, I think we were thinking of killer heels,' I tell Zuleika, but she is well ahead of me. Already she has picked out the ideal pair, and she sets to work lacing me into them, threading through the hooks and eyes until I am crisscrossed to the thigh and towering on five inches of potential murder weapon. The world looks different from up here.

Zuleika grins, her eyebrows disappearing into her bright pink fringe. 'It's a new view, isn't it?' she says. 'You look down on people.'

I've never been remotely statuesque, but my inner goddess peeks out now from her clamshell-tight hiding place. I can almost see her in the mirror. What else do I need to coax her further?

'How do you want your hair? Some dommes like it in a really tight high plait or ponytail. Or you can have it loose.'

My hair isn't really long enough to flow gloriously and luxuriantly and all that jazz, but I'm not sure the high hairline look suits me either.

'Can I just do some kind of hairband?'

A black sparkly number pushes any errant wisps out of my face. I paint my eyes black and my lips red and grin at myself.

'I have this urge to call everyone "darling" now,' I tell Zuleika. 'In a stagey drawl. Oh, daaaaaaarling, do as you're told, sweetie, or I might have to hurt your lovely little … well, you get the picture.'

Zuleika narrows her eyes and smiles. 'You're missing the critical accessory,' she says. 'What's it to be, Miss Whiplash? Flogger? Riding crop?'

'Both.'

In the dungeon, I take a good look around, mentally listing the things I might want to use. I need to prepare for this scene, since it's so foreign to me, and making a rigid plan comforts me and gives me confidence. I like the cuffs that hang from a hook in a ceiling – tick. I like the blindfold, but then he won't get to see me as a glorious vision in latex, so no tick for that. And a strap-on … hmmm. Now, that could make an interesting finale …

There is a knock at the dungeon door, an echoing clang that makes my heart thump.

I arrange myself so that one foot is on a chair, leg bent at the knee. I hold the riding crop diagonally across my chest, tapping its leather tip over my shoulder. I thrust out my breasts and hold my chin up.

'Enter.'

He pushes the door open slowly. I tense my cheek muscles so as not to smile when I see the look in his eyes. Is that awe? I think it might be.

'Christ, Sophie –'

'You're late.' I let the crop slice the air, loving its brutally efficient sound. 'And you may call me "ma'am".'

'I'm not late,' laughs Lloyd, checking his wristwatch. 'It's the witching hour, on the dot. Ma'am.'

'I don't care to be contradicted, boy, and neither do I like your tone.'

I point the crop at him, removing my foot from the chair and swaying as elegantly as I can on the vertiginous heels towards my quarry. I stop when the crop makes contact with his chest.

There is still some residual amusement in his expression, but it's quickly being replaced by a kind of fascinated dread.

I move the crop up and tap the underside of his chin, once, twice, thrice. 'You are going to learn to do as you're told tonight, boy,' I tell him. 'And you can start by getting out of those ridiculous clothes.'

They aren't really ridiculous – jeans and a dark top, suede lace-ups, dull socks – but I'm trying out the taste of belittling language on my tongue, testing it for bitterness. Besides, Lloyd deserves to suffer, doesn't he? For being such a bastard shaggable gorgeous twatface.

He hesitates, waiting for me to retract the crop, I suppose.

'Go on!' My voice rings out, twenty times more confident than I feel. 'Strip.'

I step back and slap the crop in the palm of my hand while he lifts the top over his head. The dungeon is flatteringly lit with low, flickering candle-style bulbs – not quite as atmospheric as real flame, but I guess a BDSM club needs to keep a closer eye than most on health and safety. The shadowy light casts patterns over Lloyd's pale bare chest and gives his hair a copper shine. He isn't meant to know that my mouth is watering, though, so I try to remain impassive while he removes shoes and socks then drops his jeans. After stepping out of them, his hands move to his underpants, but I wave the crop and shake my head.

'No, no. I want to take those off myself. Come over here.'

He moves closer on his bare feet until we are eye to eye. It is odd to be so much taller; we are practically the same height now.

I put down the crop and rest both of my hands in their fingerless latex gloves on his hips. I curl my forefingers inside the elastic of his boxers and then let go so it snaps back lightly against his skin.

'Why do you wear these, boy?'

'What, pants?'

'No, boxers. Why do you wear this style?'

'Er, why do I wear them? Well, they're comfortable, I suppose. Loose. I don't feel hemmed in.'

'Why might you feel hemmed in?'

He gives me a quizzical look. He has no idea where I'm going with this. I'm not sure I do either.

'Well, as a man, I have certain anatomical features, which you may have noticed.'

'You have a cock. I've noticed. I've also noticed that it seems to rule your life, boy.'

'Said the pot to the kettle.'

'Excuse me! I don't have a cock and besides, that's highly disrespectful and I'll have to punish you for it.' I give him my darkest frown. He visibly subsides. 'What I mean to say is that you wear that particular style of underwear because it doesn't hurt you when you get hard. Don't you?'

'Maybe.' Shifty eyes flick down to the floor.

'Because you're a disgusting pervert who can't look at a woman without getting an erection, aren't you? You're a sleazy sex-mad creep whose mind never leaves the gutter ...'

I have to stop. I'm going to laugh. This is so hypocritical, and if he doesn't make some wisecrack that completely kills the scene after about five seconds more of this, he isn't the man I think he is. 'Let's just have them off, shall we?'

I wrench them down, almost bending his cock out of shape so that he hisses in a breath.

'Fragile, is it?'

'Yes, ma'am.'

'Why is it hard? What are you thinking of, to make it so hard already?'

'I'm thinking of your arse in that shiny outfit, actually, ma'am.'

'Dirty, dirty boy.' I reach out and grip his balls, giving them a good squeeze. 'You've got lots of juice stored up for me, haven't you? Lots and lots of it. I expect you'd like to release a little bit of that, wouldn't you?'

'I wouldn't ... say no,' he gasps. He is looking at me with stunned respect. I think he's enjoying himself more than he expected to.

'Good. You won't be saying no tonight. Not to me – because I won't allow it. You're my boy for the night and you'll do exactly what I want.' I let go of his testicles and bat his cock from side to side with a cruel finger. 'Springy,' I comment. 'Such a nice little toy for me.'

The intent look on his face suggests that he is waiting for me to wrap my hand around it, maybe give it a few pumps up and down. No way, boy. Not yet.

'Turn around,' I order. 'Let me have a look at your arse, since you seem so preoccupied with mine.'

Since Lloyd took over the hotel management, he's been availing himself of that free gym membership like a man with an addiction to kettlebells. His backside is a piece of sculpture, firm and tight and round and biteable as an apple.

It seems a shame to harm it. But harm it I must.

I smack one rubber-gloved hand down on his right cheek, such a lovely sound. He doesn't flinch, doesn't even lose control of a breath.

'Thank you, ma'am,' he says flirtatiously, wiggling his hips. 'Do you want me to bend over too?'

'No. I want you to crawl over to where those cuffs are hanging. Get on your hands and knees. Now.'

I send my obedient serf on his way with a polished toe to his rear, stalking him and swishing the crop, making it land in light little pats on his skin.

'On your feet.' I encourage him with a slightly harder stroke.

'Are you really going to beat me with that thing?' he asks, appealing to my mercy. 'I mean, really hard?'

'Of course I am. You were unforgivably insolent just now. I have to punish you for it.'

'Oh God.' He is rueful but compliant, holding up his wrists for me to cuff.

'Regretting this? I'm not failing it, if that's what you were hoping. Not a chance. I mean to pass this test with flying colours.'

I click the cuffs shut, then pull on the length of chain that acts as a pulley, lifting his arms so that they are way over his head. It's hard work, because I'm lighter than him and have to rely on his co-operation, but he helps me tighten it until he's on tiptoes. He did this to me once and my arms were sore for two days. Revenge is sweet.

Except it isn't. Sweet is the wrong word. Grimly satisfying on only one of many levels. Aside from that, I feel sorry for him. He looks so helpless I want to rescue him.

'You can just concede this and we can go home,' I whisper to him.

'No,' he says. 'I'm going to make you hurt me.'

'You're insane.'

'Well, you can always concede this and we can go home.'

'I'm not letting you win!'

'Right. Best get to it then, ma'am. And make me scream.'

I pick up the flogger, a gentler instrument, and study its plaited strands. He is evil. He knows there's a very good chance I won't be able to hurt him.

I swoosh it against his backside.

'That tickles,' he says laconically.

I ply it harder. God, he looks good in bondage. That element of the punishment is pleasing me a great deal. His body, stretched and supplicating, cries out to be touched. But his voice doesn't cry out at all.

I keep going, doggedly, trying to change the colour of his pale bottom and not getting very far.

'I'm sorry, ma'am,' he says, 'but have you started yet?'

'Argh!' My frustration puts weight behind my stroke, and the next one hits the spot, rewarding me with a grunt.

Gradually, his skin flushes pink, but it takes a lot of flogging by me and gritted teeth by him to get to that point.

'I'm going to use the crop now,' I tell him, worried I might wear out my arm.

'OK, but you have to do it hard,' he says.

'Do you think you could stop topping from the bottom for a few moments?'

'I'm sorry, but it's important. This won't work if you don't really lay it on. I want you to make me beg you to stop.'

'Why?'

'Because I want to see what you'll do. I kind of need to see what you'll do, actually.'

'You should have a safe word, like I do when it's the other way round.'

'No, I don't want a safe word. I want you to carry on. If you want to win this, you have to carry on.'

'You're asking too much of me.'

'Fine. Then concede it.'

'No.'

'Hurt me then. Whip me till I cry.'

'For fuck's sake, Lloyd.'

'Just do it.'

Sheer frustration makes me lay the first stroke much harder than I intended.

'Ohhhh.' He howls and pants, pulling at the cuffs.

'Shit, I'm sorry! Oh, that looks sore.'

A welt rises, long and red and solemn. I touch it with my fingertips. It's so hot. But he does this to me, so why should I feel guilty? Besides, it looks good. It suits him. I make up my mind to give him twenty. I can take twenty myself. More on a good day, so it shouldn't be a problem for Lloyd. But then, I like a bit of pain. He doesn't.

'It's OK,' he puffs. 'Go on. More.'

He manages to stay silent for the second and third, but his shoulder blades are so tense that I'm the one wincing. His flesh flattens under the whip then bounces back. It's interesting to watch. I've seen video footage of him whipping me before, but it's different when the handiwork is your own. I find myself taking pride in my work, wanting to keep the strokes even and symmetrical.

At the same time, I want to look at his face. I need an angle that will show me both. I find a stance that allows me to watch his head in profile while still examining the welts that rise on his backside. With each stroke he throws back his neck and I see the curving line, interrupted by his Adam's apple, ending in a jumble of facial features contorted with pain. He starts to make noises around the fifth stroke, weird grunts and exhalations. I almost give up. Is this what I am like when he does this to me? And, if so, how can he carry on?

But he knows I want him to.

I know no such thing.

The sixth stroke is much gentler. I don't even mean to hold back, but I definitely do. It's cheating, I know, but I repeat this technique with the seventh. It doesn't even leave a mark.

'No,' he says. 'They don't count. Not hard enough. Count them again.'

'You're telling me what to do.'

'These are my rules, Sophie. Count them again or this is a fail.'

'But you aren't enjoying it. I'm finding it a bit upsetting, actually.'

'Nobody's forcing you to do it.'

'Fine.' I throw down the crop. 'You win. One fail. I can't do this to you.'

He looks round at me, almost losing balance and falling sideways. 'Why can't you?' he asks. He is smiling through the sweat, pleased with himself at finding a challenge that has defeated me.

'I'm not a sadist, and you're not a masochist. I can't make it any different. I'm not going to hurt you unless you're going to enjoy it. It's not fair to ask me to.'

'I never said I was going to play fair.'

'I can't imagine why I expected you to, to be honest.

What a mug.'

'So the pain thing is out of the window. But that doesn't mean this scene is over, does it? If you want to order me about a bit, feel free. There's a lot more to domination than whacking seven bells out of your sub's bottom, after all.'

'Yeah.' I think of the strap-on. My lips quirk upwards. 'You're right. I still have some plans for you.'

'There, you see. You can still swerve another fail.' He rattles the chains with his straining cuffs. 'I might need to get out of these, though. Feel like my arms are about to drop off.'

'You give a lot of orders, don't you?'

Suddenly, on a whim, I pick the crop back up and give him one heartfelt final swipe, scoring a beautiful deep crimson line across all the others.

He shouts out in stunned alarm. 'Oi!'

'Just making sure you remember who's running this scene, boy.'

I put my rubber-gloved hand on his bottom. The heat pulses against my bare fingertips and I enjoy running them over the slight ridges the crop has raised. I take the crop and slide it between his trembling thighs. The flat leather end nudges his balls; I push them to and fro while the handle slides over his perineum.

Now the noises he makes are different, low sighs and Os of pleasure. 'Ahhh, nice,' he manages to vocalise.

I angle the handle upwards so it parts the cheeks of his bottom, and push it up into the cleft. I grind it round and round, closer in. I wish I could see his face now. I pull the rest of the instrument through his thighs and press the handle up against his arsehole.

'Oh God,' he says harshly, urgently. 'What are you doing, Soph?'

'What do you think I'm doing?' I twist the handle against that helpless bud.

'Lube? Maybe? If you're … you know. If that's what you want to do to me.'

I laugh a cruel domme-ish laugh. 'Relax. I'm not going to bugger you. Not yet.'

I put the crop away and move around to face him. He looks strained and flushed, his normally pale face florid and shiny. His eyes are bulbous and staring.

'Sophie, please,' he whispers.

I see his cock standing erect, reaching all the way up to his navel. 'You want something?' My hand hovers around it, never quite touching it.

'Oh yes, touch it.'

'I think you've forgotten the formalities, haven't you?' I wave my fingers, trying to achieve a fanning effect that he will feel.

'Please, ma'am, please touch my cock.'

'I don't think you deserve it.'

I graze the swollen head, barely, with my fingernails. He convulses, shuddering out a long sigh.

'Like that, you mean?'

'Harder, please, ma'am, grab it, squeeze it, please.'

I drop to my knees and breathe on it.

'Oh God, you bitch!'

'That's no way to talk to your mistress.' I reach around and smack his arse, then pour more hot breath on his shaft and his tight, hard balls.

'I'm sorry, ma'am! I hate being teased. I hate not being in control. Oh God, please suck it.'

He undermines his plea by trying to twist away from me, presenting me with a pale flank instead. I smack him again and hold him by the hips, enjoying the latent power held captive under my palms.

With the very tippy-tip of my tongue I draw a slow upward line from his root to his head. I make it last. He tries to throw me off course, thrusting into my face, but he can't get the purchase he needs to succeed.

I laugh as I lick, pinching into his hips, wriggling my rubber-cased arse where he can't fail to see it. I give a taunting little flourish of tongue when I reach his frenulum and then pop off and back right away, smiling at the pained lines on his forehead.

'Oh Christ, Sophie, please ...'

'Open your eyes. I've got something to show you.'

Once his gaze is satisfactorily level, I turn around and bend over, feeling my bum cheeks strain against the constricting rubber until I worry it might split. But it doesn't and I spread them as wide as I can and shake them, then put my hands flat against them, pressing my fingertips in to the taut shiny-black second skin, peering up at him from between my legs.

'Come over here. Let me out of this,' he says.

'You *still* haven't got that quite right, have you?'

I straighten up and jump around to face him. I pull up a chair, some kind of bondage device with cuffs on the arms and legs, but I ignore those, sit myself down and sprawl with my legs over the sides.

'And guess what?' I reach down to my crotch. Velcro tears asunder, revealing my sex. 'Easy access! Good, eh?'

'Oh *God*.' He stumbles forwards when I put my hand inside the dark, furtive opening and start to rub.

'Ooh, juicy. I must have enjoyed whipping you more than I realised. Actually, it's probably the rubber. So tight and hot, holding me in, clinging.' I lift my fingers to my mouth and suck them.

He looks as if he might faint, all that colour draining away. The stiff baton obscuring his lower abdomen must be getting uncomfortable now.

But that's not my problem, is it?

'Think I'll pick myself a vibrator,' I say casually, strolling up to the toy cupboard to select a nice number with a clitoral stimulator. 'This'll do.'

I resume my legs akimbo posture, switch on the vibe and push it slowly and cleanly up inside my cunt, holding Lloyd's eyes every second of the way.

'Can you see it going in? Do you wish that was your cock?'

'Yes, ma'am,' he whispers, transfixed.

'Well, it isn't going to be. Not tonight. Your cock gets nothing tonight. It's spoilt and overindulged. It needs to learn to take turns.'

His lips are turned down and he's breathing heavily. He looks half crushed, half homicidal. I'm quite relieved that the cuffs are so effective.

The vibe slides in to the hilt and the clit buzzer begins its work. I push and thrust with it, grinding my hips in the chair, throwing back my head and losing myself in the sensation. Every now and again, I peek over to look at Lloyd.

'Open your eyes! You have to watch this!'

'I can't ... I'm so hard ... please ...'

'You concede then?'

He wrenches up his eyelids. 'No I fucking well don't.'

'Watch then.'

I work myself well and thoroughly, making sure my G-spot gets plenty of attention, letting the vibrations pulse gently through my swelling clit. I get close, and then I pull the thing out, wanting more of Lloyd's desperation and frustration before I come.

'I preferred when you were whacking me!' he yelps when I plunge the vibrator back in. 'This is way more cruel.'

'So sorry.' But the murmur is a reflex, not sincere, because I am too focused now on the tide lapping slowly forwards once more, creeping up, getting ready.

When I come, I try not to make a sound but just let the breath ebb from my body, controlled, unhurried. Although my eyelids flutter, I can still see most of what Lloyd is doing and it intensifies my pleasure to know that he is in his predicament, restrained and erect and raring to fuck me.

'I think,' I say, sounding slightly drunk as I try to swing my legs back over the chair arms, 'it's time for your treat now. I'm gonna uncuff you, but don't you even think about touching me, OK?'

'Hard to make that promise, Soph.'

'I know. That's why I'm asking you to make it.'

'All right.'

I start to unbuckle the straps of leather encircling his wrists. They are pink and a little sore looking. He lowers his arms stiffly. 'I want you to go over to that piece of furniture I got out earlier and bend over it.'

'What?' He puts his head to one side, examining me as if aiming to look into my mind. 'What's the plan, ma'am?'

'You'll see, boy. Now do it.' I let my palm ring out on that still-welted backside.

He growls, then realises that submissives are not meant to growl and lunge at their mistresses, shrugs and slopes over to the bench.

'Get that behind nice and high,' I command as he positions himself. I tie his wrists again, and his ankles. Don't want any misdirected kicks, not when I do what I'm planning to do. 'Just keep still while I go and get my equipment.'

'What equipment?'

'Aha. Wait and see. Don't move.'

'I can't bloody well move anyway. You're going to whip me again, aren't you? Oh my God, you're going to get a dildo and ...'

Now he's on the right track. But I don't want to ruin the surprise, so I simply shush him and grab the harness from the cupboard.

He must be able to hear it jingle and clink while I attach it to my pelvis. The cock part of it draws its centre of gravity down, the weight is a little disconcerting. What would it actually be like to have a cock, I find myself wondering. Does it get in the way of stuff all the time?

'Have you guessed what it is yet?' I tease, practising a few different poses, grabbing hold of the dildo part and pointing it towards his distant pink bottom.

'Something with metal ... a harness of some kind.'

'Now I just need to choose the right lube ... maybe some of this tingle gel, eh?'

'Oh, Sophie!' He says my name with such reverence. 'I never dreamed you'd go this far. Are you really going to ...?'

'Fuck your arse, darling? Yes, I am.'

'Oh sweet Jesus.'

'You drove me to it. All your goading at me to concede. All your smugness about how sure you were I'd fail. This counts for several successes at once, I feel.'

'I'll be the judge of that. You haven't done it yet.'

'You haven't done this before then?'

There's a pause.

'Actually, yes,' he admits.

'With a girl? Or a boy?'

'Boy. Experiment.'

'Good experiment? Or not?'

'Pretty good, actually.'

'Definitely the tingle gel then.' I sigh heavily. 'I was all excited about taking your virginity. That's one thing I've still never done.'

'Noted.'

'I'm going to stop telling you things. I've never been pleasured in a sheik's harem by eight naked oiled male models either. Is that noted too?'

'No, because I think you're lying.'

I'm close to him now. He needs to start feeling the seriousness of his position and he needs to start feeling it now.

I keep adjusting the harness as I walk, not sure how it's meant to sit. Like this? Like that? I pull it as tight as I can, the fake cock bowing out in front of me.

I put my hand on his bottom and he flinches. I know his sphincter has tightened.

'Dear sweet Lloyd. How do you like it? Hard and fast, or slow and sweet? How do you like your arse fucked?'

'I ... can't remember.' His teeth are gritted.

I squirt some lube on the exposed part of my fingers and slot them between his cheeks until I feel that wrinkled texture amid the softness. Tight, squeezed shut. Can I do this? Will I tear him?

I get it nice and slick and slidey then I push it forwards a tiny bit. I'm as tense as he is, every muscle of my face pulled into a grimace.

He breathes in short puffs. I know he's making an effort to remember what he always tells me during anal sex. Bear down, push back, relax.

It takes just a moment of screwing my finger left and right and I'm in. How peculiar it feels to press against the narrow walls of his passage, so hot and so tender.

He makes an incoherent noise, and I remember I need to be domming it up big style, talking him through this.

'You've got a finger up your arse, boy – how does that feel?'

'Uh, quite nice, ma'am.'

'Does it? Because you're going to have more than a finger soon enough. How's the tingle gel?'

'Tingly.'

He illustrates this with a wiggle of his arse and a tightening of the muscles, closing around my finger like a trap. Where's the prostate? Is it near here or further up? My strap-on and I will investigate its location.

'Are you ready?' I pull out my finger, watching the aperture close up again like one of those doors in space operas with multiple triangular blades that meet and seal up the exit.

'As I'll ever be,' he says with some effort.

'Right.'

I stand there, taking deep breaths. I'm more nervous than he is. Oh for fuck's sake, I should just get on with it.

'If you want to concede ...'

I attach a limpet hand to one of his hips, press the dildo between his cheeks, find the target.

'I don't think so.'

I push forward, just a little, waiting for his response.

He is gasping, but not crying out or anything. That'll be good, right? I panic slightly, wanting the reassurance of flesh on flesh, of being able to feel his passage expand to fit me. This is so foreign and so sterile. I might as well have fixed him up to some machine that pumps the dildo in and out. The most I can hope for is to press my latex-covered thighs up against his, once the thing is in completely, and hold that limited contact close.

I should say something like, 'Feel my giant dildo stretch you wide, boy' but instead I say, 'Are you OK?'

'Oh, Soph, I'm fine. I'm fine, don't worry about me. Just do what you have to do.'

If I don't finish this off, he will be insufferable for ever.

But it is still with some regret that I push the sleek black silicone deeper inside him. I stop for a moment while he groans and convulses, then carry on until I am close, closer, then all the way in, the harness straps patterning his bum cheeks, my rubbery thighs leaning into his.

'Oh my God.' I look down at where my strap-on ends and he begins. 'It's all the way in. That's got to be uncomfortable.'

'S'fine.' His voice is thick and slurry now. 'Oh, oh God. I forgot how it felt.'

'Does it hurt?'

'Not really. Do you mind … take it easy … to start off.'

'OK.'

I jiggle and circle my hips, watching the end of the strap-on move inside his opened hole. 'I want you to know,' I blurt, hardly knowing what I'm saying.

'What?'

'That … oh, I don't know. That you should let me know if it hurts you.'

'Is that what you meant to say?'

I swallow the words. 'Yes. Will you do that for me? Let me know if it hurts? And I'll stop.'

'Scout's honour, ma'am.'

I pull out, then slide it back in again. And repeat, and repeat, and repeat. I take my cues from his shuddering breath and his heartbreaking little moans, sometimes slowing, sometimes jerking it in more roughly than before.

'You want this?'

'God, yes, God, keep going.'

'Are you going to come?'

'What do you fucking think?' His breath is harsh now, so fast I almost expect steam to rise from his head. I thrust, thrust, thrust, and then he howls, loud and clear, trying to break the cuffs that hold his ankles and wrists in place with the violence of his straining.

I don't know what to do with the dildo while he is coming – I just keep it shoved up there, hoping this is the right way to prolong his ecstasy. Or maybe I should keep fucking? Oh, I don't know. I'm so glad I'm not a dominant type of person; there's so much to consider.

I wait for him to flounder into a post-orgasmic doze, then I retract my weapon with infinite tenderness and care, until his twitching gap is unfilled, having nothing but the memory of penetration to keep it wide open.

I take off the harness, fling it to the floor and unbuckle his ankles.

His legs swing, heavy and useless, together.

I move around to his front. His eyes are shut, his face gormless as it is in sleep. Perhaps he is asleep. I unbuckle the wrists, kissing each one as it is freed, then I stroke his hair while he recovers, picking plastered strands away from his cheek and forehead. I want to take him off the bench, sling him over my shoulder and drop him onto a bed. It's a weird, topsy-turvy, confusing feeling. I feel as if I'm him and he's me. It's all the wrong way round.

'Hey, Lloyd,' I whisper. The latex catsuit is fiendishly hot and uncomfortable now. I'm desperate to get out of it. 'Are you awake?'

A long 'hmmmmmm' is all I get.

I crouch down a little, cup his face in a hand (the one that didn't poke a finger up his bottom). My nose rubs his, my lips brush against the corner of his mouth, then move to his ear.

'Wake up. You're free. I'd say I passed that one, wouldn't you?'

I yelp as his hands, quick smart, land under my armpits, holding me tight. He burrows his mouth into my neck, feasting on it.

He lets go and jumps to his feet, facing me from the opposite side of the bench. 'No more ma'am?' he says, with a crooked smile. 'Who's going to clean up the mess then?' He looks down at the underside of the bench, which drips with his ejaculate.

'Oh, go on then. If you must. Lick it up, boy.'

I watch, grinning at his expression of disgust, as he obeys me on his knees.

'Never again,' he vows, looking around for his clothes. 'But it was an experience. Did you enjoy it?'

'Partly. I didn't so much enjoy it as learn from it.'

'And what did you learn?'

He turns to face me, pants in hand, eyebrows raised.

'That you're a dick,' I tell him. 'And that latex catsuits are only sexy for one hour.'

'I can't say I agree with either of those findings.' And then his hands are on my shiny arse and his mouth is on mine and the power is exchanged once more.

Chapter Four

I know the city better than I know myself. Sometimes I think its chaos and dirt are a reflection of me, feeding off me and me off it. At other times, I see its grandeur, its capacity to be everything to every person. It fulfils all dreams, including the bad ones. This is what I try to capture in my photographs: the Janus-faced metropolis, beckoning you in, spitting you out.

For every girl posing outside Oxford Circus TopShop, fake-tanned to the gills and scouting for model scouts, there's a railway station bag lady.

Innumerable coins with innumerable opposite faces, this is the gold that paves the streets.

I'm out with my camera, down by the river, when I get the text.

Challenge Time. Wherever you are, whoever's around you, take off your knickers. L x.

Suddenly our little morning scuffle makes sense.
'I think you should wear a skirt today,' he'd said.
'I'm going out, though. Pulling an all-nighter with the

camera. Want to take some shots of the urban wildlife. I told you that yesterday, didn't I? Since you're working all night.'

'Yeah, I still think you should wear a skirt. In fact, I insist.'

I turned around from the wardrobe, eyebrow poised for war. 'You *insist*, do you?'

He approached me from behind, clasped his hands around my midriff and spoke into my ear. 'I insist because I want to think about the night air circulating around your thighs and passers-by putting their hands up your skirt while you're busy snap-snap-snapping.'

'Oh yeah?' My voice betrayed my desire for him to continue with this.

'They'll ask you what's under there. Can they take a look. And you'll carry on taking your photos and just nod. And while you're capturing a pile of tyres on the canal bank or something, they'll push their hands up your thighs and get your skirt all wrinkled and rucked until it's right up under your bum. One of them gets his hand behind and squeezes your cheeks, nice and slow, while you work. The other person's fingers creep inside your knickers and feel you up. They don't ask your permission, they know it's implicit, especially when they feel how wet and hot you are up there. "Mm, think she wants it," he says. "I know that," says his mate. "Dirty, dirty girl." Their fingers meet and mix all over your cunt and your arse. They explore every crack, every space, every shallow little soaking wet fold. They carry on even when other people turn up, a bit tipsy from the pub, and form a little crowd. They make you come, over and over and over and over and when they're done ...'

'Fuck's sake, Lloyd. What's the time? Have I got time to ...?'

'I'd say so.'

We fell back into bed.

So I'm wearing the skirt.

I'm wearing the skirt in the busiest section of the South Bank, surrounded everywhere by mooching culture vultures and pleasure trippers and fire-eaters and whatnot. I'm trying to shoot those precious minutes before sundown, trying to get the exact quality of light that signals the danger in the air, the approaching shift from benign tourist trap to grimy hustlers' paradise.

Agitated, I text back: Must it be now?
Yes & I need photographic evidence.

I look around me. Nobody is paying me much attention. There is a lot of competition for that, something the pickpockets are ever grateful for. On the river, the pleasure boats cruise by, slow and stately, some of them trailing jazz music in their wake.

I let my camera rest around my neck on its lanyard and put my phone back in my jacket pocket.

I look around once more. A man dressed as Darth Vader has everyone's eyes fixed in his direction.

I put a hand on the skirt hem and sort of pat it and flutter it for a few seconds, trying to work out exactly how long this might take. No. Thinking about it will just prolong the agony.

Facing the river, I lift the front of my skirt and take hold of the elastic so quickly my fingers seem to double in quantity. Looking fixedly ahead at the palatial facades on the opposite bank, I yank the knickers down, hoping that they'll just fall themselves once they reach a particular region of thigh. They are stubborn, though, and I have to lower them to my knees before they oblige me. I shut my eyes as they drift to my ankles.

Stepping out of them, I'm tempted to just take off at speed and leave them lying on the bare concrete, but that won't do. Photographic evidence, he said.

I make a point of not checking to see if anyone's watching me this time. Do anything brazenly enough, and the chances are you'll get away with it.

Instead, I crouch down to pick them up then hold them at arm's length and take a picture on my phone. A boat sails by and some of the trippers wave and take pictures of me. Well, probably not me. Probably the South Bank complex and the fairground and the aquarium that used to be County Hall. But I'll be in there somewhere, waving my polka-dotted cotton briefs like a flag, representing Britain.

Once the picture is taken, I send it to Lloyd, then I stuff the knickers and phone into my jacket pocket, sigh heavily and resume my original work.

A text interrupts me.

Well done. You're on the South Bank?
Yes.
Did anyone see you?
Not sure.
Nobody hovering over your shoulder with propositions?
Not yet.
OK. Next task.
Another one?
Yes. It's a treasure hunt. I'm sending you all over the city with little tasks to complete. Fun!
Hmm.
Don't be like that! Next task. Go to Buckingham Palace and flash a sentry.

Game

What? How am I going to get a photo of that?
After you've shown him your arse, leave those
knickers in his sentry box and take a picture.
I'll get arrested!
You won't. They aren't supposed to react, are they?
Go on. Bet it's been done a million times before.

The light is fading now, the sky an amazing violet grey.

I take a few photographs then I decide to walk the distance between here and Buckingham Palace. If I walk everywhere, perhaps there won't be so much time for these damned challenges, I reason. Besides, I like walking.

So I head over Westminster Bridge and past Big Ben, chiming the half-hour, through St James's Park to the Palace.

The Queen is away, according to the flag, which is a faint relief. Don't want Her Majesty catching a glimpse of anything untoward, after all.

Drawing closer, I notice that the crowds aren't too thick now. The museum part of the palace has closed for the day and it seems to be mainly people coming off the park and heading into Victoria, passing through rather than stopping.

I take myself to the extreme right side of the pavement, wanting to get a good run up so that my little flash will be a blur of speed that leaves the sentry wondering if it really happened. I compose myself, do a few breathing exercises, like an athlete preparing for a race. I wait for it to get a little darker and the crowd a little thinner. Then, once I have a clear path ahead, I pitch myself at speed towards the gates, weaving between the milling groups of tourists.

At the crucial moment, I perform a balletic quarter turn, flip up the back of my skirt and lean forwards, before completing the full pirouette, the fabric falling back over my bottom.

A couple of squeals and some hysterical laughter follow my onward progress to the far side of the palace. I hide myself around the corner and gasp for breath, once, twice, three times, before part two of my mission.

It has to happen quickly. I take out my phone, put it on camera mode and hold it in front of me, running back through the same crowd, some of whom are still commenting on what they just saw, if they saw it.

They part before me, curious to know what I'm doing.

I stop dead in front of the sentry box, grab the knickers from my pocket and fling them at the feet of the soldier. He doesn't move a muscle.

I take the photograph and hare off again, barging past an American man who entreats me to 'Show some damn respect!'

I take cover back in the park.

Done. I text Lloyd the photo.
Impressive! He'll be sleeping with those tonight.
He'll probably hand them over to the police.
Lol, I think not. Ready for the next phase?
Not really.
Of course you are. It's the cocktail hour. Take your-
self off to the Ritz, buy yourself a cocktail and find
an attractive woman to snog. Get a photo.
A woman?
Yep. Pulling a man in a hotel bar would be shooting
fish in a barrel for you, wouldn't it?
True.

The Ritz isn't far away. I walk purposefully past the doormen and up the steps, under its shimmery glimmery awning and into the bar.

I forget why I'm there for a moment, and imagine I'm on an industrial espionage mission, looking for ideas for my own hotel. Their drinks are pricier than ours but then they have the history and the prestige behind them and they can get away with it.

I order a Cosmopolitan and scope the place for likely talent.

In one corner a group of impeccable young things giggle and snort among themselves. They are pretty, but they just seem wrong somehow. And what should I say to them? 'Excuse me but would you mind most awfully if I kissed one of you?'

I figure I'll play this the same way I always play it.

I'll sit alone at the bar, make plenty of eye contact and see what happens. It's as good a way as any to waste some challenge time.

I spin the cocktail out, watching the bar staff – no Lloyds among them – do their stuff. They're good, efficient, polite, personable. Maybe I could poach one of them.

Several men approach me, but I reject them. I tell the fourth one straight. 'I'm looking for a woman.'

He blinks. 'Any woman in particular?'

'No, just a woman I can kiss.'

'Well, you know, Soho is just around the corner.'

'It has to be here.'

'Has to be?'

'Yes.'

He checks his watch. 'Well, you know, I'm meeting a girlfriend here. Maybe she'd be interested.'

'You're meeting a girlfriend? So why are you all over me?'

'We're open-minded. She's not my only girlfriend. I'm not her only boyfriend. If you catch my drift.'

'I catch it precisely. I'm in a similar set-up myself.'

'My name's Brad, by the way.'

75

We fall into an easy, flirtatious conversation about our unconventional sex lives. When the girlfriend arrives, in a cloud of perfume, I am regaling her lover with an account of the time I took three cocks simultaneously. He's impressed.

'Hello,' says the girlfriend, whose name is Kristen. 'What have we here?'

'This is Sophie. She'd like to kiss you.'

Kristen is certainly kissable, with full, slightly sardonic lips and a cascade of shiny brown hair. She looks sleek and expensive but there's a glint in her eye that I recognise. There are other people like me. I sometimes forget this.

'Just like that?' she laughs.

'Just like that. Shall we retire to that corner?'

Four leopard-print bucket chairs surround a table in their own niche. It's in view of the bar, but slightly secluded from the rest of the room.

We take our drinks over. On the way, I give my camera-phone to Brad.

'So then.' I turn to Kristen, feeling it's time I got down to business. I put a hand on her thigh.

She smiles. 'Forward, aren't you?'

'Yes. I am forward. How about you?'

I lean in a little. Her perfume is surprisingly floral, not the predictable knockout musk. Her skin is so perfect it almost shimmers.

Her smile fixes in position, her cheekbones quivering a little with the effort. She has a gap in her front teeth. I find it sexy, imagining my tongue seeking out the groove.

'Love your shirt,' I say, brushing the silky sleeve.

'Thanks. It's Stella McCartney.'

She lets my hand come to rest around her upper arm, my fingers stroking its soft inner side.

'So, this kiss, then,' she says, looking over at her boyfriend. 'Is it for a bet?'

'Not a bet, but similar. I don't want to mess up your lipstick, but ...'

Small talk is starting to bore me. It's not like I want her for an enduring friendship. I put my free hand on the side of her neck opposite the arm I'm holding and brush my thumb under her ear. She tilts her head in Pavlovian pleasure, bringing it closer to me.

'OK,' she murmurs.

Her lipstick is luxuriously creamy without the distracting taste the cheap stuff leaves in your mouth. She has been chewing spearmint gum in the fairly recent past, and perhaps before that she smoked a cigarette.

Her lips are firm, but she offers no resistance, letting my tongue slip in to investigate that delightful tooth gap. The cameraphone flashes as our breasts touch, her silk against my cotton. Her nipples are hard.

Screeches of laughter from the girl group bring us to our senses and we draw apart, mission accomplished, shy smiles on our faces. Her lipstick must be the stay-put kind. She looks no different.

'Thanks,' I say, getting back my breath. 'Thanks for helping me out.'

I turn to Brad, reaching out for my phone. 'Can I see?'

He hands it over and I examine the five pictures he has taken of the kiss in every stage. I select the most flagrant of the in flagrante poses and forward it to Lloyd.

'So, Sophie,' says Kristen, checking her face in a mirror compact. 'Do you have plans for tonight?'

Brad's ears prick up. He leans forwards.

'You enjoyed yourself there, huh?'

'We could make that table for two a table for three, couldn't we?'

'Oh, I think I'll be busy,' I say. 'Sorry. I'm just waiting to hear from my boyfriend.'

'He can come too,' says Kristen swiftly.

'Er ...'

The text alert bleeps.

'Nice work,' says Lloyd. 'Are you hungry?'

'I've just been invited to dinner by this couple. I gather a threesome could be on the table. Well, not the restaurant table, obviously. But you know what I mean.'

'Never mind them,' comes the reply. 'Thank them politely and get yourself out of there.'

I do so, after they insist on giving me their number 'in case I find myself at a loose end later' and find myself on the pavements of Piccadilly in a late summer early evening fug of exhaust fumes and street pizza stands.

I lean on a lamppost, recreating in my head that rather delicious lipstick kiss, waiting for Lloyd's next directive.

When it comes, it makes me clench my thighs.

Get something to eat, then find a pub garden or similar open public space and get yourself felt up in it. Photos required.

My stomach churns, but I buy myself a slice of carcinogen and pepperoni and chew my way stoically through it before heading towards Mayfair. If I'm going to be felt up outside a pub, it might as well be by a high class of feeler-upper.

Amidst the art galleries and celebrity eateries, I find a classic old Victorian pub in pink sandstone with pavement tables.

This will have to do. The additional element of being seen to in the actual street appeals to me on a very base level.

The pavement is thronged with crowds of well-heeled tourists and the smart post-work crowd, none of whom seem to mind paying Mayfair prices for average tipples.

I scope out the different groups and settle on three good-looking young men in rugby shirts and sunglasses, drinking lager and talking animatedly.

I buy myself a mineral water – that cocktail in the Ritz has given me enough head-fuzz for the time being – and lean on the wall, ostentatiously looking over at them every few seconds. I make a big deal of checking my phone and my watch in between sly glances.

After about ten minutes of this, one of the guys, who has been following my progress fairly avidly, calls over to me. 'Has he stood you up, love?'

He's Australian, big and beefy, with a blond crop and a square chin.

'Looks like it. I guess I'll finish this and go home. Unless ...'

Bingo! He pats the bench beside him. 'Sit yourself down. He's a loser anyway.'

I scurry over and plonk myself beside the large lager-drinker. 'Do you know him?'

He laughs. 'If he's stood you up, he's a loser. Trust me.'

This is going to be easy.

It takes the duration of one more pint.

There's five or ten minutes of general chat about London, then his hand lands on my thigh, heavy as a brick.

Then, another five minutes discussion about Australia with specific reference to his home town of Melbourne while his hand moves up and down and he shifts ever closer along the bench, his two friends looking on in amusement.

An intensely boring description of the rugby tour of Britain they are on provokes me to put my hand on his and move it to the hem of my skirt, encouraging his thick fingers to pull it slowly up to thigh level.

I don't know how many pints they've had, but I guess four or five, because inhibitions don't seem to be anywhere in evidence. Soon enough, he has managed to wedge my skirt almost to the top of my thighs.

Granted, they are under the table and nobody else outside the pub would be able to see – even the passers-by wouldn't be looking so low. The Mayfair streets are not busy, the main traffic being taxis gliding past at a stately pace.

Their passengers will be the ones who might catch a glimpse and guess what's what. From their windows, they will be able to see my legs, sideways on, bare to the very top, with a large man's hand wedged between them. They'll catch a flash of the image, but not for long enough to know that what they saw is what is actually happening. They might look back, but by then the backs of the other drinkers and the table will obscure their view.

I think we can get away with this. But how the hell am I going to get a picture?

I widen my thighs just a fraction, enabling his big ham of a fist to make its way to the apex. Just as it does, I take my phone and snap a photograph.

I am examining the rather disappointing shot of some bunched fabric and a wrist, when Jayden's fingers whizz back down my thighs as if my pussy has actually burnt them.

'You … no panties!' he exclaims, loud enough for his fellows to hear and crease up with laughter. 'And what's with the photos?'

'Just a little hobby of mine,' I say, as matter-of-factly as

I can muster. I need to keep him on task, get him hot and bothered so he'll carry on regardless of his pals.

'Hobby?'

'Yeah. I like to take photos of myself getting fingered. Does that seem weird to you?'

His eyes are so confused, bless him. He runs a hand over his buzz-cut hair and says, 'In a word, yeah.'

'I know I'm different,' I tell him, placing his hand back on my bare thigh. 'But I just love the feel of a strange man's fingers between my pussy lips. I just love the way they stroke and rub and make my clit want to burst with heat. When I look at the photos after it gets me so wet to see how I let a man get his hands right up there, pushing his fingers all the way up inside my cunt ...'

I break off. All three of them are like waxwork figures captured in a state of hypnosis, leaning over their pint glasses.

'Is that so wrong?' I finish, pouting at Jayden.

'No,' he breathes, letting me push his hand down the slope, into the dark place in the gap of my legs. 'You're a special girl, Sophie.'

I smile at his friends, who lean further, trying to see over the ledge of the table. Jayden's fingers find my slit, confidently this time, fitting themselves between the lips with ease.

I hand my phone over to Sean, the lad on the left.

'Get under the table,' I suggest. 'And take a photo.'

Jayden's fingers push against my clit and my bottom squirms on the wooden bench.

'You might need to put the flash on though.'

Sean looks at his friend, looks at Jayden, looks at me, looks at the phone. 'Is this a set-up?' he asks uncertainly.

Jayden's fingers slip and slide. I lean over the table so as to make sure it's invisible to anyone standing behind us.

He's getting close to my cunt, readying himself for the full impalement.

'I mean, like a porn version of *Pranked*. This isn't like that, is it?' He cranes his neck, looking for a nonexistent camera crew.

'Trust me,' I say in a strange gaspy voice. Jayden has found a very good place to rest his weary fingers. 'It's just me and my little foible ... ohh.'

Those thick fingers feel so good, even if they blunder a little bit around the opening. What he lacks in technique, he adds in enthusiasm, though. He wiggles them around inside me while I sit on the bench like butter wouldn't melt. It would though. It would melt in the time it took to place it on my clit.

My thighs already feel as if butter is running down them, warm juices clinging to my skin. Luckily the cigarette smoke in the air neutralises any telltale odour.

Sean bobs down beneath the table. His friend makes to join him but Jayden holds up his free hand.

'Don't draw attention, mate,' he says. His voice is slow and syrupy, like somebody caught in a dream.

'Are you really doing it?' the friend contents himself with asking. 'Really getting your fingers in there?'

'I'll show you the picture,' says Sean from his low-down position. 'Hang on.'

I put my hands under the table and spread my pussy lips wide, hoping that they will show up in shot along with Jayden's knuckles and his big fat thumb on my big fat clit.

The flash of light is brief and a few heads turn towards us.

Nobody can see, I tell myself. Nobody. Except Sean, who has the ringside view.

'Fucking hell, you're really doing it. She's not wearing panties either.'

'Really?' The friend compromises, leaning to the side to get a swift peek under the table. 'Wow, she's dripping, man. That's one wet pussy.'

Jayden bends to speak in my ear. 'Do you want to come?'

I hold back from screaming *Of course I do!* Retrieving some brain cells from somewhere, I consider the question.

Lloyd didn't say I had to come. In a sense, it might be easier if I don't. I'll be on edge and horny as hell for the next task, whatever it might be. Something tells me it won't be vanilla-sweet.

Oh, but can I really turn down an orgasm? One I'm so close to?

I make my decision. 'I want to come,' I tell him. 'But not here.'

'Your place?'

'Wait. Take your fingers out. I'm going to go to the loo.'

'You better not finish what I started in there!'

'No, no, I won't. Wait a moment.'

'I'll come in there with you, if you like. We can …'

But I've pulled down my skirt, snatched my phone off a still-crouching Sean and I'm on my way.

'Photo for you,' I text Lloyd from the stall.

Impressive! Where are you?
Mayfair. What shall I do now?
Buy a hotel?
Is that what this is? Monopoly but with sex?
Yes! Shall I send you down the Old Kent Road next?
I'd rather you didn't.
OK, wait a moment and I'll give you your orders.

I tap my feet impatiently. I've been in here long enough. I ought to get going.

I can hear taps running, hand dryers blowing, the capping of lipsticks. I shift a little on the toilet seat. Jayden's fingers were sufficiently thick and undecorous to have left a mildly stinging sensation in my pussy.

The phone bleeps.

Right. Last mission. Get yourself to Soho. Go to Tied and Trussed. Jerome will give you your instructions there.

Tied and Trussed is a place Lloyd and I know well, and the staff know more than they would ever need to about our tastes and interests. We have bought a lot of their stock and the owner, Jerome, sometimes socialises with us. So I allow myself grounds for optimism as I stow the phone away and emerge from the Ladies'.

Jayden stands right outside the door, ready to catch me like a rugby ball. I duck away from his hopeful embrace and break into a speed walk along the bar.

'Gotta go,' I shout over my shoulder. 'Urgent business.'

'I've got urgent business myself!' he shouts back, dismayed.

The last thing I hear as I barrel through the door is his enraged bellow of 'Pricktease!'

I let the word melt into the evening air and hurry away, across the city again, leaving the strangely bland and anti-septic vibe of Mayfair behind.

I'm more at home in the fleshpots.

Soho is alive in the dark, all neon-lit, boozy and crowded. Tied and Trussed sits between an upmarket Italian restaurant and a clip joint – respectability and criminality on either side. It represents a place between these two extremes, and yet its depraved pleasures might be enjoyed by patrons of both establishments.

The window display is elegant – an elaborate flower fashioned from various lengths of leather and chain, its stem wrapped in ribbon. I admire this for a few moments, then head inside.

Jerome is at the counter. A huge blond Dutchman with a substantial moustache, he is chatting with a gay couple about Shibari rope bondage. He pauses when he sees me and waves me over.

'Ah, Sophie, you are here.' He turns to his customers. 'I will have to put you in Margi's hands – she is an expert and will be able to help you.' They wander over to the assistant, Margi, who is putting the finishing touches to a wall display of manacles.

'Well, Sophie, we have an interesting evening ahead.'

'Have we?'

'Yes. Come through to the back room.'

I've been in the back room before. Jerome sometimes lets me and Lloyd 'try before we buy' in there. Provided he's allowed to watch.

Bondage furniture lines the walls and box after box of cuffs, chains, cords and straps are piled high in the corners. The overwhelming smell of leather is intoxicating, and Jerome adds to it, in his head-to-toe cowhide.

'So what's on the agenda then?' I ask, remembering to be nervous. 'Lloyd says you have instructions for me.'

'Yes, I do.' Jerome is busy scanning his stock for something. 'You'll need to take off your clothes.'

His matter-of-fact tone piques me. He isn't even looking at me.

'What for?'

'No questions.' He turns and wags a finger at me. 'You don't have to, of course. It's just what Lloyd said.'

I shrug, a bit sulkily, and take my camera cord off. I turn my back to Jerome for the rest, shivering in the unheated air.

Once I am nude, I turn back to him, thrusting my bare breasts towards him as if in challenge. He has located what he was looking for – a set of fur-lined leather cuffs – and he shoots me a lascivious grin.

'Well, Miss Martin,' he says, holding them out. 'You want to put yourself in these?'

'I suppose.' I can't get out of this mindset that I ought to resist Lloyd's plans for me, even if they are to my taste. Sometimes I hate that he knows me so well. The sense of having nowhere to hide, at least sexually speaking, can be overwhelming.

Jerome lumbers over and fits the cuffs to my wrists, pulling each one tightly into the soft yet demanding embrace of the fur. He buckles them then links them together at the metal loops.

'Put up your arms,' he says and I raise them over my head, my bound wrists creating a graceful pinnacle to my sloping arms. Beneath them, my body is naked and vulnerable. There isn't much I can do to fight off any unwanted advance.

Jerome consults his boxes again, emerging with a long roll of shiny black tape.

'Now then,' he says, and begins unwinding it. He sticks one end to my shoulder and commences wrapping it round me. He doesn't cover my breasts, leaving them exposed and continuing his bondage-bandaging at my ribcage.

'Does this rip off like a plaster?' I ask warily, watching as the ribbons of shiny black take over my waist and hips.

'No, it is not painful,' he assures me. He cuts the tape off when he reaches my bottom and recommences on my left leg. 'It is a good seller, this stuff. Easy to apply, easy to take off. Looks really something.'

'Nice and shiny,' I comment. Looking down at myself, the gap that exposes my pussy is somehow far ruder than simple nudity. I am signposted for sex, all the major access routes clear. Anything lickable or fingerable is uncovered – the rest hidden from view by line after line of the tape. He arrives finally at my left foot and I'm done. Only my head, breasts, bottom and pubic triangle are left open to view. There can be no doubt as to what my purpose is. I am a collection of erogenous zones, with a face.

'OK.' He surveys me proudly for a moment then drags one of his fetish furnishings, a kind of padded stepstool affair, away from the wall and into the centre of the room. 'Now put yourself over this, Sophie.'

'Are you going to fuck me?'

I've never fucked Jerome, not because I dislike him or find him unattractive, just ... haven't. Somehow.

'I can't answer that,' he says, prodding me onward with a finger in the small of my back. I let him arrange me over the stool, on my knees, with my stomach leaning on a nice fat cushion, locked wrists tied to a crossbar in front. He smacks the insides of my thighs so I part them hurriedly, then he straps my knees to the step. There's no way out of this now.

'Why not?'

'Orders. Now, I may or may not fuck you, but I do get to warm you up. Just wait there one moment.'

To my considerable astonishment, he opens the shop door and calls, 'Gentlemen? Are you ready?'

I'm facing the wrong way and I'm too firmly strapped

down to turn my head, so I don't see who comes in, or how many of them there are.

'Sophie,' says Jerome after shutting the door again, but he is introducing me rather than addressing me. Introducing the spread cunt and outthrust arse that must be pretty much all they can see of me anyway.

'Now this is a little quiz for you,' he continues, talking to me this time. 'I have three gentlemen here with me. All of them are friends of yours. What you have to do is play a game of Guess Who. First of all, though, I get to make your ass red, which is one of my favourite games.'

'What's that got to do with it?' I complain.

'Nothing. Just the payment I demanded for my services. Come on. I'll be nice.'

Nice isn't really the word for the tingling teasing pain of the flogger as it lands, briskly and sharply, on my defenceless posterior. Jerome enjoys his work, though, and he flicks the strands all over my untaped rear until I gasp and squeak with humiliated outrage. At the same time I am working on riding out the sting, my brain is calculating the likely identities of the three witnesses. Is one of them Lloyd? Surely, it must be. So Lloyd and two of his friends. Which two? Ouch!

My mind abandons its machinations and I am given over entirely to the attention-grabbing heat in my backside.

'She's getting wet now,' observes Jerome, pausing for a moment. 'Your work will not be too hard.'

'What work?' I ask.

'Do I have to gag you? Your input is not required.' He gives me one more thwack of the flogger to make his point, then puts his big hands over my burning globes, absorbing their warmth. 'OK, I think she's ready for her first. Concentrate, Sophie. As soon as you know who this is, tell us.'

I hone my senses, putting myself on red alert. Footsteps approach, but their sound alone isn't enough to give me any clues.

One hand lands on my hip. It's medium sized, maybe? It glides up and holds one of my breasts. The touch is familiar, slightly tentative. Not Lloyd. This is a gentle caress, a considerate circling of my nipple.

I try to get his scent. It's fresh, vaguely piny. A burst of this coupled with the distinctive tenderness of his touch gives me my answer.

'It's Jake,' I state confidently.

'Aww.' I'm right. 'I wanted to last a bit longer than that! Do I still get a shag?'

This appeal is presumably met with a shaken head. My hotel lifeguard pats my flank and retires, injured.

'Well done. I don't know if there's a prize,' says Jerome. 'I guess that's up to the governor. Now for number two.'

My second candidate's technique could hardly be more different. He is almost rough in comparison. Before I realise he's there, he has pushed two fingers inside me. I yelp and try to push them off, but I am held fast.

'Take it easy!' I snap.

He removes them with an apologetic rub of my clit. His hand, which is even bigger than Jerome's, flattens against my pussy lips and he jigs it back and forth, giving my clitoris a quick spark every few moments. It's the perfunctory going-through-the-motions of a man impatient to get to the main event. A man who thinks he doesn't need to make an effort. A man who is arrogant and also built like Atlas on steroids.

'Lincoln.'

'What the fuck? You must have eyes in the back of your head.'

'No, but I've got nerve endings, like all women. Remember that.'

'This is fucking fixed, man.' My personal trainer slinks off, muttering.

I'm so sure that number three will be Lloyd that I almost call it out before Jerome says anything.

But then I think about it. Here I am, all taped up, wet and horny as hell, strapped in position. Do I really want to leave here without a fuck? I smile to myself, deciding to pretend not to recognise Lloyd until the final thrust hits home.

'Well, you are on a roll, as they say,' chuckles Jerome. 'You obviously know these gentlemen well. They didn't even need to get their cocks out. Let's see if you guess our third contender as quickly.'

I can almost smell him before he approaches, the Lloyd-ness of him. To me he smells of pure sex, but somebody else might identify subtle aftershave, extra-strong mints masking the faint evidence of cigarettes and something else, something I've never been able to put my finger on but which must be pheromonal.

But the third man, when he finally hovers behind me, smells of very strong and unfamiliar cologne – reeks of it, in fact. My senses rebel, disappointed in the extreme. I clench my pussy tight, unconsciously repelling the unwanted cock.

Hang on, though. I still have enough working brain cells to figure out that this could be a deliberate ploy. It could still be Lloyd, in olfactory disguise.

Working on this theory, I relax my pelvic floor and hold my breath, the better to recognise further clues.

What would Lloyd do, confronted with me in this position? Firstly, he would be riveted by my bum. He would grab handfuls of the reddened cheeks and squeeze them. Maybe he would kiss them – in fact, he certainly would. And he would give them an extra smack for luck while his tongue sought out the juices running below. Then he would take advantage of my helplessness to tease me, fingers almost hitting the spot but not quite, breathing over my clit but not allowing the all-important tongue tip to reach all the way. He would spread me wide and just look at me until I began to quiver and buck in my bonds.

I know he is trying to trick me now, because he does none of those things.

Instead, I feel knuckles graze the back of my thigh, the small exposed part at the top, very gently, tickling them. I try to wriggle away but he continues. I can't gauge hand size or anything from this – it could still be someone else. He isn't standing close enough for me to detect the underlying Lloyd-fragrance.

The knuckles move up and rest themselves in the crease between bottom and thigh. They sit there for a while, sinking in. I feel him shuffle forwards, closer.

I hear him take a breath.

It's Lloyd. Definitely, beyond doubt. That's the way he breathes.

He can't see my face-splitting smile, which is good, because I don't want him getting any ideas.

I think he deduces, maybe from the exhalation or the sudden relaxation of my shoulders, that I have figured out who he is, though, because from there on in he makes no attempt to hide his sexual identity.

His fingers uncurl and his Lloyd-sized hands flatten over the curve of my bum. There's a squeeze and I picture his lustful expression in my mind's eye. His thumbs reach between my cheeks and press into the tender inner flesh, making my sphincter jump in tense expectation.

Next I guess he has dropped to his haunches, because the sudden gusts of warmth on my clit suggest his breath in close proximity. I sigh with pleasure as his hands reach forwards to fondle my breasts. It's the way he does it, that unerring knowledge of what it takes to make my nipples unbearably tight and send waves of buzzy desire from them to my crotch.

He keeps them in hand and then there is one broad lick between my pussy lips, scooping up the juices, then his tongue circles my vagina, round and round, moving further in with each rotation until he is fucking me with it, shallowly and tormentingly, while I strain against the straps.

I can't take too much of this, and it isn't long before I start to protest, little whimpers that I hope convey the sentiment 'get on with it and fuck me, soldier'.

He buries his face in me, releases my breasts and moves his tactile investigations to my cunt, concentrating on that area with intense focus.

If I come, if he makes me come, it seems important that he should know I know it's him. But I don't want to let that information slip before I get his cock in me.

I mustn't come yet. I must get his cock in me.

'Please,' I mutter, hoping this will suffice.

But he doesn't reply, just keeps the finger and tongue pressure right up.

'Please,' I shout this time. 'Please. I need cock. Fuck me, please.'

He makes me wait a few seconds longer, but I know he won't be able to resist this direct plea, and my gamble pays off.

Even then, he maintains the pretence by putting on a

condom, even though we only use them for other partners now. For a split second, I panic that this is just someone who is very, very like Lloyd but not him. What if that's the case? What if Lloyd is watching me now, watching me mistake another man for him?

In my confusion, I try to close up my vaginal muscles, but when I feel the tip of his cock and his firm grip of my hips, the momentary anxiety is dispelled. This is Lloyd's cock. Even in its rubber sheath, I know its precise curve, weight, girth.

He knows I know.

He penetrates with exquisite slowness, as if making sure there is no room for error or doubt. If this doesn't give it away, he seems to be saying, nothing will. How many times have I felt this hard length stretch me until it is deep inside?

Not enough times. It could never be enough.

Now I can tell him. Now I must tell him.

Once I've clamped my muscles around him so tightly he can't escape, I whisper his name.

I hear his delighted intake of breath. 'You knew?'

'I knew. But you aren't going to stop now, are you?'

'You don't want me to pull out?' He makes a mock tug backwards and I moan.

'Nooo. Do me. Now, you bastard.'

He pulls almost all of the way back.

There is a second of unbearable tension.

Then he reaches for my hair and pulls it hard, slamming himself all the way back in simultaneously. My endorphins all whoosh together and race around my body, scalp to toes, filling me with wildness.

Halfway through the fuck, a skilled combination of hard and fast and slow and steamy, I realise that I am laughing. I am so stupidly delighted to be here, with Lloyd, in this grim stockroom in Soho, getting banged into the ground that it feels like my life's high point.

I know it's just my brain being strange, but I go along with it, let the joy surge and the rhythm guide me, all the way to an orgasm that starts small and builds, up and up and up, until it's too big for me and it spills out.

I am joyously impaled, happily immobile.

He comes almost immediately – my orgasm seems to have this effect on him a lot of the time – and lets go of my hair, putting his hands on my shoulders then clasping them around my neck. I feel his head drop on to the nape of my neck, resting there. His heartbeat pounds into my back, even through his shirt.

For a blissful moment, only our heavy breathing can be heard.

Then a spell is broken, and Jerome speaks. 'Well, that's three out of three,' he says. 'I guess you got your prize. Guys, shall we …?'

I'd completely forgotten they were there. They troop out and shut the door on us, leaving us to our recovery.

'What the fuck's that aftershave?'

'Cheap stuff on special offer in Superdrug.'

'You're not keeping it.'

'No.'

We yawn back into trembly pleasurable silence.

'When did you know it was me?' he asks just before I nod off in my restraints.

'When you breathed.'

'When I breathed? I was under the impression I did that fairly continuously.'

'No, you dolt. I didn't hear a thing for ages, then you took this breath, just – the way you do. And I knew.'

'Really?' I can hear the smile in his voice. 'You know me pretty well.'

'I think we've spent enough time in close proximity to be fairly clued up on each other.'

'Yeah. I'm wondering now if I'd recognise you that way. I think I would.'

'It was smell as well. Even underneath that terrible aftershave.'

'Ah, so that cunning plan didn't work.'

'Nope. Plus, it was so obviously going to be you anyway. It's like a classic fairy-tale plot. Three of these shall ye shag, or something. And you're the handsome prince all rigged out like a malignant goblin.'

He snorts. 'Thanks. Handsome prince, eh?'

'I'm not talking literally.'

'No, I suppose not. Well.' He raises himself, pulling out of me with slow care, and discards the condom. 'As far as handsome prince behaviour goes, there's one thing I haven't done.'

I hear buttons, belt buckle.

'What's that?'

He comes around to face me, crouching so our eyes are level. God, his are so blue. I sometimes forget how blue they are.

'Kiss the princess,' he says then fastens his lips to mine.

Corny as fuck, but it makes me feel annoyingly gooey, in amongst the kissing and the tonguing and the breathing in of his more familiar scent, now overpowering the cheap crappy cologne.

'Who are you calling a princess?' I croak, once he has kissed me into oblivion.

He just smiles and starts to untie me.

'I passed that one then?'

'I suppose you did. What was going on in that pub in Mayfair? That looked spectacular.'

'I'll tell you all about it at home. Oh shit!'

'What?'

I called his flat 'home'. But I can't draw his attention to that. 'I was supposed to be taking photographs tonight.' I flex my wrists, freed from their bonds.

'Well, the night's young.' He scoots behind me, unstraps my knees. 'It isn't eleven yet.'

'Yeah, but ...'

I stand, tentatively. Lloyd catches me when I sway, unsteady on my feet. I miss the drips on my thigh, the unmistakable evidence that Lloyd has been up to no good inside me. I want to do it again, sans condom.

'But?' He smoothes my hair, cups my face, kisses me again as if he can't help it.

'I'm in the mood now,' I murmur into his ear. 'Not for photography. I want to do it in a bed, without a condom, after you've removed that fucking awful aftershave with paint stripper if necessary.'

'Sounds like an offer I can't refuse,' says Lloyd. Once the last strip of tape has been peeled off, he slaps my bum. 'Get dressed then.'

Back at his flat, after politely taking our leave of Jerome, Jake, Lincoln and the collected clientele of Tied and Trussed, we shower and then pore over the pictures I'd sent to Lloyd on his phone.

'I really liked those knickers,' I sigh, looking at them fluttering in the South Bank breeze, then crumpled inside a sentry box.

'I'll get you new ones.'

'Do you think they're being used as evidence right now?' I muse. 'Military police swabbing them for DNA to find the identity of the Buckingham Palace drive-by knicker-thrower.'

Lloyd chuckles. 'Yeah. It was an opportunist crime, they'll say. Is it a one-off or is she a serial offender? They'll have you down in the barrack dungeons if they ever get hold of you.'

'Oh God, do you really think so?'

'Of course. There'll be an interrogation, but they've got you bang to rights, haven't they? If the knickers fit …'

'Like a lingerie-based Cinderella.'

'But there's no ballroom dancing with Prince Charming. Instead, you'll be convicted and sentenced.'

'To?'

He holds my eyes for a second. I watch his pupils skitter from side to side.

'What do you think you deserve, prisoner at the bar?'

Ah, I know and love this game: crime and punishment, without the crime. Just the fun part.

'Isn't it your role to pronounce sentence, Your Honour?'

'Well, I do believe it is. Wait there while I find my black cap.'

'Death? That's a bit harsh.'

'Hmm, you could be right. I might commute it to three hundred and seventy years of sexual slavery.'

'Penile servitude?'

'I wasn't going to say it …'

'But you were.'

'Yeah.'

Chapter Five

My skin looks like silk and my hair isn't the colour I always think of it as being and I had no idea the gap in my teeth was that prominent.

But none of these things jump out at me half as much as ...

'Look at your eyes, Soph. Look at the way you're looking at me.'

I can't think what to say. Instead, I laugh self-consciously. 'Velociraptor.'

'No, not that. Well, partly that. But there's something so ...'

'I need to tone up my arms.'

He puts the photograph on the desk and stares at me across the broad walnut surface. 'That's not all you need,' he mutters, picking up the envelope full of proofs and emptying the rest out.

'What do you mean by that?' I pick one up, one of me masturbating, and cringe at myself. 'What do I need?'

'A reality check.' He snatches the snap from my hand and waves it in front of my nose. 'What are you seeing here, Sophie? I don't think it's the same as what I'm seeing.'

'You really want me to answer that?' I feel sulky, as if I'm being told off. I slump in my chair and push out my chin.

'Yes, I do. Tell me what this is a picture of.'

'Me, wanking.' I say it aggressively, trying to make it as crude as possible.

'I need more detail.'

'Me, reaching my delicate fingers down to my slick intimate folds and manipulating them in order to achieve orgasm.'

'Forget the masturbation part. Who's the woman?'

I click my tongue and huff at him. 'What the fuck, Lloyd? I don't have time for bloody riddle-me-ree. What do you want from me?'

'Describe her.' His voice has got louder and more strident. He's going to shout at me in a minute. I'm preparing my walking-out-in-a-huff reflex.

'Describe her? Not as young as she was, not as tall as she'd like to be, flabby arms and thighs plus too much round the middle, hair needs cutting, pulling a really stupid face.'

Lloyd holds my eyes for a moment then turns the picture round to look at it.

'It's weird,' he says after long ruminations. 'I always thought you were really confident.'

'Nobody's really confident though, are they? Everyone puts it on.'

'I don't. I really am. I think I'm a pretty stand-up guy. I mean, I acknowledge that I have faults, principally my filthy mind, but I have an outlet for that. No, I mean, I would never describe myself in the terms you just used.'

'What, you'd say you were a handsome, buff stud, would you?'

'I think I'm looking pretty good these days, actually. Better than I did when we met. And do you know why that is?'

'No.'

'Because I think that's what you deserve. A man who

takes care of himself, who you can look at and think, Give me some of that.'

'Well, good for you. Thanks for your efforts, and all that. Much appreciated.'

'I know it is, Sophie. But why are you so down on yourself?'

'I'm not! I'm just modest and self-effacing, you know, like people are meant to be. I'm not in a black hole of self-loathing or anything like that.'

'I wish I could be sure of that. I had to trick you into getting these pictures taken. What is it about your own image that frightens you so much?'

'Lloyd Freud.' It's my 'shut up now' phrase whenever he gets too close to the bone.

'Don't. I'm not messing about. I want to know you, and I don't feel I really do.'

'Trust me, you're better off that way.'

'Why would I trust someone who won't let me know them?'

'So you don't trust me?'

He shrugs, flips the photograph aside. 'I do, in many ways. Most ways. I don't think you're sneaky or dishonest. But you're hidden, and there can only be one reason that you hide, and that's fear. What are you afraid of?'

'Monsters.'

He smiles against his will. 'I'm not a monster. Do you think I'm a monster?'

'Only in a good way.'

'Speaking of monsters …' He pushes another photograph towards me, one of the pair of us in the throes, but this one has something else paper-clipped to it. A business card.

'What's this?' I hold it up and read. '"Yours For the Night. Sexy, sophisticated brunette, new to escorting, will service your every need. To discuss rates, call –".'

I put the card down, eyebrows raised. 'You want to pimp me out?'

'What are you worth, Sophie? How much should I charge?'

'You know the answer to that. You know what I used to charge the guys in the hotel bar.'

'Yeah. Nothing. Is that what you're worth?'

'I'm not a commodity. That's why I didn't charge.'

'Well, for this task, you have to commodify yourself. So how much are you going to be worth?'

'I don't think I can say. Isn't it a buyer's market?'

'What are you selling?'

'My cunt.'

'No, you aren't. Not for escort work. You're selling a service to the purchaser's ego. He wants to be seen with a bright, smart, attractive, sexy woman. That's what he's paying for. If he wants cheap meat, he'll go to a cheap meat rack.'

'That's a horrible way of putting it. I haven't said I'll do this.'

'So a fail then?'

'No.'

'Right then. Put a value on yourself.'

'What's the market rate?'

'I don't know. Sky's the limit. I believe the average for an overnight is around seven hundred pounds.'

'Go for that then.' I shrug, not wanting to prolong the conversation.

'Sophie, are you thinking about this? I want you to really think about it.'

'I don't want to really think about it. Just line up the schmuck and I'll screw him. Task over.'

'No, that's not what the task's about.'

'It's about sex, isn't it? Like they all are. Lead me to the sex and I'll have it.'

'You really think sex is always about sex? Just that? The meeting of genitals?'

'I'm an uncomplicated girl.'

He laughs. 'That's the last thing you are, my love. Come on, now. Figures. Name your price. What's a night with Sophie Martin worth to a man so tragic that he has to pay for female attention?'

'What do you think? What am I worth to you?'

He shakes his head. 'Don't you dare.'

'You can't answer that?'

'No, I can't. And I don't pay for it. Never have, never would.'

'Well, look, I'm going for the market average. The seven hundred pounds. Though I can picture the guy asking for his money back. You can get one and half iPhones for that.'

'I wish I knew that you were joking.'

'You really want to do this?'

'Yes. I think it'll be … enlightening. Look, come around here.'

I wheel my chair round to his side of the desk, where he is firing up a website. I gasp and drop my jaw, as a large photograph of me naked – scanned from one of Sash's pictures – appears on screen. My face is pixelated, but the body is definitely mine.

'What the fuck, Lloyd?' I look around wildly, as if expecting a legion of sex-crazed punters to burst through the office door at any minute.

'Relax, it isn't live yet. This is the preview. When you give me the OK, I'll unleash it on to the World Wide Web and see what happens. Take a look at the site and tell me if you want to make any changes.'

I scan the text, but find it hard to process. I'm reading an advert for myself, essentially, but I don't really recognise the goods described.

'"Sophie is a classy, stylish young professional woman, able to hold her own in any social situation. She is well informed on a wide range of conversational topics, holding a university degree and possessing a dry sense of humour. Scratch the smartly suited surface, though, and you will find an uninhibited slave to pleasure."' I make a face at Lloyd. 'Did you write this?'

'What? I thought it was quite good.'

'"Sophie's sensual nature will delight and impress you. You will be back for more."'

'I just need to add in the rates.' Lloyd taps away on the keyboard. 'Overnights only. I'm not doing any hourlies. Not for this task. It's important that you do the full escort schtick, including conversation. Though probably the man will just want to talk about himself, if I know my high-end johns, which I do.'

'How?'

'That gambling den I used to work in was always full of them.'

'Right.' I squint at the screen. 'Have you airbrushed that picture?'

'Nope. It's one hundred per cent Sophie.'

I bite my lip. 'It's actually quite nice.'

'Yes, it is. Isn't it?' He turns to me and smiles, as if in pity. 'I'm almost sorry to give you this task. I think it's going to be ten times more difficult than any pure sex game would be. But I'm going to have a question for you at the end of it, and I want you to keep it in mind throughout.'

'What is it?'

'I charged seven hundred pounds for this. What should I have charged?'

'Is there a right or wrong answer to it?'

'Yes. And if you answer wrong, you fail.'

* * *

'His name's Conrad.'

Lloyd has cornered me on the third-floor corridor, where I have just emerged from the room of a guest hysterical about the lack of park view from her west-facing window.

'Conrad? German?'

'No, I don't think so. Anyway, that's his name, and he wants you.'

'Do I want him, though?'

'It doesn't matter, does it? He pays for you, he gets you.'

'So, where, when?'

'You're meeting him here, in the bar. He's a delegate at the Futures for Futures Traders conference.'

'A banker.'

'I suppose. Or a gambler. Actually, I have a feeling I might know him from the casino. Anyway, the cocktail bar at seven, then dinner at eight, then ...' He gives me a knowingly grotesque wink.

'That's only an hour from now.'

'I know. Better get ready, eh? He asked for a businesslike look with sexy underwear beneath. High heels, pencil skirt type of thing. Maybe put your hair up.'

'Did he have any other requests? Besides dress?'

'He gave me the impression he expected his money's worth.'

'Oh. And what's that? What's included for seven hundred pounds?'

'You decide.' Lloyd's hand lands on the small of my back. He doesn't exactly pull me close or hug me, but it's still a reassurance.

'I can say no?'

'Of course you can. But it'll probably mean a fail, that's all.'

'I might not tell you about it.'

'Conrad will tell me. My agency values feedback and offers partial refunds for clients who give it.'

'What a great agency.'

'Yeah, I think so. And I'll be in the room next door, OK? There's an interconnecting door. So if you need me ...'

'I won't need you.'

We knock foreheads, bump noses. It seems like the prelude to a kiss, but at the last moment he ducks to the side and whispers in my ear, 'One day you might.'

Then the lift pings and he hastens off to the ground floor, leaving me to contemplate my whoredom.

I go to change in Lloyd's apartment, a suite of rooms behind the ground-floor office. I have plenty of my own clothes and belongings there – I am an almost-resident. I wonder, while I select scant silky stuff from a bedside drawer, why this isn't enough for Lloyd. What difference would a formal change of status from frequent guest to cohabitee make? How long would it take for one or both of us to get complacent? At the moment we see each other because we want to. If I moved in properly, we would see each other because we had to. Surely living *and* working together would incur that kind of contempt-breeding familiarity I dread.

I choose an oyster shade for the basque and thong, having read somewhere that men find this 'classy' as opposed to the more obvious red and black stuff. But then, if he is paying for a whore, will he not expect me to dress like one?

106

I put back the oyster silk and bring out a truly tacky basque with scarlet satin and cheap black PVC panels. The matching knickers are crotchless, shiny and black, with a garishly red strip of lace running along the top. I snap some seamed stockings to the suspenders and pose, hands on hips, looking like a two-bit hooker, not that I understand what 'two-bit' means. To which two bits does the phrase refer? If it's T&A, then I am giving plenty of that. I twirl, impressed by the amount of flesh I flash, surprised as always at how much more naked than actual nudity really bawdy underwear makes you look.

Over this I don the aforementioned pencil skirt with crisp white shirt, pearls and three-inch-heeled black patent pumps. I twist my hair into a chignon and reapply my make-up so it is a little less subtle, the lips redder, the cheeks glowier, the eyelashes thicker and blacker.

Pouting in the mirror, I suddenly realise that I am going to be wining and dining with my purchaser in full view of my staff. While many of them know me of old, and remember the days when I used the hotel bar as my own personal pick-up joint, this is still a strangely squirm-inducing thought.

I have the feeling Lloyd will be partaking of an early evening libation in the cocktail bar, and I am right. As I swan in on my spike heels, I spot him in a corner with two off-duty waiters, drinking bottled beer and playing games on their phones.

I avoid eye contact and instead scan the bar, looking for likely woman-buyers. Almost immediately a man in a dark-blue suit rises from his barstool and nods at me. I walk towards him, taking in the swept back dark hair with its scattering of silver, the expensive tan, the watchful eyes. Between forty and fifty in age, well upwards of 100K in salary.

'Sophie?' He puts out a hand.

'You must be Conrad.'

We shake, like colleagues, business partners. Essentially, that's what we are. I try to view it as an equal relationship, but his next words undo my optimistic imaginings.

'Not bad,' he says, and those two words are like a deluge of cold, dirty water. *Not bad?* 'The picture was quite accurate for once.'

'Good.'

'I'll get you a drink, but I know you girls like your money upfront, so let's get that out of the way first.'

Somewhat to my alarm, he reaches into an inside pocket and pulls out an enormous wad of twenty-pound notes tied up with an elastic band.

'Oh God! Couldn't you have paid with a credit card?'

He stares, then sneers. 'Give my details to your pimp? I think not. Here.'

He hands me the money. I make to put it in my handbag, but he waves his hand and stops me.

'No, no, Sophie. You're new to this, aren't you? You count it. Make sure I'm not trying to fleece you. Here, come and sit at the bar to do your adding up and I'll get you a drink. What do you want?'

'Mineral water.' I snap off the elastic band and begin riffling through the notes. The barman is watching me from the corner of his eye. I shoot him an evil glare and he goes back to filling the glass washer. 'It's all there. Thanks.'

Again I reach for my bag, and again I am stopped, this time by Conrad's hand on my elbow.

'No. I have something I like my girls to do with that.'

My girls. I am one of many, a disposable cunt. I feel a little wet, perversely relishing the exquisite humiliation of my situation.

'With the money?'

'Yes. I want you to go to the ladies' room and stuff it into your underwear. Bra, knickers, stocking tops – I want them filled with notes. Go on then.'

I am mute for a moment, considering his outlandish request, but something about it appeals to me and I obey without question.

In the stall, I put the lid down on the toilet, fearful of flushing away a considerable sum, unbutton my shirt, take five twenties and arrange them, fan-shaped, in the left cup of my basque. The paper corners catch on my nipple, the notes being new and crisp, as if fresh from the mint. Was it good manners on his part to give me unused notes to put next to my most intimate areas? Perhaps I should take it as an act of consideration. Another hundred adorns my right breast. Five more to dispose of.

A circle of queens peer over the top of my left stocking top, while I reverse the notes on the right side and give five Michael Faradays a view of my skirt lining. The stripperish look this gives me is somehow satisfying.

I still have three hundred pounds to distribute. They will have to go in my knickers. That is what the money is going on, ultimately, after all.

I put five notes in the front elastic, the dry paper crackling over my shaved pubic triangle. The penultimate hundred flaps over my buttocks, the central twenty creasing into the crack of my arse.

There is only one fitting destination for the final hundred. I weave it inside the gaping PVC split, creating a kind of

DIY money gusset. I will have to make sure none of it works its way back out and falls between my feet, but the initial feeling is that the notes are secure, covering my pussy lips like prissy purple guardians of my virtue. I think this will please Conrad, and I know it will enhance the effect he wants – of my never, for one minute, being able to forget that he has bought me.

Between the front, back and bottom nests of money inside my knickers, my entire sex is papered with filthy lucre. Now I feel like a whore.

While the room is still empty, I emerge from the stall, walking carefully, rustling with each step, tiny prickly darts from the bill corners piercing my skin every time I move. I feel the notes inside my knickers shift, rubbing against my labia and my clit, while my nipples grow harder, pushing against the sharp edges.

The door bangs open and I hurriedly make a show of washing my hands, bending low over the sink, trying hard not to look turned on.

When the new arrival disappears into a stall, I put back my shoulders and prepare for my return to the bar.

Conrad watches me walk over, approving of my extra-careful sashay. If my thighs get too close, the notes rub together and threaten to pull each other out of their stocking-top cradle. I mustn't hold them too far apart, though, because that will threaten the delicate set-up in the crotchless part of my knickers. As for my breasts, their purple-stamped covering almost shows through the light silk of my shirt.

With a leafy shushing sound, I mount my bar stool, sitting down squarely on a couple of hundred quid.

Conrad smiles. 'Where did you put it?'

'Two hundred in my bra. Two hundred in my stockings. The rest in my knickers.'

'Nice. How does it feel?'

'Stiff, papery, dry. The corners are a little bit sharp.'

'Good. What about the money in your knickers? Do you have any inside, or is it all around the waistband?'

'Mostly around the waistband.' I pause. 'A hundred interleaved around the crotch. Because my knickers don't have one.'

He raises his eyebrows. When he speaks, his voice is very low. 'You're wearing crotchless panties?'

'Uh-huh.'

'Why did you choose those?'

'They seemed appropriate.'

'Why? I'm paying for an escort, Sophie. For the company of an attractive woman. You seem to imply that I'm paying you for sex. If that's what you think, why don't you work in a brothel?'

'What do you think this place is?' But I feel deflated even as I make the wisecrack. He is playing mind games with me, determined to make me feel as trashy and low as possible.

'Maybe, Sophie, I should swap you for a sophisticated lady. I'll hand you over to those sweaty-looking boys in the corner. They look as if they could use a good rummage in a willing cunt. What do you say?'

He indicates Lloyd and the waiters.

For that moment, I'm enormously tempted to say, 'Go on then. Give me to them.' Then I can disappear with Lloyd and fuck him raw while this entitled tosser talks bonuses and braggadocio with a real working girl.

Lloyd's half-smile when I look at him gives me nerve though.

'Who says I'm wearing them for you? I just happen to like a bit of fresh air, that's all.'

Conrad likes this answer. He laughs. There is a telltale lump at his crotch.

'Are you ready for some sophisticated dining then?' I wave a hand towards the Michelin-starred restaurant.

'Yes, I think I am. And I'm ready to start getting what I've paid for, Sophie. In full. Are you ready to start giving it?'

'Absolutely. Just say the word.'

He proffers an arm and we glide out of the bar, causing everyone we pass to look after us and mutter curiously about what's making that strange rustling noise.

In the restaurant, I sit with my knees half a foot apart, trying as hard as I can to minimise the noise of commerce emanating from my groin.

'Tell me about your other clients,' Conrad requests, though it's not really a request, more a sort of command. 'What was your last one like?'

I have to think. Before Lloyd, there were so many men. Which should I choose?

'My last one? My last two, I should say. A pair of clients. Professional footballers.'

'Misers. Couldn't they splash out on one each?'

'They weren't Premiership. Pretty low down the league, I think.'

Conrad puffs up his chest. 'I could afford a much more expensive girl,' he hisses, as if I have implied that he's poor. 'But value for money is what I'm all about. It's how I make my cash and it's how I keep hold of it. So, your two footballers? How did that play out?'

'They were strong, powerful men, but not very bright. They made me talk about *The X Factor* and other TV shows

I don't really have time to watch. Frankly, it was a relief to get to the bedroom.'

'And when you got there?'

'You want the full post-match report, or the highlights?'

'Highlights will be fine.'

'Champagne, Jacuzzi, then they took turns. Oral, straight sex, bit of sixty-nine.'

'No double penetration?'

'There was some talk of it, but they were both too drunk to get it up again.'

'I love the way you talk about it. As if it's just another boring night down at the local. I could listen to whores talk shop forever. It turns me on.'

'What expectations do *you* have for tonight?'

The waiter appears, pours a good wine and takes our orders. Once he leaves the table, Conrad leans forwards. 'I expect to fuck you. Tell me now, are your nipples hard?'

'Yes.'

'And your pussy – is it wet?'

'A bit.'

'Are you creaming all over those twenty-pound notes? They were pristine when I gave them to you. Bet they aren't now.'

'Can I ask you about the other girls you've paid?' I feel a need to turn the tables on him. Does he expect his girls to desire him? Does he think my wetness is for him? I want to tell him that it isn't – it's for the situation, purely and simply.

'No. But you can tell me what you like doing in the bedroom.'

'Aren't we supposed to be making light conversation? Dinner table chitchat?'

'I'm calling the shots, Sophie, or had you forgotten? He who pays the piper ...'

How is getting fucked for money the same as taking requests for a tune? But I don't challenge it.

'You name it, Conrad, and I'll do it. If it's legal and won't result in illness or injury, I'm probably up for it.'

'That's good to know. Sometimes I can be a little … unusual in my tastes.'

'What are your tastes? Costumes? Kink? Role-play?'

'I think I'll wait until we get to the bedroom, if you don't mind.'

'It doesn't matter if I do mind, does it?'

'No.'

I finish my wine and make to pour myself another, but he puts a hand over my glass, shaking his head.

'Can't have you getting tipsy, Sophie,' he says lightly. 'That's not what I'm paying you for, now, is it?'

So what is he paying me for? If it isn't for sex, or companionship, or pleasure? What is it?

***

In the bedroom, I am ready to find out.

Lloyd is next door. I am not in any danger. I repeat this to myself when Conrad sits himself on the bed and makes me stand in front of him. He stares at me for so long that I feel distinctly spooked.

'Still nice,' he says to himself. 'Very. Take off your shirt, Sophie.'

I unbutton it and pull it from my waistband, shrugging it over my shoulders until it falls on the floor. The garish basque with its topping of twenties is revealed.

'Nice, I like the way you've arranged the money. I like it even better when I make the girls crumple it up and stuff it in like that. The last girl's tits looked huge and there was a big spare-tyre effect where her knickers were full of balled-up paper. She was so embarrassed.' He laughs. 'Some of them went right up her cunt. Take off your skirt.'

The pencil skirt slips down. Black PVC, scarlet satin and purple paper clash together over my pale skin.

'I like that. And you put it in your crotch, you say? Come over here and show me.'

I move closer. He motions me around so I turn my back to him then bend over, exposing the money-patched split to his view.

'That's superb.' He reaches out and runs his fingertips over the paper, pressing it against my hidden clit. 'I'm going to ask you to get on all fours on the bed, just like that. No, keep the heels on, they're fine.'

I watch Conrad through my arms and legs as he picks up his briefcase and opens it. He doesn't seem to be in a hurry to undress. Is he not going to fuck me?

From a fabric pocket in the case lid he withdraws a long thick dildo. He did ask about double penetration – it seems that must be an interest of his. I tighten my sphincter in anticipation. Should I charge more to be fucked by two cocks, even if one of them isn't real?

Lloyd's question: *How much should I have charged?*

As Conrad approaches, dildo in hand, I notice that the bulge in his trousers has flattened somewhat. Where is his erection? Why am I posing here with my arse up and money stuffed down my knickers if it doesn't even give him the horn?

He reaches over and removes the money from my crotch, exposing my pussy to his gaze. I wait for a finger to touch me or pinch my clit or penetrate my vagina, but that doesn't happen.

I look over my shoulder, curious to know what he is doing.

He is wrapping the money around the dildo, securing each note with the next one, until the entire implement is plastered with purple and images of the Queen's head. Then he takes a condom and slides it over the top, holding the money tight in place, keeping it clearly visible through the transparent latex.

'Head down,' he growls, noticing my interest. 'Bum up. Thighs wide.'

He joins me on the bed, introducing the tip of the dildo to my widespread labia, rubbing it around in my juices, lubing it up ready for the long journey into inner space.

I want to talk, very badly, to make some remark about this being the ultimate metaphor for capitalism, but something tells me he doesn't want to hear my opinion. I take it in silence when the broad rubber-clothed invader is shoved none too gently up inside me.

'This is what I like, whore,' he says in a low hypnotic voice, sending his thick hard representative up to the hilt. 'I like to watch your cunt used for money. By money. Watch you getting fucked with the dirty cash you're going to take from me. You won't be able to spend it without thinking of what it did to you.'

He thrusts hard and I start to pant. I can't work out whether or not it feels good. At the moment, it feels so strange, so disconnected, that I don't think my nerve endings have worked out whether they're meant to be experiencing pleasure or discomfort.

'Touch yourself.'

My nerve endings know how to play when I put a finger on my clit. They veer happily over to the pleasure side of the street. While I flick, Conrad speaks again.

'This is the only thing that gets me hard these days. To buy, to pay, to watch my money fucking a whore. To have, to own, to take, to possess. Do you know how that feels, Sophie? Of course you don't. You're a whore. You get had, owned, taken, possessed. You're the item on the shelf. I choose to take you or leave you. Choice is such a turn-on, Sophie. Choice, power. You'll never know how sweet it can be.'

His dildo slides over and over my G-spot, pushing me beyond the capacity for speech. If I could speak, what would I say? *Fuck you* is all that springs to mind. Perhaps it's just as well I'm mute at the bottom of my familiar path to orgasm.

Fuck you, asshole, tattoos through my mind as the combination of clit-strumming and dildo-fucking does its damnable work. And then I realise that there is something I can do to take some power away from him. An easy thing, a passive thing, a thing he won't even know about, but will make me feel happier.

I can fake it.

'I'm going to keep doing this, Sophie,' he says, 'until you come. You're going to come, right there, full of a wad of my money, come all over it. Dirty, dirty whore.'

I shout, then sigh in a creditable imitation of how I sound when I'm coming on all fours with a dildo in my cunt. I have a large bank of memories from which to draw.

'Ooh, hard, fuck me hard, you banker.'

I hold my breath for a moment. Too much? Will he cotton on to my dramatics?

No. He chuckles, obviously pleased with himself. 'Think of that when you're handing a twenty over at the bar later. Think of what else it bought. I love watching whores come with my money inside them. Love it more than anything. Get up and suck me.'

The dildo is withdrawn. Still tense and tight with the need to come, quashing it down as hard as I can, I get up on my knees and face Conrad.

He's hard now all right. Apparently, this is what it takes to get him there.

My resistance turns, for a moment, to pity. What a stunted person he must be. But then I wonder how I can have the brass neck to judge another, given my own limitations in the field of normal human behaviour. He's just a cock. I'm just a mouth. So, let's have oral sex.

He frees his cock, puts his hand on my head and pushes it down.

I suck and lap at it while, overhead, a commentary on how he amassed his fortune bores me enough to make me concentrate hard on giving a truly A-grade blow job. My tongue tip flits and glides; my throat opens to accept his full length. I perform a full-scale ravaging of this dick's dick until, somewhere in the middle of a story about ripping off another trader, his voice breaks and he spurts into my mouth, filling it with salty cream.

I'd like to say his semen tasted of wealth or power or something, but it didn't. It tasted like spunk.

I swallowed it and looked up. 'Was that to your satisfaction?'

'Not bad. You can do it again later.'

I remove the money from my bra and throw it down on the bed. 'Actually, I won't.'

I repeat the action with the notes – not so neatly arranged now – in my stockings. Money drifts and floats around the duvet.

'I beg your pardon? I've paid you for the whole night.'

'I'm giving you your money back.' I relieve my knickers of Her Majesty's disapproving face.

'You can't do that. Don't you need it?'

'No. I don't. Sorry to disappoint – better luck with the next woman you buy. Only please don't kid yourself you're buying the woman. You're buying her cunt, her mouth, maybe her arse. That's all.'

I hum a few bars of 'Can't Buy Me Love' as I pick up my clothes from the floor.

Conrad, still post-coital and visibly flabbergasted, doesn't move from his station on the bed.

'That thing with the money in the underwear, though,' I tell him, turning from the interconnecting door, which I'm about to knock on. 'That was good. Creative. Turned me on. I might do that one again. Bye.'

'I'm going to have strong words with your pimp!'

I knock on the door. 'Please do. He's right here, as it happens.'

Lloyd answers the door. I'm never exactly displeased to see his face, but I could kiss it all over fifty times right now.

'Is there a problem?' he asks, peering out at Conrad, still kneeling on the bed with his deflated prick on his thigh and a beet-red face.

'She's walked out on me. I won't be recommending her. I'm going to put a one-star review on your website.'

'I'm very sorry, sir. I see she's refunded you. May I recommend Especial Escorts if you still want company – here's their card.' He tosses one over and shuts the door on the outraged banker, locking it behind him.

'Sophie, Sophie, Sophie,' he says softly, holding me at arm's length, his eyes bright with all kinds of things. It occurs to me that I'm still tautly pre-orgasmic. I hook an ankle around his calf, trying to bring him closer. 'Do we have a fail?'

'Never mind that,' I whisper, rubbing my head against his

shoulder. 'Something started that didn't get finished.'

'Was he lousy?'

'He was bad. The situation could have been hot, but he took it too far. You would have done it so much better.'

'Would I?'

'Yeah. Do it, Lloyd. Pretend to pay for me.'

'What's pretend about it? You've just lost us seven hundred quid. You're going to be paying that off, starting now.' He spins me round and gives me a gentle shove towards the bed.

I can't get there fast enough.

I bounce on to the bed in my basque, stockings, heels and crotchless knickers – all minus the money now – and kick up my legs.

'Fuck me!' I implore, flinging out my arms like an operatic diva. 'How many unnatural acts add up to seven hundred pounds?'

Lloyd, undressing a few feet from me, his eyes trained on my lewd display, simply curves one side of his mouth upwards, calculating. 'That's going to take years to pay off,' he says. 'I'm very mean, you see. I won't pay more than a pound for any given act. Perhaps you should seek a better-paying client?'

'Nah. I'm cheap as they come.'

'Good.' He notices something. 'Crotchless? Classy.'

'He didn't like them. He didn't even fuck me. Well, he used a dildo, but does that count?'

Lloyd positions himself above me, looking down the length of my tackily attired body. 'What else did he do?'

'He made me put all the money in my underwear. Not in the bedroom – while we were downstairs in the bar.'

'Really? That's why you were walking in that weird way. I like it. Proper kinky.'

'Can you fuck me now, please?'

'I'll fuck you when I please. Since I'm the buyer. First, I want to inspect my purchase.'

He pulls down the cups of the basque, before running fingers and then tongue over my tight, hard nipples. I shudder and arch my back underneath him, spreading my legs in silent, urgent invitation, but he takes his time, assessing the span of my waist, the curve of my hips, the angle of my collarbone, before moving lower.

'So far, I'm impressed,' he says.

He lifts my legs to better explore my most intimate spots, makes me keep them bent with pussy and arse on display.

'Was the dildo big?' he murmurs, digging three fingers inside my vagina. 'Did it go all the way up here?'

'Yeah,' I gasp. 'And there was money wrapped round it.'

'Money? What the fuck? Weird.' But his fingers are so smooth, so sensitive, so perfectly attuned to my quivering, pulsing cunt that I feel the first surges of orgasm again.

'Lloyd!'

'I know. It's OK. Come.' He adds a slowly circling thumb to my clit, ensuring that I can't do anything else.

I toss and turn energetically, while his hand continues coaxing the climax out of me, not releasing me until the very dregs of ecstasy have leaked from their source.

'Don't go to sleep,' he chides, tapping my cheek until I open my eyes.

'Sorry,' I mumble, lifting my arms to wrap them around his neck. 'You'll want your money's worth.'

'Are you going to answer my question now?' he asks. He lifts my bum and opens me wider, ready to penetrate.

'Your question?' My mind is blurred, full of heat and skin and lust and satisfaction.

'How much should you have charged for that?'

'I think I answered that, didn't I? When I gave the money back. Oh, please.'

I try to push myself on to him, but he holds back.

'So you think you're worth nothing? Is that what you were saying?'

'You know it isn't. I was saying that no money was worth what he wanted from me.'

'You're worth more than that?'

'I suppose.' Suddenly, I am doubtful. Am I? Is that what I meant?

'So you should have charged more?'

'No. I shouldn't have charged anything. I'll only do it if I want to. And if I want to, I won't charge. That's always been my way, Lloyd, you know that.'

'I know that. I just needed to know if it was because you thought you were worthless ... or priceless.'

'I don't think I'm priceless, but ...'

'Don't argue about it. It's the right answer. I'm going to pass you on that. Even if you did fail the rest.'

He smiles down, looking so idiotically proud of me that I want to slap him. It's hardly a Nobel-winning achievement, is it?

'Thanks, so can you get on and fuck me now?'

'Your wish is my command.'

Chapter Six

'Do you ever see that guy Dr Lassiter these days?'

Lloyd's question appears idle, but I've learned that Lloyd doesn't waste words, and there will be method behind the chitchat.

I think back, trying to recall the last time I had an appointment with the professional disciplinarian.

'You know, I think it's been a while. Maybe eight, nine months. Since we got together, that vacancy has disappeared. Why?'

'Just wondering.' Lloyd shifts on the sofa, switches TV channels.

'No, really, why?' I remove the remote control from his hand and keep my fingers twined in his, literally pressing for information

He clicks his tongue. 'Suspicious mind, Sophie. I bet Dr Lassiter knows a cure for that.'

'Dr Lassiter's cures are all the same. They always involve a sore bum.'

'I know. I've consulted him myself.'

I'm shocked for a moment. What does that mean? 'What? You've met him? He only takes female submissives.'

'Not like that.' He shakes his head in disbelief at my unlikely presumption. 'I mean, he's given me some good advice. I've spoken to him in the bar after a couple of his ... sessions. When we first got together, I knew you liked a good beating, but I was no expert in giving them, so I thought I'd ask one.'

'Did you really?' I'm fascinated to think of Lloyd as a pupil of the dry corporal punishment fetishist. I try to imagine how the conversations went ... were there lessons? Practical sessions?

'Yeah. While you were off comparing cane stripes with Rachael, I was taking instruction from the don. He knows his stuff, doesn't he?'

'I ought to call Rachael, meet up for a drink with her. Haven't seen her in yonks.'

'Ah well.' An impish grin breaks out. I have learned to fear these. 'That might be on the cards already, actually.'

I knew it!

'What have you done?'

'I bumped into Dr Lassiter in reception the other day. We got talking. He gave me the best idea for the next challenge.'

'Oh God. Go on.'

Lloyd's arm creeps around my shoulders. He pulls me tight while he whispers the details of my doom into my ear. 'Dr Lassiter and Rachael are members of a club.'

'I don't think I need to ask what kind of a club, do I?'

'I think your first guess would be accurate. It's called Kinky Cupcake.'

'Kinky what?'

'I know, weird name. Apparently there's a coffee shop attached. Anyway, he said, he and Rachael were big fans of this club and had had several amazing nights there. Was I interested in joining? It's by recommendation only, but if I were up for it he'd put my name forward. I said, "Why the hell not? Can Sophie join too?" Of course, he said. So he's gone there today to register us.'

'I see. And the challenge?'

'We've done bondage. We've done spanking. We've done domination and submission. But we've never done it in public. Have we?'

'That time you handcuffed me to the balcony ...'

'That doesn't count. It was dark. Nobody could see you.'

'So, you want us to go to this club so you can do stuff to me while people watch?'

'Essentially. Does that appeal?'

Of course it appeals. I have a well-developed submissive side, so this has been a long-term fantasy. Whether it will be quite so exquisite in reality remains to be seen.

'It could do. I need more details.'

'We have to go to the club to meet the owners – kind of an interview. Dr L. will let us know when we can do that. Then, I guess, we pick a club night and just turn up. Anything goes, apparently. I'll make a list.'

'I know your lists.'

'I think you'll find this pretty easy, compared to that last gig at least, so I'm going to have to get my diabolical thinking cap on.'

'The one with the skull and crossbones.'

'Yeah. That one. In the meantime, perhaps we should rehearse. A dry run. Though dry might not be the right word.'

'Ho ho.'

'I don't like your tone. Fetch the hairbrush. And be quick about it.'

The resounding smack on the bum with which he sends

me on my way stings pleasantly all the way to the bedroom. But that's not the only cause of the tingly throb in my pussy. The ghost of future kink hangs over the immediate scene, heating it up with the promise of depravity.

***

'I know they'll accept you with open arms. It's me I'm worried about.' Lloyd smoothes down his hair for the thousandth time and practises a cold-eyed stare into my mirror compact. 'I don't even own a pair of leather trousers,' he complains. 'They'll see straight through me.'

'Don't be stupid. There's no correlation between the amount of leather worn and the effectiveness of the dom.' I lower my voice a little. This tube train is packed.

'Don't call me that. It makes me feel weird.'

'What, a dom? That's the part you have to play.'

'I know. But it sounds inhuman. I don't like it. I'm just a person who likes to mess about with whips from time to time.'

'So you're a dom. Don't make such a fuss about it. At least you don't have to be a sub! That's even worse. Makes me sound like a baguette.'

An unforced laugh chases away Lloyd's nervous witterings. 'Yeah, it's pretty horrible. Can't they think of some better names? Sexier? Can't I be a ... tetherer. A cuffer. A whipper. No, there isn't anything, is there? I'll stick with dom.'

'As for me, what can I be? Pain slut? Fuck toy? No, it's all horrible. Submissive it is.' I sigh. 'What about master and servant?' I start humming the Depeche Mode tune. 'I quite like that.'

'So do I. Except you'll never in a million years be my servant. Or my slave. Alas and alack.'

'You can whip me all you like but I'm not ironing your bloody shirts. We've had this conversation before.'

'No we haven't. I've never asked you to iron a shirt. Why would I run a hotel with a massive laundry and then iron my own shirts?'

'OK then, you can whip me all you like but I'm not ... er ...'

'The point, Sophie, is taken. Like you will be.'

'Sh. That man's looking at us. I think he knows where we're going.'

'Maybe he's going there too. Maybe he knows that, underneath that coat, you're wearing nothing but a rubber dress and thigh-highs.'

'*Lloyd.*'

'Oh, this is the stop. And he's getting off here too, how about that?'

We follow the gentleman in question along the platform and up the escalator. I am grateful for my long coat as we ascend through a draughty hall, past ad after ad for West End shows and exhibitions.

Thankfully, Kinky Cupcake is not too distant from the tube station, tucked away in a warren of tight-knit streets and alleyways full of transformed warehouses and industrial buildings. Sweatshops are now art galleries, grain stores have become artisan cheese shops. The raggedy waifs and strays who used to wander these cobbles have been replaced with students and young professionals trying to use their iPhones and ride their bicycles simultaneously.

We swerve one such, Lloyd pulling me into the wall and saving me from a knickerless sprawl.

'You OK?' He pats my hips, rubbing the lining of my coat against the smooth rubber that encases them.

'Yeah, think so. Is this it?'

We look up at an archway over a large black door. There is no name on the wall, nothing to identify the building. But it's the right address.

'What do we do? Knock?'

'I suppose.'

Lloyd knocks on the battered black door, then stands back and smoothes his hair down yet again, waiting for admission.

'I wish I knew what this interview thing was about,' he mutters, then there is rattling and jangling from the inside lock and we grip each other's fingers instinctively.

The door opens a crack – a face appears above us, impassive and silent.

'Oh, the password!' says Lloyd. 'Um, Lacoste.'

The door opens a little wider and a hand, presumably belonging to the owner of the face, waves us in.

'Names?' asks the doorman. Maybe Lloyd could borrow some leather off him – he certainly seems to have the full set.

We supply our identities, which are ticked off against a list.

'You have an appointment,' the doorman tells us, which we already knew, but we follow him up some stairs to a very ordinary-looking waiting area. At least, so it seems, until I realise that the magazines on the table aren't exactly *Woman's Own*.

'Nice gimp mask.' I pick one up and show it to Lloyd. 'That'd suit you.'

'Don't. I feel naked. Do you think I should get a tattoo?'

'Lloyd, you're really nervous, aren't you?' I take his hand and hold it tight. It's clammy.

'I feel like I'm going to be asked to prove something. I feel like I'm going to be found out.'

'What could they possibly find out about you? We do this stuff! We do it for real. You're as eligible to join this place as Lassiter is, or Max Mosley, or … anyone.'

He smirks. 'I'd rather not end up on the front page of the papers.'

A door opens and a sleek, beautiful woman in a perfectly cut trouser suit smiles out at us. 'Lloyd? Sophie? Please come in. We're always so delighted to meet new members,' she continues, as we cross the deeply carpeted floor of her office. 'Take a seat. My partner, Mal, will be up shortly. Can I get you anything to drink?'

Neither of us wants to be nursing glasses or hot cups while we discuss the most intimate aspects of our fantasies, so we both shake our heads.

'You were recommended by Dr Lassiter, I see.' She reads from a computer screen. 'One of our most distinguished members. He runs a Sunday evening class in disciplinary techniques – perhaps you'll find that of interest?'

'We've both learned a lot from Dr Lassiter,' I say.

She looks at me – a proper head-to-heels sweep of the eyes – and smiles. 'I'm sure. So you're a couple?'

'Yes.' Lloyd answers this one, with a really piercing glance in my direction.

'Are you lifestyle players?'

'No, just bedroom dabblers really. Looking to go a bit deeper.'

'Oh, lovely, I do like it when we have relative newbies to the scene. So many delights to be found.'

She has the kind of throaty, theatrical delivery that could very easily sound false, but I believe her. Her enthusiasm for this seems nothing but genuine.

'Which way round is your dynamic? Or do you switch?'

Lloyd clears his throat. 'We did try switching, actually, but it wasn't something we really went for. So I do and she's done to.'

'Oh, yes, a nice way of putting it. But of course, the gifts are reciprocal. This balance of power can't work with partners who don't respect each other as equals.'

'That's so true!' I'm quite excited by her words, more so than I would have expected to be. 'One thing I hate is when people assume that the submissive partner is weak. That's such a simplistic, wrong-headed way of looking at it.'

'Oh, I couldn't agree more. Submission takes a great deal of courage and strength. For one thing, as a woman in today's world, it's so often considered taboo to admit that you like a man to take control in the bedroom.'

'I kind of buried that side of myself for years,' I continue. I'm so excited I can hardly get the words out. I feel close to this woman, whose name I don't even know – it's like an instant infatuation. 'I felt guilty and disloyal for even thinking it.'

'And yet, what do you have to feel guilty for? A preference that may well be innate and, even if it isn't, there's nothing you can do to change it. Perhaps one day we'll be able to enjoy our sexuality without fear of judgement. Until then – here we are.'

She leans over sympathetically, and the door opens to admit a man with vampire teeth.

This throws me off my stride a little.

'They're real.' He answers the unspoken question with a big flashing smile. 'I had them filed down. So many subs go for a vampire.'

'But you don't actually ...?' Those fangs could do some damage.

'Ah ...' He smiles enigmatically and proffers a hand. 'Mal. Not short for Malcolm.'

'What is it short for?' asks Lloyd, standing to shake the guy's hand.

'Malfeasant.'

'Nice name,' I observe, taking my turn to glad-hand him. 'I'm Sophie. This is Lloyd.'

'Great to meet you. So, how are we playing this?'

The question is addressed to O, who notices my slight stiffening at it.

'Dr Lassiter will have told you, I assume, that we require a small demonstration of your commitment to this practice,' she says. 'It helps keep the dirty sniffers of the press off our doorstep. With our elite membership, there's rather a lot of potential for blackmailers within these walls. Of course, we trust Dr Lassiter's judgement. All the same, it's a rule of the house.'

Mal clarifies the issue. 'So what's it going to be, my dears? A spanking? Nice bit of bondage? Maybe a spot of humiliation?'

I hope Lloyd has something prepared. We haven't discussed this. I thought it was meant to be an interview, not a practical.

'Bloody hell, baptism of fire,' I mutter, shooting him daggers.

'You can say no,' he reminds me in a whisper.

'I'm not falling at the first fence. What are we doing?'

He raises his voice to answer. 'Sophie, I want you to stand up and remove your coat.'

I stand up. The tops of my boots tickle my naked thighs, reminding me of the pale expanse stretching from there to the too-high hem of the rubber dress.

I shrug off the coat and hand it to Lloyd, turning away

from my audience as I do so and maintaining my huddled half-crouching stance, trying to make myself as small and invisible as possible.

'Up straight and face our examiners,' he orders briskly. This means I have to break my eye contact with Lloyd. I really, really don't want to do this. But I do it.

'Oh, we're not examiners,' coos O. 'Don't make the situation more formal than it needs to be. You do look lovely, dear – gorgeous rubber. Call us by our names, Lloyd, if you're comfortable with that.'

'OK,' says Lloyd from behind me.

I look at a distant spot on the wall behind O and Mal, blurring out their rapacious smiles and lustful eyes. My shoulders are back, thrusting out my tightly confined breasts. The bottom of the dress barely skims my pussy; it would only take the fractional raise of a leg to expose everything.

'Put your hands on your head, Sophie.'

The movement lifts the dress ever so slightly, just enough to give my new friends a glimpse of shaved lip. The tension created by the latex is unbearably sexy, as is the knowledge of my inescapable exposure. I feel the wetness, the unruly pulse of desire. Lloyd was right. This challenge is going to be easy after all.

'Now turn around slowly.'

I perform a slow rotation, trying hard not to stick my bum out too far, though I'm sorely tempted. With one hundred and eighty degrees completed and Lloyd's face back in my register – an evilly intent, highly focused face – he commands me to stop.

'Bend over,' he says.

I won't look at him. I won't make a face at him. I mustn't give him failure ammunition.

So I lower my eyes to the ground and carefully let my upper torso follow suit. I feel every upward millimetre of my hem's progress over the curve of my bottom until it sits nice and square in the middle of my outthrust cheeks, showing everything beneath.

'I'd value your opinion of her arse,' says Lloyd politely.

'Wonderful shape,' purrs O. 'So full and round.'

'The most spankable I've seen in a long time,' is Mal's verdict. 'Though it's a bit pale for my taste. I prefer them redder.'

'That can be arranged.' *Lloyd!*

'Of course, it's your call.' Thanks, Mal.

O has a question now. 'What kind of things do you like to do to that delicious bottom, Lloyd? How much use does it get?'

'Oh, plenty. Obviously, like Mal, I like to see it turn red. I like the heat, especially if I put my cock inside afterwards.'

'Ah yeah, there's no beating the feeling, is there?' says Mal yearningly.

Never mind red arses, I'm pretty sure my face is that shade of which they so approve. Just as well it's beyond their view. In the meantime, my cunt is dripping. Surely they'll notice soon? Oh God. I clench and unclench the muscles, praying that this will help me keep my secret.

'Fucking a good hot red arse, you mean?' says Lloyd, still in this insane polite chitchat kind of tone. 'Absolutely. My favourite.'

'Do you use butt plugs?'

'Oh yes, she loves those. For pleasure and for discipline. She wore one behind the reception desk all morning once after one particular episode of naughtiness.'

Oh, I remember that. Remember the squirming on the

chair, the growing pool of liquid lust in my knickers, the perma-blush on my face as I greeted each guest. He's such a glorious pervert. They really are going to see the shining evidence of my arousal very soon.

'I must visit your hotel,' remarks O. 'Dr Lassiter recommends it very highly.'

'Thank you,' says Lloyd, then his tone changes and I know he is addressing me. 'Stand up. Turn back around.'

Rather than slide back down over my curves, the latex remains, slightly rumpled, halfway up my bum. As my eyes find that distant spot on the wall once more, Lloyd reaches out an idle hand to caress the bared skin. I only just catch the moan in my throat, replacing it with a shuddery exhalation.

'Spread your legs, Sophie. Yes, that's it. Little bit wider. Good.'

My pubic triangle is on display, lips parted to uncover the swollen red bud within. Lloyd, stroking my bottom and running a finger up between the cheeks, pushes me forwards an inch or so.

'Show them,' he says softly. 'Show them how wet you are.'

I tilt my pelvis, angling it so that my sex is as fully viewable as possible.

'Take your hands off your head and hold your lips open for them.'

I obey, feeling as if all my blood is rushing from crotch to face and back again, draining every other part of my body. My legs feel weak and my arms start to tremble.

'She's very wet,' he tells them, dipping fingers lightly into my juices.

'She likes to be put on show.' Mal is leaning forwards, his face livid red. 'That's a great sign. She'll be brilliant at the master/slave events. Tons of potential.'

Lloyd, standing behind me now, lifts his fingers to my mouth and has me lick them, tasting myself on his warm skin. 'You're doing so well,' he whispers into my ear. 'I'm proud of you.'

I hate that his expression of pride makes my chest swell and my heart constrict. I hate that. I want to be indifferent to his fucking pride. Why can't I be indifferent to it?

'O, Mal, do you like her dress?'

Mal grunts his approval while O repeats her assertion that it's 'gorgeous'.

'Perhaps you'd like to see it at closer quarters, then. Would you like to feel it?'

They don't need asking twice. Like big cats on the veldt, they stalk and circle their prey, drawing closer.

Lloyd stands aside to let them surround me. 'Touch her,' he invites.

O's elegant hand runs along my side, from my shoulders to my hips, snagging at the rumpled part of latex and moving beyond to land flat-palmed on my naked flesh.

'I'd like to feel her tits,' she says to Lloyd. 'Are they heavy?'

'Find out for yourself.'

She weighs them in considering hands, tending to them so gently. She has to be a submissive. There is no pinching or squeezing from her fingertips.

Meanwhile, Mal is all about my arse. He crouches behind me and I can feel his stare boring into the tops of my thighs. He holds me by the top of my thigh-highs and sniffs the leather. I feel his nose drift upwards on to my quivering flanks. When he buries his face in my bottom, Lloyd calls time.

'I see you approve.'

'Thank you for letting us examine her,' says O, releasing

my breasts and planting a daring quick kiss on my cheek. 'She's delightful.'

'Delightful,' echoes Mal, sounding a bit strained. When he comes back around to the front, I note a bulge in the tight leather pants.

'One more thing,' says Lloyd, to me. He puts one hand on my shoulder from behind and delves between my legs with the other, giving my clit a good rub, swishing his fingers in the surrounding gush. 'You need to come, don't you, love?'

It feels so heavy, so tender, so shamefully needy. I do, I do, but must it be in here?

It seems it must.

'Oh,' I whimper. 'Please.'

'Show our friends how you like to touch yourself,' he says.

It sounds like a request. It sounds as if I can say no. But I know different.

I hide my face in his arm at first, then the command tone comes out.

'Sit in the chair, Sophie, legs apart. Now.'

He releases me so I can obey the order. My half-naked bottom meets the cold wood of the seat. I widen my thighs, show my glistening wares to these two complete strangers while Lloyd hovers over my shoulder, his hand on the back of my neck.

'Show them. Masturbate for us, love. We want to see you come.'

I shut my eyes. Part of me wants to be in this scene so very much, and yet another part of me wants to run away. Lloyd, helpfully, cuts down my options. He strokes the nape of my neck with gentle knuckles, leaning behind me, murmuring supportive filth.

'You want this, Sophie, you want to be watched. Get your fingers on that big fat clit and give them a show.'

I follow his instructions blindly. He's right, it's so fat and full and juicy, so ready to be touched.

'Would she like a vibrator?' offers O.

'No, fingers only this time. Come on, Sophie. Show them what a willing wanton thing you are. She'll do it with anyone, you know? She's the whore you don't have to pay for. Everyone knows it. Everyone knows they can have her just by looking at her. She's opened her legs for so many men, she's the town bike, the good time that was had by all, aren't you, Soph? But despite all that, she's still mine, when it comes right down to it, she's still mine because I know how to do it right, because I know her.'

His words and my fingers work together, a key and lock, opening my exquisite shame, setting fire to it until it combusts into an orgasm of such complex potency it blows my mind. What makes me come? Is it the simple manipulation of my clit? Is it Lloyd's words, his voice, his savagely accurate summation of me? Is it the fact that I am watched and laid bare to two strangers, who will now know exactly what I am? Is it all of it together? I can't separate the strands. I give up trying and deflate on the chair, limbs hanging heavy, juices growing cold, cunt twitching in tiny aftershocks until it comes to rest.

Lloyd has his arms around me from behind. He is hugging me quite fiercely into his chest, kissing my hair. He knows me.

I wonder if there's a handy hospital trolley, because the only way I'm leaving here is on one. It seems like the kind of place you might find such an item. With plenty of straps attached.

'Did you enjoy that, Sophie?' O is solicitous, sympathetic.

I aim a drugged kind of nod in her direction. 'Mmm, thanks.'

'I know I did,' says Mal. He reminds me of a drunken uncle making inappropriate remarks at a family gathering. I can't imagine this *Carry On* vampire being authoritative, but I guess he must be. O doesn't seem the type to settle for a dud.

'Thank you for being such a lovely audience,' says Lloyd unctuously. I dredge up the energy for an appreciative chuckle from somewhere and Mal and O join in.

'Well, if you'd like to wash your hands and sort yourselves out, why don't you take a little tour of the club? I think everything's open just now. We have a lovely café and bar area just next door.' O has moved on from the scene, brisk and businesslike once more.

It's our signal to straighten up, shake the lust fog from our heads and pretend nobody ever watched anybody getting off in front of them.

My rubber dress covers my bum once more. I squirt my hands with that spirit gel stuff they have in hospitals, a bottle of which O keeps handy in her desk. She lends me a mirror to fix my hair and make-up. Lloyd loosens his collar, pulling the tie off and stuffing it in his pocket. His neck is damp. He was more nervous than I was.

We make polite noises and leave for the aforementioned café area. It's substantially less gothic than I expect – no upright coffins in the corners, just pot plants.

'So then,' says Lloyd, once we have ordered coffees and sunk down into a deep leather couch in the corner. 'How was that for you?'

'It was good. Weird, but good.'

'And do you think you'll be able to do something similar, but on a grander scale, at the play party tomorrow night?'

'There'll be lots more people there.'

'Yeah, but they're all kinky. They get to watch you, but you get to watch them as well. We're all voyeurs and some of us are exhibitionists too. Come on. You can't tell me you aren't an exhibitionist, Soph.'

'No, I can't tell you that. But what are you going to do?'

'Haven't decided yet.'

I cast my eye around the room at the other customers. Will they be the witnesses of my shame? It's mid-afternoon, so those that are here are mainly students or people who work nights. While there is a smattering of leather, most are dressed according to a more bohemian template. A few suits here and there. The idea of having all their eyes fixed on me is exciting.

A woman in a clingy jersey dress crosses the room and I jump up.

'Rachael!'

My old friend and partner in submission turns to face me. 'Ah, I was looking for you.' She comes to sit with us. 'I heard you were going to be in for you induction this afternoon. Lloyd told me. How did it go?'

'Pretty good, I think. They didn't throw us out, at least.'

'What did you do? Spanking, bondage?'

I don't want to say. Lloyd helps me out.

'I made her finger herself in front of them.'

'Oh, gosh, I don't think I'd have been able to do that! Not when I was a newbie anyway.' Rachael puts an arm around me. 'You're so brave.'

'Am I?' I never think of myself as such. I just go along, let the tide carry me. What's brave about that?

'I'm glad you're here,' says Lloyd to Rachael. 'I could use some advice.'

'Yes?'

'What shall I do? Tomorrow night? This is the first time I've done anything like this for an audience and I don't want to mess it up. What would you suggest?'

'Hmm.' Rachael frowns, as if surprised Lloyd should need guidance. I'm quite touched at how anxious he is to do things right. Mr Cocky Cocksure has stage fright. 'Well, I'd start simple. If you enjoy the experience, you can always build it up.'

'What did you do, your first time?' I ask.

'It was a simple spanking scene,' she reminisces. 'I wasn't alone, actually. Me and two other girls played a little scene where we were lazy housemaids caught showing each other our underwear.'

'Do elaborate,' drawls Lloyd. His hands are clasped ever so casually over his crotch. I think I know why.

'It was fun,' she says. 'Me and the other two – O was one of them – dressed up in these teeny-tiny French maid outfits and pranced about in the boudoir with feather dusters. Have you seen the boudoir?'

'Not yet.'

'It's lovely, you must. Anyway, we pretended to dust, and O and the other girl, both more experienced than me at that time, started making out. We ended up lifting each other's skirt to see all the frillies underneath, touching each other. O was licking this other girl out while I watched when the Mistress caught us.'

'Who was the Mistress?'

'You'll meet her, I expect. Danuta, she's one of many here. She bent us all over the end of the bed in a row, took down our knickers and flogged us, one at a time. Then we all had to stand in the corner while she got the Master – that was Mal – to come and join in. He caned us, then I had to stand in the corner while O and the other girl carried on. I think they had to do oral sex on each other again, then Mal fucked one while Danuta did the other with a strap-on. Something like that.'

'Blimey.' I'm impressed. 'It sounds quite complicated. It must be planned out in advance then?'

'Yes. You'll need an idea of how you want things to go.' She addresses herself to Lloyd.

'I can see that. So, you didn't get involved in the sex, your first time?'

'No. The second time I didn't have so many inhibitions to lose though. It all got easier after that.'

'What do you think, Soph?' Lloyd turns to me. 'Would you want to go a bit further? Are you shy? Retiring?' His sharky smirk makes me flap a hand at him.

'You know I'm not.'

'But I shouldn't be discussing this with you. Why don't you, uh, go and buy us a cupcake each while I have a quick word with Rachael. Here.'

He hands over a ten-pound note.

I linger over the glass-fronted counter, admiring a cake which features a naked body made of chocolate buttons. Liquorice bootlaces trail from a Twix whip handle. How inventive. I peek over my shoulder every now and then, to watch Lloyd and Rachael, deep in confabulation about what sinful things will be done to me tomorrow night.

'Can I get you anything?'

The barista, handsome and obsequious in an apron and a black silk shirt beneath, gives me what seems like a knowing look. I wonder if he's a sub. Does getting ordered around the coffee machine turn him on? Are there people who work in service industries because they love to serve so much that they get a thrill out of it? I grin to myself, imagining an alternative workforce, role-playing the country back to economic ascendancy.

'I'm not sure,' I tell him.

'When you've identified your whim, please let me satisfy it,' he flirts.

'Oh, aren't you precious? I'll take three of those flapjacks, ta. Have you ever considered hotel work?'

He blinks.

'Never mind.'

He puts the flapjacks on a tray, gives me my change.

'Is it safe to come back?' I hover around Lloyd and Rachael's vicinity, not wanting to interrupt them mid-plot.

'I think we've got everything covered,' says Lloyd.

'Unlike your thighs,' comments Rachael. 'Great boots. Where did you get them?'

We lapse into chat until the last flapjack crumb is consumed and Rachael confesses that she is late for her date in the dungeon and scurries away, though scurrying isn't easy on six-inch heels.

'I guess we go back to the hotel and wait for tomorrow night,' says Lloyd, rising to his feet.

But he missed something out of his guess, because the moment we are out of the building and back in the dingy backstreets, he finds the first disused side alley he can and pushes me up against the wall. He parts my coat with urgent hands and presses himself into my rubber curves.

'Do you really think,' he whispers in my ear, 'you can get a man all hot and worked up, showing yourself off in front of strangers, and expect to get away with it?'

I bite my lip, grind into the hardness he must have been

d, gesturing me away. I am to be prepared.

n the office, she takes a bag from under O's desk and mages through it.

'o,' I say, faux-casually, 'is the set up all done?'

think so.'

'Where's Lloyd? What's he doing?'

'Mal's lent him some gear. He's getting dressed. I think was going to give him a few pointers about tonight too.'

'ointers? He's not doing knife play, is he?'

'achael laughs, emptying the bag so that the contents le and clink on the desk. 'Don't be daft. I might do a though.'

'Really? You're into that?'

'Only with one dom. I wouldn't let just anyone near me a blade. Don't look so scared, Soph. It's all about limits. e might be a bit further out there than yours.'

'Blimey, no one's ever said that to me before.'

'here are all sorts of things you might do that I wouldn't omfortable with either. It isn't like "Oh, she's into BDSM he must want to do x, y and z." It's different for everyone.'

'Do you like being watched?'

'Honestly? Not really. I'm self-conscious about my looks. n't enjoy it, but I enjoy the feeling of doing something scares me, for my dom, to please him.'

'don't really get that.'

'You're in a different headspace than me. You play the you do because it's what you want. If Lloyd wanted it you didn't, it wouldn't happen, would it?'

'No.'

'Because you don't have that kind of relationship. I get on the idea of service, of subordinating my own desires omebody else's.'

nursing for at least half an hour. 'What are you going to do about it?'

'Three guesses.' His hands are at my hem, yanking at the latex. The wool of his suit trousers chafes my thighs.

'OK.' I dart out my tongue and flick it along his lower lip. He catches it for a moment, sucking it in, then releases it so I can speak. 'Guess one: pick me up and spread my legs.'

'That'll do for starters.' He jolts me upwards so I have to cling to his neck, my breasts pushed into his chest, my legs wrapped tight around his hips. The wall is hard and uncompromising against my spine, but I don't care, caught in a forceful kiss that knocks my senses sideways.

'Next?' he demands, drawing away with a bite of my lip.

'Guess two: get your cock out of your trousers.'

His hand bears my theory out, fiddling with belt buckle and zip for an intense moment, while I start to wonder how secluded this spot really is. It's getting late. Soon the offices will release the workers and they will flow and flood through the streets, bound for stations and bus stops all over town. Maybe this alley is a cut-through.

'Guess three,' I rasp, more urgently. 'Fuck me into the wall.'

'Oh, you're a mind-reader,' he says, nipping my ear.

He gets his cock gets into position underneath me, holds me up by the undersides of my naked thighs and enters me. It's a quick and effortless first stroke, impaling me without fuss or struggle. He pushes in to the hilt and stands, crushing me in place, still for a moment. I can tell by his breathing and the twitching of his face that he won't be able to hold himself in for long. He's already close.

I want to unhook an arm from his neck and touch my clit, catch up with him before he streaks ahead and leaves me behind. He helps me, bracing one of his forearms underneath me while he releases my arm. I tense for a moment, feeling my body drop an inch, my coat scraping against the cold brick, but then I am hoisted back into position, with my hand free to self-pleasure.

For the second time that afternoon, I start to rub my clit. I love the feel of his thick hard stalk underneath, keeping me filled and tight while I finger myself.

'Don't take too long,' he gasps. 'I don't know if I can …'

'It turned me on,' I tell him in brief bursts, panting in between, 'when you made me show myself to those people. Doing what you told me … having to do it … knowing they thought I belonged to you … it got me off … oh God, it did.'

'You like people to think you belong to me? You do. You do belong to me. This hot, wet little cunt I'm in is mine. Do you get that?'

'Yeah. I get that.' I begin to wriggle, trying to provoke him into a thrust.

'Patience, sweetheart. You made me wait. I'm returning the favour.'

'Nooo, I can't. Can't wait. Do it. Fuck me.'

He won't be able to resist it. He can't resist it. He screws his eyes shut and gets to work. My back will bear the bruises, my cunt will sting and simmer with sweet remembrance for the rest of the day and night.

You are his, it says, when I lie in bed feeling the burn. *Why do you fight it?*

Chapter Seven

Lloyd leaves me in the café with a shot glass of while Rachael and O whisk him off to 'set u

The party doesn't start for two hours ye setting up do they need?

The people all around me are preparing to pa high spirits, brandishing their riding crops ar while they down expensive bottled beers. None nervous. I guess they are all old hands at this

'You look lonely,' says one man, his bare up in some kind of harness. 'Want to join us

His coterie stops behind him – three girls leather miniskirts and very little else.

'I'm waiting for someone,' I tell him, cro I'm still dressed for work – Rachael promise get changed in the office later.

'Are you sure you're in the right place?'

Am I? Good question.

'Quite sure, thanks.'

'OK, well, enjoy your play.' He drifts off to with his acolytes in tow.

Rachael appears from the stairway door a

I pause for a moment, unsure what to say. 'Each to their own,' is my lame conclusion.

'Exactly. Each to their own. Now look, are you going to get dressed or are we going to stand here debating kink psychology all night?'

'Sorry. I'm nervous. Love your outfit, by the way.'

Rachael is wearing a black velvet number featuring a cleavage with more plunge than a bungee jumper and a huge slit up both sides of the long skirt. She appears to be nude underneath.

'Thanks. Get a shimmy on then.'

I begin to rid myself of the sharp trouser suit, inspecting the contents of the desk while I unbutton.

It looks like a corset.

'Is it a corset?'

'Yes, and I hope it fits you. Really, they should be custom-made. But I reckon we're about the same size, even though I'm taller, so I thought it was worth a try.'

'What if it doesn't fit?'

Rachael shrugs. 'There's a load of costume gear in that cupboard over there. Something will.'

As it happens, the corset is hideously uncomfortable, but for reasons that are nothing to do with the fit, which is fine.

'Not so tight,' I gasp as Rachael reins me in so fiercely I expect to hear the cracking of bones.

She relents and lets the laces out a bit. I breathe again.

'I forget sometimes that you aren't a veteran at all this,' she says. 'Sorry.'

I look down at myself. I seem to nip in and flare out much more than usual, in a sleek black and red satiny kind of way. My breasts spill up and over the cups, two indecent pale pillows, thrust out and ready for handling.

'It's like my rubber dress,' I tell her. 'But more so.'

'You could try a rubber corset. They're awesome. Now, I have this skirt thing for you.'

The skirt thing is a tiny lacy scrap that barely covers my arse. Not that it matters. I can't imagine that my arse is going to stay under wraps for long tonight. Suspenders emerge from the high-set hem to link up with lacy stocking tops.

Looking at myself in the mirror, I see the classic saucy sexy minx. I practise a look of wide-eyed innocence, a pout, a wiggle of the bottom.

'Do you think Lloyd will like it?' asks Rachael, grinning.

'Are you kidding? Lloyd likes anything and everything. A hairy gorilla suit would turn Lloyd on.'

'Only if you were wearing it.'

I tut. 'Nah, I don't think so. He's just a horny bastard.'

'No, I think you're wrong. I think it'd have to be you in the gorilla suit. I even think it'd have to be you in the sexy corset.'

I turn away from the mirror and put my hands over my exposed collarbones, my throat suddenly tight. 'D'you really think so?'

'God, yes. Don't you?'

I wander over to the desk again, not trusting myself to answer. Wrist cuffs. 'Do I have to put these on?'

'I would, since they're there. I guess it's for a reason.'

She buckles them on for me, nice and tight. The leather is heavy, which is both sexy and reassuring. Instantly, I feel closer to the headspace I'm aiming for.

I pull on high strappy shoes and then I'm left with the last thing: a collar, with dog leash attached.

'I don't know about this,' I say, picking it up.

'Why not?'

'Because it makes me think of dogs, and dogs don't turn me on. I don't really want to be treated like an animal.'

'I guess I won't invite you to the pony farm then.'

'I guess you won't.' I snort. 'You're serious? That place really exists?'

'I've told you! I went there the other month. I had a brilliant weekend. Look, put the collar on. Don't think of it in relation to dogs. Think of it as a slave collar.'

Slaves? Isn't that worse?

Rachael puts a hand on my shoulder. 'It doesn't symbolise anything you don't want it to. It's just a weird-looking necklace. It's a piece of leather with some metal links attached. Whatever you want to make it, that's what it is. And it's a damn sight less uncomfortable than that corset.'

'Where's Lloyd? Is he coming to fetch me?'

'Yeah, he'll be here soon.'

I pick up the collar, weigh it in my hands. It's just a thing. It can mean what I want it to mean. I'm not a dog, not a slave, I don't belong to anyone. I do what I want, because I want to do it.

I put it on. It's supple, the leather moulding itself to the contours of my neck. The chain dangles between my breasts, chilling them.

Rachael picks up the end of the leash and tugs on it playfully. 'How does it feel?'

'It's OK. It's good. Where's Lloyd?'

'Here's Lloyd.'

He stands in the doorway – I pivot on my teeteringly high heels and look him up and down.

'Wow. It's a dom makeover.'

He looks like a sexed-up cat burglar, in black leather trousers (Mal's?) and a black silk shirt, billowing and open to about halfway down his chest. Most fun of all, he is wearing an eye mask and a flogger in his belt. And shiny, shiny, shiny boots of leather. His hair is slicked back and his smile is deadly.

I put a hand on a jutting hip and ask in my best husky purr, 'Who's *this*?'

He shuts the door behind him and crooks a finger. 'Let me look at you.'

I swing the leash, burlesque-style, as I approach him, but he grabs it as soon as it's within reach and uses it to hold me still and close, the length of chain wrapped around his fist.

'Gorgeous,' he says, putting his other hand to my neck, sliding it down over my bare shoulders. The intensity of his attention makes me want to step back, to make a jocular remark, to puncture the moment. Something stops me, though, holds me still just as the leash does. 'Turn around.'

His hand on my shoulder steers me lightly. He lifts my skirt, the two pathetic flounces of frothy net, and checks that I am naked underneath. I look at the ground, conscious of Rachael watching us, conscious of Lloyd's eyes on my bottom and pussy. There will be more eyes than his later, but I don't think I could feel so naked if a million eyes were trained on my sex. I have never felt more laid bare.

With a tug of the leash, I am facing him again.

'Are you ready?' he says softly.

'Are you?'

'Not sure. Shall we skip all this and go home?' His fingers caress my jawbone, his thumb drifting over my cheek.

'Would that be a fail?'

I don't even care. I don't even care about the silly game. I want to tell him, yes, let's abandon this, let's go, let's be lovers.

But when it comes down to it, I just can't.

'I suppose,' he says. 'Maybe.'

'No, let's do this.'

'You're sure?'

'I want to. I'm sure.'

He pulls me tight, really tight, into his chest and whispers in my ear, 'I'm going to make you beg tonight. One way or another.'

'We'll see,' I whisper back.

O and Mal arrive, cooing and smiling at our little tableau.

'Getting into the mood?' enquires Mal, searching the cupboard for his Dracula cloak. 'It's going to be a hot one tonight. Very well attended. Lots of the top players in.'

'Who's domming you, Rachael?' asks O. 'Won't they be wondering where you are?'

'Oh! Yes.' Rachael gives her hair one final primp in the mirror and dashes off. 'See you later. Good luck.'

Mal pours us all a glass of port and we stand around, slightly awkward, O and I baring expanses of flesh that seem to preclude polite chitchat. It's left to Mal and Lloyd to banter self-consciously about fire regulations and door policy.

Mal raises his glass. 'Well, I think a toast is in order,' he says. 'To beautiful submission. And the two very fine examples of it here in this room.'

Lloyd echoes the toast while O and I simper.

'First night nerves, Lloyd?' asks Mal.

'Yeah, a few,' he admits.

Mal slaps him on the back. 'You'll ace it, bud,' he says. 'Just remember what I taught you.'

'And what was that?' I ask, but Mal taps his nose.

'Curiosity killed the cat. And did quite a lot of damage to the pussy too.'

He laughs uproariously. O shoots me an apologetic

eyebrow raise. Life with the Benny Hill of bondage must be wearisome sometimes.

Our drinks consumed, our inhibitions mildly lowered, we prepare to enter the circus ring.

I reach for Lloyd's hand and squeeze it, the squeeze lasting a little longer and ending up a little tighter than I intended. I want to tell him to break a leg, or something. Should I be wishing luck to a man whose immediate future involves visiting intense pain on my backside? All the same, I prefer my position to his. I don't have to exude confidence or authority. I just have to obey orders.

Mal and O, in front of us, open the door. Lloyd removes my hand from his and takes hold of the leash. I am to walk behind him.

We process through the café, where bodies turn and eyes swivel to follow our progress. It feels unlike anything I've ever done before. I'm so used to displaying myself, yet I've never been put on display like this. My skin crawls, but at the same time, my cunt moistens, feeling puffy and heavy almost immediately. Lloyd's arse looks fine in those leather trousers, so I concentrate only on its tight outline, swaying from side to side in front of me.

Down to the dungeon we go, down, down. The stairs are hard to negotiate in heels and Lloyd takes the descent considerately slowly. People mill in the flame-lit corridors. There are submissives kneeling at their master or mistress's feet all over the place, even more so when we enter the dungeon.

A cross, a pillory and a spanking bench are all in use, small crowds and queues of people lining up to watch or wait their turn.

I peek from the corner of my eye at all the naked, willing flesh on show. At first, I'm drawn to their bottoms and thighs, their spread slits and marked skin, but after a while what I want to see is their faces. Twisted in pain, lips bitten, eyes popping desperately or screwed shut, none of them looks as if they're enjoying the experience at all. There is none of the 'ecstasy in agony' one might expect. They look like I feel when Dr Lassiter or Lloyd is on the cruel end of the cane. True physical masochists are rare, I suppose.

But behind those tormented faces, inside their minds, there must be fierce efforts of self-control and dedication to their dom/mes going on. I think of what I get from a good whipping – the endorphins, the tumble into the luxurious embrace of submission, the sense of being dealt with and controlled and made use of and yet cared for all at once. Really, there is nothing like it.

The man at the cross is untied and released. Now he has the beatific expression, dropping to his feet and kissing his master's boots. O steps up and stretches her limbs in the required X-shape while Mal ties the ropes.

At the pillory, they seem in no hurry to finish their exhibition. The dom has finished flagellating his submissive, but he is rubbing something on her bum cheeks that seems to be exacerbating the soreness, by the look on her face.

The domme at the spanking bench releases her male submissive and leads him away by means of a leash attached to a cock ring. He is fully hard, gasping for breath, and, as she yanks him past us, I admire the deep crimson shade of his paddled bottom.

I wait for him to be replaced, but then a tug at my leash makes me stumble and I realise that it's my turn.

'Now?' I whisper as Lloyd takes hold of my upper arm and turns me to face the amused onlookers.

'Speak when you're spoken to,' he mutters from the side

of his mouth. 'Unless it's to safe-word.' He raises his voice, addressing the crowd. It's not enormous, as most people are interested to see what's happening at the pillory. Nine or ten people give Lloyd their polite attention. 'Masters, mistresses and their devoted submissives, I'd like to introduce you to Sophie. Before we start, there's one thing you need to know about Sophie, and that's that she's a very, very bad girl.'

There is an amused ripple from the crowd. He puts his hand, which is now gloved in thin leather, underneath my lacy skirt, and rubs it up and down my arse.

'Tell them, Sophie.'

His gloved finger draws a line up my crack, squiggling between my cheeks. My pussy gushes.

'I'm a very, very bad girl,' I falter.

'And I think we all know what very, very bad girls get, don't we?' More chuckling. 'What do you think, Sophie? Any ideas?'

My mouth is too dry to answer. I think my cunt has used up all the moisture in my body and there's none left.

'Hmm?' He pats my bottom gently with his gloved hand, still expecting his answer.

'Do they get spanked, sir?' I finally manage.

He joins in with the general revelling in my humiliation that's going on around the bench. 'Do they, Sophie? Are you asking me? I thought I was asking you.'

His head is cocked to one side, his lips curled in amusement, his eyes gleaming with lustful purpose. I want to slap him and jump on him, both at once.

I take a deep breath and try to edit the natural sulky tone from my reply. 'They get spanked, sir.'

He claps his hands, making my collar wobble as the leash swings between them. 'That's right. They do. Now, I'm going

154

to throw this open to the audience. I'm going to ask them exactly what kind of spanking a very, very bad girl deserves. The answer I like best wins a prize.'

'What's the prize?' asks a domme in a peaked leather cap.

'The prize, ladies and gentlemen, is that you get to administer the whipping.'

I wheel around, stunned.

They like that. The laughter is more than a chuckle this time.

I open my mouth to form a word, but then I remember what he said. Only when spoken to, unless to safe-word. Of course, I *could* safe-word now, in theory.

But why would I? Lloyd is offering me the chance to take my thrashing from a practised, experienced top. In a way, he's doing me a favour. And himself, of course – I suspect his offer is driven by the fear of wielding a less-than-steady hand under public scrutiny.

I have to hold my nerve, that's all. I have to beat him at his own beating game.

I press my lips together and lift my chin, staring ahead at the crowd, daring them to think I'm scared.

'Eyes down,' he orders, and the accompanying pat on the bum is less gentle this time, though the gloves add an extra dimension of sensuality. 'What am I bid?'

Some hands go up in the crowd, which is growing. The action at the pillory appears to have ended.

'Three minutes with a flogger,' somebody suggests.

'The birch,' says another. 'Has she been birched before?'

'No.'

'Oh, then maybe not this time. She's been caned?'

'Yes.'

'Six for a bad girl, twelve for a very bad girl.'

'And for a very, very bad girl?'

'Maybe eighteen. Has she taken that many before?'

'No, twelve is the current record.'

'What's she like with a wooden paddle?'

'Oh, she hates that! With a passion.'

'I guess I'd recommend the wooden paddle then! Maybe twenty.'

'I like the tawse,' says the peak-capped domme. 'Gorgeous impact on a round female bottom.'

'I like it too,' says Lloyd. 'I'm giving you the prize.'

Ugh, the tawse, horrid. Better than the cane though, and the paddle, so I congratulate myself inwardly while the domme is being congratulated outwardly.

Until Lloyd speaks again. 'OK, how I'm going to organise Sophie's punishment is like this. I'm going to strap her to the bench and warm her up myself, using my hand and the wooden paddle.'

Oh, you bastard! How can a wooden paddle be considered a warm-up implement anyway? It's a travesty.

'When I think she's done, I'll hand over to you, ma'am, and this rather wonderful Lochgelly tawse here, and you can give her, let's say, twelve of those. After that, well, we'll play things by ear.'

Lloyd's improvisational skills are altogether too good, and I assume that, by the time the whipping is over, he will be well over his nerves. Perhaps mine should start kicking in now.

He unclips the leash from my collar and stretches out an arm towards the spanking bench in silent command.

Its design makes it obvious how I am to position myself. I straddle with my knees on padded shelves, my stomach over a large bolster that lifts my bottom high. My wrists are cuffed together behind my back while my neck rests on another padded insert, keeping my face in full view of the crowd.

The lacy skirt is barely worthy of the name now. It slides frothily and independently towards my lower back, baring my bottom in its corseted, suspendered frame to the view of the audience. Once I am secured, Lloyd moves the bench so that I am looking outwards at the crowd. Only by shutting my eyes can I avoid their gaze. On the other hand, they won't see my bottom and my widespread pussy lips.

Except they will, because Lloyd invites a select group behind me, promising to change the aspect later on.

'Now, Sophie, you are to keep your eyes open and face the good ladies and gentlemen who have come to join in your discipline. If anyone reports to me that you have shut them at any time – except to blink, or if there's a very hard stroke – then you'll get the cane on top of all this. Do you understand?'

'Yes, sir.'

My pathetic squeak draws another laugh from the crowd, who are loving Lloyd's showmanship.

I shiver and let out a little moan as his shiny, smooth hand rubs itself all over my bottom and thighs, grazing the soft inner flesh, taking a few sly pinches that make me jolt, as far as I can.

'Ready, Sophie?' he says very quietly.

'Yes, sir,' I whisper. I wish I could see him. I feel like one of those hog roasts on a spit – a piece of doomed meat, stripped of all dignity. But I like it. I want it.

I want it even more when Lloyd's palm falls, stinging but sweet, on my arse. Those gloves soften the blow and give it a sexy edge I haven't felt before. I want to squirm and offer myself up, higher, more. Give me more. He does.

He spanks firmly and thoroughly until every inch from

the bottom of the corset to my stocking tops feels warm and glowy.

'She likes that,' says someone in the crowd, knowing I can hear, knowing I am watching them speak. 'Dirty girl. Bet she's wet.'

'She is,' says one of the people behind me.

I am.

'Well, that's nothing new,' says Lloyd, his hand falling over and over again, speeding up the pace until I start to bite my lip and dig my fingernails into my palms. 'A spanking always gets this little trollop good and wet. Sometimes I've had to fuck her first, so she doesn't get too excited by it. Anyone else tried that?'

They start swapping topping anecdotes while their submissives blush and flutter their eyelashes. I'd be amused, if Lloyd's hand wasn't starting to really hurt. A gasp jerks out of me, then several cries.

He stops, indulges in a bit of chat for a while, leaving me to process the heat and soreness of my arse and lament the fact that my first public spanking is far from over.

The people behind me are sent away again, and a new clique takes their place. They admire my bottom and my juicy pussy while Lloyd taps the paddle upwards from the backs of my thighs, preparing me. I am a little relieved to feel that it isn't one of those ping-pong bat shaped numbers that wham themselves into the whole of your bum with each stroke, but a slightly wider version of a ruler. It'll hurt, but not in such a universal and overwhelming way.

The first stroke is mild, but the second is not. I notice the audience cringing in advance of the ruler's impact and I know it's going to be hard, so I shut my eyes.

Busted!

They all rat on me in chorus and Lloyd tuts.

I'm too busy trying to absorb the sharpness of the blow to care. It fell right at the curve of my bottom and it throbs.

'I'm going to let you off that one,' he says, 'because it was a little harder than I intended. I seem to have the spanker's version of an itchy trigger finger. But make sure you keep your eyes open for the rest.'

He manages to keep his paddling arm in check for the remaining strokes, which fall with an even sting across my already warm bum, taking the heat deeper, broadening the pain.

I know that a bigger and bigger crowd is watching my shameful treatment, but somehow that seems to help me take the pain. The encouraging, somewhat wistful smiles on the faces of the submissives remind me that this is what we all love, what we come here for. They all understand the dynamic, which very much lessens the potential humiliation factor. What they see is a girl having a great time with her lover, where someone outside the scene might see a girl being exposed and punished.

The tops are seeing it differently, though – I can tell by their flushed cheeks and cruel smirks. They are enjoying my pain, silently judging Lloyd's technique, hoping he'll make me scream, or beg, or cry. I avoid their eyes and focus on the peak-cap domme's very handsome sub.

Lloyd's final stroke – a doozy – coincides with my sudden recognition of the handsome sub as the barista from upstairs. He gives me a heart-melting smile of sympathy when I yelp inelegantly and puff out my cheeks.

Lloyd puts down the paddle and rubs my other cheeks all over. The leather is not cool enough to soothe but I don't care. I want those slick smooth fingers inside me. He fails to oblige, though.

'Warmed up now?' he asks me, leaning down over my ear.

'Yes, sir.' My voice is syrupy, breathy. I am well on my way.

'Good.'

He puts a hand on my neck, standing beside me. I can almost make him out in full profile if I strain my eyes.

With his other hand, he beckons the winning domme.

She pats her sub on the head and orders him to behave himself before crossing the floor and taking up her position behind me.

'Lovely leather,' I hear her say.

Then Lloyd shifts the spanking bench around one hundred and eighty degrees, so my arse faces the crowd and I am looking up at the domme, watching her stroke the triple tongues of the tawse with blood-red taloned fingers.

She lowers the strap and brushes it across my face. 'Kiss it,' she says.

I do. Its smell makes my clit bloom. I want to breathe it in forever. But she withdraws it and removes herself from my line of vision.

'Did we say twenty?' she asks from my rear.

Lloyd laughs. 'Twelve, I believe.'

'Worth a try, wasn't it?'

Lloyd drops to his haunches in front of me until our faces are level, then puts his hands on my shoulders. 'I want you to watch me,' he says. 'All the way through. I want to see your face.'

I'm not sure I can do this. I try to shake my head, but he shakes his back, chewing on his inside lip. He smiles, a kind of scared rabbit-in-headlights twitch of the mouth.

'Please,' he whispers. His fingers press into my flesh.

The tawse whooshes through the air and cracks down hard. Raw, hot pain flares from my bottom and radiates outwards. I cry out, scrunch shut my eyes.

'Look at me,' insists Lloyd.

I look at him. He is making this happen to me. This is all his fault.

I can't be angry with him for it. But I can be angry with him for this – for trying to turn a good strapping into some kind of fucking love-in. Why does he want me to look at him?

I ask the question. 'Why?'

The space I leave for his answer is usurped by the tawse, falling for a second agonising time on the same spot she marked before.

'Oh God!' I pant, wanting to break free of the cuffs and defend my bottom. Ten more of these? Impossible.

'You need to think about why this is happening,' he says, while I wriggle in my tethers. 'You need to remember why you're here. I want to give you a constant reminder.'

'I'm here because you're a bastard,' I hiss, tensing up for the next lash.

'No, you're here because you can't make a decision. You're here because you're scared.'

'Shut up.'

'You really want me to punish you, don't you?'

'Shut up! Owwwwwww!'

The third stroke is lower down, lighting up my lower bum. I imagine it vivid scarlet, glowing into the crowd so that they can warm their hands around it.

'What do you want me to do to you?' he asks, his face even closer, his lips almost brushing mine. 'After this?'

'I don't know.' I really don't. I can't think now, all other considerations pushed out by the dread knowledge that another stroke is on its way.

'I'll do anything you want.'

I take the next stroke with a belligerent cry. I'm getting close to swearing. I have to be careful.

Lloyd takes one hand off my shoulder and strokes my hair instead. 'You know that, don't you, Soph? Anything you want.'

'This isn't … I can't talk … don't make me talk.'

He cocks his head and smiles this insanely soppy smile. His eyes are misty-blue inside the mask, as if he might cry. He has that look I've seen in paintings and films, the look denoting Mad Love. Is it real? It's certainly unnerving.

It's more unnerving even than the prospect of eight more of Mistress Nasty's worst shots.

I revise this opinion after the next one, which makes me shout, 'Fuck!' really loudly into Lloyd's adoring face.

'That's not your safe word,' he points out. 'Use it, if you can't bear it.'

'I can,' I insist through gritted teeth. 'I can bear it.'

'You're not going to let her get away with that language, are you?' asks Mistress Nasty. I watch Lloyd's eyes flick upwards to her.

'Sophie never gets away with anything,' he says. 'I see to that.'

'I should think so too.'

Another swingeing smack knocks the breath from my body. I moan, my voice cracking, horribly near tears.

Lloyd puts both palms flat on my cheeks – not the ones undergoing the ordeal, the other cheeks – and lays his forehead against mine.

'Halfway there,' he says, which makes me moan even more. Only halfway!

'Let yourself go,' he says, then, taking me by panicked surprise, he fastens his lips to mine.

I try to shake away at first, but he holds me.

Is he serious? Kissing me while I am being strapped? Is this even possible?

But the tawse falls again and the burn drives me into a kind of hot, sensual fog where anything becomes possible. Lloyd's ravenous mouth and probing tongue carry me out of my tense self-consciousness, even though I keep on whimpering and snuffling each time the leather falls. It is soft and lush at one end, hard and fierce at the other, or sometimes interchangeable. A murmur of heartfelt aws from the onlookers laps against my ears. I feel like I'm drowning, but that the vortex will lead somewhere good, better than life.

Lloyd, leather, pain, warmth, luxury, shock, lips, teeth, tongue, bite, lust, need, want. These things float in and out, up and down.

It takes me a while to work out that the twelve strokes have been given.

Regretfully, Lloyd breaks lip contact, stroking along my cheekbone with a butter-soft fingertip. 'You did it,' he says. He kisses my forehead then stands to shake hands with the domme. 'A fine job,' he says. 'Exemplary. Thank you very much.'

'Pleasure was all mine,' she says, laying a hand on my burning buttocks. 'Well, maybe not *all* mine. I think you might find her quite ... receptive ... to whatever needs you might have.'

They can all see how wet I am. I wish I could clamp my thighs together, but it just isn't possible.

Mistress Nasty departs, with a brusque, 'Daniel! Heel!'

Lloyd uncuffs me and helps me to my tottering feet. The room swoops and blurs around me. There seems to be a lot of fire and shadows.

When the skirt falls back down, he clicks his tongue with disapproval and takes it off. Everyone is to see what has been done to me. I am not to hide it.

I let him pull me into his arms for a tight embrace. I don't know what to feel. Am I angry with him? Am I grateful to him? Am I happy or am I traumatised? Something about this experience has thrown me into confusion; its power lingers, seeping into every move, every thought. I wonder if this is what he wanted.

But I don't have to ask what Lloyd wants. I know what he wants. I just don't know if I can give it.

'Where shall we go?' he asks, holding me close.

'Somewhere private.' I hide my face in the whispery silk of his shirt.

'I'm not sure there *is* anywhere private here.'

'I want to be alone with you.'

'OK. I'll see what I can do.'

He leads me out of the dungeon, not on the leash this time, just hand in hand. I imagine the number of double takes from people turning to check out my bright red bottom, and the thought makes me realise how very much I would like to come soon. I need to find a private place with Lloyd and have him screw the wits out of me – not that I have many left.

Our best solution is a compromise – a divan in an upstairs room called the Boudoir that isn't quite as exposed as the others, tented beneath a large expanse of parachute silk. People will be able to see our outlines moving beneath it, but not our faces.

He puts me on my back and fingers me with those wicked supple leather gloves on before I can utter a word.

'I should have done this back down there,' he says, spearing two, then three of the slim black intruders inside my cunt,

164

keeping a thumb on my fat clit. 'I should have made you come while they watched you. Would you have liked that?'

'Mmm.' I try to lift my sore bottom up so it doesn't make contact with the mattress, but he won't let me.

'I asked you a question, Sophie. Would you have liked that?'

'Yes, sir,' I gabble, wanting the head of steam released quickly. He keeps slowing his pace, though, every time I think it's coming.

'Another time, maybe,' he says, speeding up again. 'I think you should get your arse whipped in front of strangers again. I think I should do it often. I think it's what you need.'

I come hard, onto those shiny fingers, my bottom chafing on the velvet.

'I don't know though,' he says, wrenching down the leather trousers, pulling wide my legs. 'Maybe you'll be better behaved now.' He pulls me upright, moves me on to my knees, pushes my head down into the prickly pile. 'Maybe you'll do as you're told.'

He fucks me hard, bruisingly, gripping my hips and pummelling my hot bottom until it's even hotter and stings even sharper.

'Maybe you'll see what's staring you in the face,' he pants. 'And stop giving me the run-around.' He smacks my thigh in what seems like genuine punishment.

'Don't hurt me.' My alarm is genuine. There is something a little bit feral about Lloyd tonight.

He sighs, slows down, strokes the hand-shaped glow on my thigh. 'Don't be stupid. You know I'd never hurt you.'

A strange comment from a man who has just beaten seven bells out of his girlfriend's arse, perhaps, but it makes a kind of sense. The pain he inflicts is no more than skin-deep, and it isn't even real pain. It's pleasure pain, play pain.

He's telling me my heart is safe with him.

He's telling me he wants my heart.

I give him the next best thing, my orgasm, and he gives me his. The sex is good, hot, fast, hard, passionate, amazing, but is the orgasm enough any more?

Into the dying throes of my climax, a knot of fear intrudes. Have I found the point of no emotional return?

Chapter Eight

'I think you should always wear those gloves in bed.'

I'm lying with my head on Lloyd's chest, semi-mummified in rumpled bed sheets while his leather-gloved hand strokes my sore nipples.

'Maybe I will then. That sounded like one heck of an orgasm.'

'It was. You're a genius. I don't know where you can go after this. Any stronger and my head'll blow.'

'Well, make the most of the afterglow, madam, because it's your last for a while.'

I try to sit up, but my cotton cocoon prevents me. 'You what?'

He waits for my confusion to hit its peak before deigning to reply. 'The next challenge. No orgasms for a week.'

'That's a shit challenge! How's that even ... ugh, Lloyd. Why?'

He laughs, pulling me down, ruffling my hair. 'Because I don't think you can do it.'

'You don't think I can go a week without coming? It's easy and, what's more, it's really boring. Come on! You can do better.'

'I don't think you'll find it easy at all.'

'What's difficult about keeping my legs crossed and my thoughts pure for seven days?'

'Quite a lot, I think you'll find. There are challenges within the challenge. All will become clear.'

I crane my neck to look up at him. 'You're serious about this, aren't you? Nothing I can say to change your mind?'

'Not a word.'

'And what are you going to do for these seven days? Won't your right hand be worn to the bone by Sunday?'

He shifts a little, retracting his softened cock from my bottom. 'I don't remember making any vow of celibacy,' he says lightly.

I manage to sit up properly this time, bolt upright. 'You mean you're going to …?'

'Why don't you wait and see? While you're up there, put the kettle on, eh?'

***

I know I'm a hypocrite. It's not as if I own Lloyd. I'm not even a possessive type of person. We've done threesomes, we've done swinging, we've added people to the mix and then multiplied. But all of that has made us stronger – if we can get everything we need from each other, why would we ever go elsewhere?

I suppose what I find so hard is the thought of Lloyd having sex that excludes me. When he's had other women before, I've watched or joined in. What if he finds he likes the novelty? What if he wants to extend the openness of our relationship still further? Would I be OK with that, if it was what he wanted?

Goddamn, he was right. This challenge is hard, and it hasn't even started yet.

On Monday I throw myself into my work, making sure I wear my most conservative trouser suit and lowest heels. If I don't look sexy, I won't feel sexy. Or so I hope.

It seems to do the trick, at least until I retire to Lloyd's apartment for the evening.

'Have you eaten?'

'Yeah, got something in the kitchen earlier. What are you watching?'

Lloyd is lounging on the sofa in his dressing gown watching some kind of CCTV footage. When I get closer and recognise the feather-patterned hotel wallpaper, I realise it's a film we made a few months ago. Of us.

'Sit down and watch,' he invites, making room for me beside him.

'Uh, I think I'll take a shower.'

'No, it isn't optional. It's compulsory. Sit down and watch or you incur a fail.'

'Oh, I get it.' I grump and huff, but I take my seat beside him, dodging away when he tries to put an arm around me.

'No you don't. Come here.' He pats his thigh imperiously.

I discard my jacket and grudgingly allow myself into his embrace. On the television, there is the crackling of a cheap microphone and some giggling off-camera.

'So, Sophie,' he murmurs into my ear, 'have you been a good girl today? No crafty hands down pants, I trust.'

'Shut up. I've been working.'

'Working the johns in the bar?'

'No, you twat. Working in my workplace.'

'Give us your fingers.' He takes my hand and sniffs the fingertips. 'Hmm, I suppose you'll pass. Strip down to your underwear.'

I remove the black trousers and plain jersey top. I didn't

dare risk the silk camisoles this morning – the feel of silk next to my skin would not have been helpful.

When I sit back down I am wearing large cotton knickers from a Marks and Spencer multipack and a matching boring bra.

'Very utilitarian,' says Lloyd admiringly, capturing me in his arms again. His dressing gown is silky, slinky, against my skin.

I see myself saunter on to camera, rather more exotically garbed in a sheer black lace-edged mesh dress that leaves nothing to the imagination. It has suspenders and stockings sewn on to it. I give the camera the finger and shake my hair over my face. God, I hate cameras. I was drunk when we made this film – it was the only way I could do it. 'Look at you,' says Lloyd, giving my thigh a squeeze. 'What a sexy little tramp, eh? Look how hard those nipples are.'

I stiffen. How am I going to get through this? I could pretend to be a film censor, who watches skin flick after skin flick all day long and has become desensitised to it. But desensitisation can't happen just like that, so I abandon the idea. Perhaps I could just keep my eyes unfocused, or slightly to the right of the action.

I try it, but it'll be tough to sustain for longer than five minutes.

The only other option is to concentrate on fooling around with Lloyd – but where will that get me? Up arousal creek without an orgasm, that's where.

Lloyd pulls me onto his lap and starts kissing my neck while the TV-me bends over and shows the split nutmeg of her – my – whoever's – pussy to the room.

'You were wet,' whispers Lloyd. 'Tight, hard nipples – oh!'

He touches mine, which are prodding the M&S cotton with some force. 'Are you cold, Sophie?'

'Fuck off.'

'The opposite? Aw. All lubed up and nowhere to come.'

TV-him is in shot now. He drags TV-me over to the bed and we start making out. It occurs to me that I don't know what happens in this film. I can't remember. I am glued to the sight of his lips on mine. Kissing is so sexy; I could watch montages of kissing scenes all day. When his tongue slides in, I squirm on Lloyd's lap.

He mirrors his TV-self, tipping my head back and giving me his most thorough attentions, all the time keeping one eye on the screen. I hadn't realised that the challenge would involve touching, or any form of intimacy. Suddenly, I am flooded with the realisation of exactly how difficult this is going to be.

Especially when the flood of realisation is accompanied by a different kind of flood, in my knickers.

Lloyd kisses like a bandit, all plunder and bravura confidence, taking what he wants because he wants it. I've always found that hotter than hot, and I'm not about to stop.

He breaks off when TV-us stop writhing. TV-him has got me over his lap. There's no way I can watch this without the prickle of heat between my legs turning full forest fire.

'Oh, you're going to get spanked,' he crows. 'Just the way you need it. Look at that little white arse – it won't be that colour for long. That dress doesn't even cover it. Tut.'

I've never watched myself get spanked before and I'm fascinated. Part of me wishes I could see my face, but a bigger part is relieved that I can't. I'm pretty sure I'd screw an already sketchy collection of features into nightmare configurations.

'What am I getting spanked for?'

'Duh. For having a little white arse.'

He tightens his grip on me. TV-him raises his arm and brings his hand down hard. The sound is lovely. I never hear it properly when I'm on the receiving end; maybe it's muffled by my own mind working overtime on sensation analysis. But on TV, it comes across beautifully, a sharp, crisp percussion.

Of course, it's interesting to see my bottom under the palm, the way it flattens and then springs back into shape, the way it blushes pink, then pinker, then red, then redder. But what I really can't take my eyes off is Lloyd. His face, his intent focus, the set of his jaw, the determination. Christ, that's sexy. Sexier than the strong arm rising and falling, sexier than the hand printing its emblem onto my heating skin. His missionary zeal makes my hairs stand on end.

'I think you're enjoying this.' His voice cuts in to my reverie.

I take the breath. Hadn't realised I needed to.

'Do you wish you were her?'

'I am her.'

'Do you wish you were in her position?'

'No. Today I like watching. And besides, what's the point of a spanking today? A spanking without sex. It's like a birthday with no presents.'

TV-him stays his hand. TV-my bottom is cherry red. He rubs it considerately, saying words I can't quite catch, low croons of post-spanking pre-sex seduction.

I'm saying something, fussing – I think I'm refusing to show my face on camera. He gives me one more smack to my bottom, then shrugs and says, audibly, 'OK then, if you insist.'

He kneels up on the bed and I, with my back to the camera, lower my head to his cock. He holds my shoulders while I suck, throwing his head right back so his Adam's apple juts out.

I like watching his breathing quicken and his neck flush. I like watching my head bob up and down while my spanked bum jiggles with the effort I'm putting in.

Back on the sofa, the flesh-and-blood Lloyd moves the hand that has been resting flat on my stomach down, gliding over the cotton knickers until he reaches my crotch.

'Oh, these are damp,' he says. 'Oh dear.'

'Can we watch something else? *Antiques Roadshow*, perhaps.'

'No way, it's just getting to the good part.' He slides his fingers inside my knicker elastic, planting them firmly inside my pussy lips.

That's where they stay for the rest of the tape.

TV-Lloyd removes my mouth from his cock while it's still hard and lets me hide my face in the duvet, presenting my thighs, bum and cunt to the viewer instead. He gives the invisible audience a guided tour of these, spreading lips and cheeks, pointing out little crevices and areas of interest. Chief among these is my vagina, which he then pushes some fingers inside, coating them in juices, which he smears over my thighs.

'What do you think?' Lloyd whispers into my ear.

'The lighting could be better.'

'No, what do you think is going to happen to her?'

'Shall we make a bet?'

'I think you'd win. Come on. What?'

'Well, at an outside guess, I'd say you stick your cock inside her.'

'Inside her what?'

'Ah. Good point. I seem to remember a sore pussy the next day, so ...'

'Well, look, you win.'

TV-him has inserted his cock into the correct orifice. I feel like a winner. I also feel like an enormously sexually frustrated person, watching the way he bangs into me. Because of my self-imposed restriction on shots of my face, all we get to see is Lloyd's back view, but the way his gluteal muscles tense and flex is a sight I feel privileged to behold.

I start circling my hips, very subtly, hoping he won't register my sly efforts to press my clit into his resting fingers. It occurs to me that I could sneak an orgasm without him knowing it – would that be possible? If he doesn't know about it, do I have to declare it?

But that wouldn't be in the spirit of the challenge. After all, there's nothing to stop me hiding away in the toilets at work and seeing to myself. He'd never know. All the same, the daring naughtiness of doing it right under his nose appeals to me. So I work the hips in infinitesimal rotation, increasing the clitoral pressure in tiny degrees.

'You want to come, don't you?' he says, just as his TV incarnation collapses on my back.

'No,' I say, but my breath is all weird and catchy.

'You're such a liar. I know what you're doing. Well, you can come if you want. Be my guest. I'll finger you if you like. But it just means a fail.'

'You think you're such an evil mastermind, don't you? This is nothing.' I try to wriggle away from the hand planted in my pants, but I can't.

'I'll have to up the ante then.' He starts kissing me again in that full-blooded Lloyd way. I try harder to elude him but it's useless. My pulse is hammering, my blood raging around my body in a race to get to my cunt. I start to feel light-headed and desperate.

When he breaks the kiss, I gasp as if I've just run a marathon.

He takes pity on me, removes his hand.

'You passed that one. OK. Well done. But I'm not finished. Not by a long way.'

***

I have to spend the next day at work without any underwear.

In the morning, Lloyd lays out my silkiest shirt, my shortest, tightest skirt, a pair of lace-topped hold-ups and nothing else.

'What's this?' I frown, emerging from the shower to find the clothes I'd brought back in the wardrobe.

'Second challenge within a challenge. Spend all day commando.'

'Ha. Won't be the first time.' I pick up the blouse and let it sigh over my skin.

'No. But it's the first time you've done it with no expectation of an orgasm in your near future.'

He's right. And it does make a difference.

Feeling a gentle draught waft up my skirt and bathe my nether regions is bliss when I'm anticipating a good shag over the desk in due course. When I know nothing like that is likely to happen, it's torture.

I can't cross the lobby floor without a barrage of lustful looks – mainly people trying to get a glimpse of the stocking tops that peek from the hem of the miniskirt. My jacket covers the worst indiscretions of my nipples, but I can still feel them, fizzing away against the silk, sending urgent messages to my pussy.

In the bar, a former 'gentleman friend' spies me and stops

me to chat about inconsequential things. While he talks about his promotion, one of his hands slides down my back and onto my arse, rubbing it.

'Hey, I'm working,' I warn him. 'And not available like that, not today.'

'But I miss you, Sophie,' he mourns. 'And that tiny skirt ... don't you want it?'

'No. Sorry. But great news about the promotion.'

'Whoever he is, I'm jealous.'

The man's voice follows me across the bar and into the kitchens, where I try to escape, only to face the porters licking their chops as they look me up and down.

In the back yard, I find Lloyd smoking a cigarette.

'Ah,' he says, smirking. 'Comfort break?'

'I need to get away from all the lechery. It's starting to do my head in.'

'Well, if you must dress like a whore ...' He stubs out the cigarette, grinning, and reaches out for me.

I hang back, suspicious of his motives.

'C'mon, Soph. I was just wondering if you'd come out here to relieve some ... urges.'

'Yeah, because I find the food bins are an ideal environment for self-pleasure.'

He catches me, winds me in. 'Any port in a storm,' he whispers. His hands are all over me, instantly, under the jacket, feeling their way up my thigh.

'Lloyd!'

'I just need to make sure you're not cheating.'

He drops to a crouch, nudges up my skirt and peers into the darkness. His nose nuzzles my thighs as he takes a deep inhalation.

'For fuck's sake, Lloyd! Anyone could come out.'

Half laughing, half mortified, I try to push him away, but he clings to my thighs, keeping his face close to my private parts.

'God, so wet,' he says, his words warming my sex. 'Dripping. And your clit is huge. You really want it. Poor Sophie. But you aren't going to get it.'

A rustle and a cough come from the direction of the kitchen doors. Someone has seen us and ducked inside again.

'You bastard,' I hiss, managing to dislodge him this time.

He loses his balance and falls backwards, onto a stray potato peeling. He stands up and brushes the seat of his good suit trousers, looking wounded. 'These had better not need dry cleaning,' he moans. 'If they do … oh yes. Good idea. I'm definitely going with that one.'

'What?'

'You'll see.' And he stalks off back to the kitchen door, leaving me to wonder who it was that saw Lloyd sniffing my crotch in the bin yard.

The rest of the day is accordingly uncomfortable. My clit feels like a lead weight, dragging me down wherever I go. I want to squirm and scratch when I'm seated. When I stand, I want to squish my thighs together hard.

But somehow I make it through.

It's a relief to get back to my own flat, minus Lloyd, and even more of a relief to put on my sensible, matronly underwear the next day.

Despite the growing undertow of frustration nagging at my nethers, I stay professional, even with Lloyd, who continually hints at some dark future event every time our paths cross.

Finally, I corner him in an ill-lit corner of the cocktail lounge. 'Go on then.'

'What?' He looks up from the menu he is annotating.

'What's today's challenge? Hit me.'

'That's exactly it.'

'You can't. I mean, you can't mean … you aren't going to spank me?'

'What else would I mean?'

'You can't. I don't consent to it.'

He shrugs. 'Fail then.'

'No, I only fail if I have an orgasm. This is different.'

'Excuse me.' He looks up, eyes wide, arms folded. 'I think I set the terms, don't I?'

'It doesn't give you carte blanche to do exactly what you want.'

'No, Sophie, because if it did, you'd be moving in with me. Tonight.'

This is where I have to back down. 'Just give me time,' I mutter.

'That's what I'm doing. So. Tonight. My place. Your arse, my lap. OK?'

'Fine. That's … fine.'

He nods, dismissing me.

The rest of the day passes very slowly. Time to think, time to think. The thing is, he could give me the rest of my life to think. I'd still get nowhere. I'm paralysed, deep down. Paralysed and inadequate. Perhaps I should let him go. Could I let him go?

When it comes down to it, this is the only way I can make a decision – to have it made for me, or brought down to a test or lottery of chance.

Lloyd knows this, but he doesn't know why.

I don't want to talk about why.

***

The spanking is given on the pretext that I ruined his suit trousers by pushing him over in the yard.

It's long and expertly sensual and administered to my bare bottom in my favourite position – draped over his lap. It has the obvious hoped-for consequence of making me insanely horny, which he, of course, relishes.

'There's a correlation between the heat on your bottom and the wetness in your cunt, isn't there?' he says, running his hand over my throbbing skin.

'Very scientific.' I try to push up my bottom, to lure his hand between my soaked lips. I get nowhere.

'Tut tut.' He accompanies his clicking disapproval with two light smacks. 'You know the rules. Now, I think you can stay like that while I watch this DVD. Just like that, over my knee, and I'll rub some lotion into you. Would you like that?'

'Nooo,' I moan, though normally I would love it.

His lotioned fingers torment me for the entire duration of the film until, by bedtime, my cunt is twitching in bemusement, wondering when the hell the cock is turning up.

Not tonight, Josephine. Not for a few nights yet.

Day four involves a butt plug. On day five I'm tied to the bed and tickled with feather dusters until I scream.

But what really worries me is day six.

On day six, he does nothing at all.

I wake up in his bed on day seven insouciant and breezy.

'Almost there,' I crow, ignoring my morning fog of lust and jumping out of bed.

'Almost,' says Lloyd, watching me from the bed. 'Not quite.'

'What have you got planned? I can't believe you didn't try anything on yesterday. You must have some kind of massive finale prepared.'

'You know me too well.' He's quiet for a moment, watching me scoop my shower things out of my overnight bag. He's told me thousands of times I should keep some on his shelf, but I've never got round to it. 'I've invited some friends round for dinner.'

I stand straight, watching his face for a moment. 'Oh?'

'Close friends.'

'Who?'

'Rachael and O, from the club.'

'For dinner?'

'Yeah. It's our day off. Thought they could come round in the afternoon and hang out.'

'And by hang out, you mean …?'

'You'll see.'

His smile is not reassuring.

In the shower, I daren't even apply the gel to my pubic area, I'm so scared of turning myself on. I wash my hair for what seems like hours, digging my fingers into my scalp, then pulling them back when I realise that the sensation is too sensual. I lather up my arms and stomach and legs and back and leave the rest to the suds. Some of them slide over my breasts and bottom and dissolve in my crotch, but it's nothing to do with me. I didn't touch them.

Goose bumps pucker my skin when I get out and I quickly scrub myself dry and wrap my treacherous body in its bathrobe. When I dress, I put on the only pair of jeans I own and a shapeless jumper. Pure thoughts, pure thoughts.

At the farmers' market, looking for things to cook for our guests, I try to draw Lloyd out on the subject of his plans, but he distracts me with vegetables and artisan cheeses and slaps on the rump until I give up. I think he likes my jeans.

All the same, I have a sick, anxious feeling about it.

It doesn't help that every single thing at the market makes me think about sex. Ripe fruits, firm cucumbers, rich scents and luxurious textures. I want to smear the berries all over me. I want Lloyd to turn me into an Eton mess.

The urgent tug at my crotch continues when we get back to the flat and start chopping and preparing. My fingers stained with juice, the sharp blade slicing and dicing, Lloyd skinning the fish with such practised skill that I want to stop what I'm doing and just watch those hands at work. It's a symphony of sensuality, and I want the crescendo. Except I can't have it. My night can't end with a bang or a whimper. Just a head of steam that might well burn me.

'What's for dessert?' I ask, slicing the last potato for the dauphinoise.

Lloyd indicates the large variety of fruits we bought at the market. 'Isn't that obvious?'

'No, I mean –'

'I know what you mean. Let's just call it Bombe Surprise.'

'No, let's not. What can I actually expect?'

He reprises his exaggerated Clouseau accent and disappears into the bathroom, waggling a finger at me in what he must think is a Gallic style. *Twat.*

'What shall I wear?' I call after him, desperate for a clue.

'Nothing,' he shouts through the door.

Seriously? Nothing?

I put the ingredients together, cover them with foil and slide them into the oven.

I wander into the bedroom and look at the dress I brought for the occasion. Lloyd can't expect me to sit at the table eating in the nude. What if I spill hot sauce on myself? He's just joking. I put on the dress and a pair of stockings and make a start on my make-up.

'What do you think you're doing?' Lloyd emerges from the bathroom in a towel, hair wetly tousled.

'Duh! Getting ready. They'll be here in twenty minutes.'

'You're wearing clothes.'

'Yes.' I hold the mascara wand steady, half an inch from my eyelashes. 'And?'

'I told you. Unnecessary.'

He strides around the room, gathering shirt and trousers from the wardrobe, socks and pants from the drawer.

'Unnecessary? Maybe in the Stone Age, but I'm no cavewoman.'

'Ah, but you are.' He locates his deodorant stick and applies it with a will. 'You are a cavewoman. And I'm Captain Caveman.'

'You aren't hairy enough. Besides, I always hated Captain Caveman. Can't you be Dick Dastardly instead?'

'Yeah, OK. And you can be Penelope Pitstop. Naked Penelope Pitstop.'

I give him a look while he buttons his trousers and loops his belt through them. 'I don't remember that scene in *Wacky Races*.'

'I must have daydreamed it. Get that dress off. Chop chop.' He claps his hands then returns to buttoning his cuffs.

'But why?' I complain. 'Why must I be naked?'

'Because I said so.'

'It is only Rachael and O coming tonight? Nobody else?'

'Just me and you. Though you might not be coming.'

'Hur hur.'

'But if my calculations work, you will be.' He sprays cologne beneath his chin, grinning demonically.

'OK.' I take off the dress. 'Will that do?'

'And the rest,' he says. 'No knickers required.'

'I wish you'd mentioned this before,' I grumble. 'I'd have gone to the beauty salon, or done a spray tan or something.'

'You're perfect as you are,' he says, gliding dangerously near and running a hand down my spine.

'I'm far from it. But thanks.' I struggle out of my knickers and pull a face at my somewhat untended pubic triangle. No doubt O and Rachael will be porn-star smooth. But, then again, I'm not a porn star. So why should I care?

I return to the dressing table and my mascara while he stands behind me, putting stuff in his hair. I wonder if any other couple has ever prepared for an evening out like this? Him all spiffy and suave in his expensive shirt, her butt naked in full maquillage?

Our reflections in the mirror give me that dreaded flush of lust. Tonight is going to be difficult. I wish I knew how difficult.

I wait for them in the living room while Lloyd answers the door. I am discreetly arranged on the sofa so that my legs are crossed and my arms folded over my breasts, but all the same, I can't help feeling a little ... what's the word ...?

'Oh, Sophie, you're naked!' trills Rachael, bursting in with a bouquet of bright orange and yellow flowers.

That's the one.

'It's the new black, apparently,' I say, taking the flowers from her and going to put them in water.

Lloyd joins me with two bottles of wine that O has handed over and uncorks the red to let it breathe.

'I feel really weird,' I mutter to him. 'Really really weird.'

'Good,' he says, beaming. 'Just put those in the sink and come and sit down. I want to get this show on the road.'

On opposite ends of the sofa, O and Rachael sit, chatting, both looking a million dollars in skimpy dresses and strappy shoes. They were obviously given a dress code too.

My assumption had been that I would be made to watch while Lloyd romped with the two submissive stunners, but my own nudity has thrown me and I no longer know what to expect.

On the one hand, it would have been enormously difficult to watch Lloyd fuck two other women with no chance of being asked to join in.

On the other, it's what I was prepared for. And now it isn't going to happen.

'Sit between them,' Lloyd suggests. At least, it's phrased as a suggestion, but I don't think it really is. He watches us for a moment while we all look up at him.

'Sorry,' he says, reviving from a trance-like few seconds. 'I just don't think my sofa has ever looked quite so sexy. Anyway. I thought we could start with cocktails. I'm going to do a little trick I used to sometimes show off with in my mixology days. I'm going to make you each a personalised cocktail.'

'Ooh.' O and Rachael are impressed, though I've seen him do this a hundred times.

'Starting with you, O, I think you're a sophisticate who would go for something stylish and classic, not too sweet, perhaps a little citrusy – am I right? And you'd go for lighter spirits rather than dark. The drink's appearance is important to you. Tell me if I'm wildly off base.'

'No, no, you're not.'

'OK, then. It's a classic, but never a cliché. I'm going to make you a Cosmopolitan.'

'Lovely! I'm just in the mood for one.'

'Great. Now, Rachael ... you're adventurous and well travelled with a taste for the exotic. You like new flavours and experiences. I'm going to give you something with a horrible name but a great kick – a Monkey Gland.'

'What the hell's a Monkey Gland?'

'Gin, Pernod, orange juice, grenadine.'

'Yummy. Go for it.'

'As for Sophie, well, I know what she likes.'

'I know what you're going to say,' I warn him. It's an oft-repeated gag in our relationship.

He beats me to it. 'Sloe Comfortable Screw!' he shouts in triumph, hastening to the kitchen. 'Against the wall,' he adds from over his shoulder.

'Lloyd's funny, isn't he?' says Rachael indulgently.

'Funny peculiar,' I reply.

'No, he's a sweetie. I love the relationship you have. I envy you sometimes.'

'Really?'

'He's so in love with you. And you're so in love with him.'

'Do you really think so?'

O weighs in. 'Well, I don't know you as well as Rachael does, but I'd certainly say so.'

'When you work together every day, you have to get on with each other,' I say, but I'm talking to myself. I don't know why I have this need to play it down, to make it seem less than it is. The feeling that I don't deserve him – getting louder and clearer each day – makes its unwelcome presence felt in my consciousness. Hello, old friend.

Lloyd returns with the drinks, plus what looks like a Whiskey Sour for him, and takes a seat in the armchair. Again, he can do little more than look at the three of us, lined up like the three submissive monkeys.

A sip of his drink galvanises him.

'OK,' he says. 'We've discussed this beforehand, O,

Rachael and I. I think it's time for the appetiser.'

Appetiser? I don't know what they mean, but they certainly do.

O and Rachael rise from the sofa and pull me up by my hands.

O sits back down in the middle and beckons me down on to her lap. I sit between her thighs, leaning back on her chest, her large pearls bumping against my shoulder blades. Her hands, heavily beringed, move around my front to cup my breasts.

'Spread your legs, dear,' she whispers into my ear.

I look up at Lloyd, who is entranced, running one fingertip round and round the rim of his glass. My naked thighs splay until my legs hang outside O's stockinged knees, spreading my pussy wide.

O caresses my breasts and it feels reassuring, gentle.

'That's the girl,' she croons. 'Nice and wide. Lovely pert nipples here.'

She kisses my neck. She smells glorious, one of those old-school Parisian fragrances that were banned for being too close to the smell of sex.

Lloyd can't seriously expect me to …

Rachael kneels down in front of us and skims perfectly manicured nails along the insides of my thighs.

'Oh.' I can't help the little exhalation of helpless, fearful desire.

When her tongue curls inside my lips, her feminine touch and knowledge is so acute that I gush into her. O, holding on to me for dear life, begins to nip at my neck. Rachael really knows how this is done. She might lack Lloyd's muscularity and firmness of purpose, but every lick hits home, deadly accurate, while my clit grows and my juices run ever thicker.

My body trembles, moving out of my control.

Lloyd's face is almost too hard to look at. The expression of utter intensity frightens me. I shut my eyes, feel O's rings snag at my nipples, Rachael's nails dig into my skin. I try to take myself away from physical reality, find a place where I am not aroused, not exposed, not being eaten out by a beautiful woman while my lover watches. But the place can't be found, the reality can't be denied.

I begin to squirm and surge on O's lap, trying to escape Rachael's tyrannical attentions.

'It's no use, darling,' whispers O. 'If Rachael doesn't make you come, we're going to swap places. And believe me, I have never left a woman unsatisfied.'

'It ... isn't ... fair,' I pant, and then I have to give in.

The orgasm is huge and tears me into pieces. I kick and wail until I fear for the women's safety, my eyes tight shut, my hands flapping, my bare body undulating all over O.

When I come to, I find Lloyd standing over us, smiling down, his eyes all shiny.

'That wasn't fair,' I say, my voice coming out as a harsh whisper.

'No, but it was amazing.'

He holds out his hands. I swing my legs off O's lap and let him hold me, too weak and shivery to knee him in the groin as I rightly should.

'Failure never looked better.' He kisses the words into my ear, then addresses our guests. 'Wonderful work. Truly wonderful. You are artists of erotica.'

They go back to sipping cocktails, still as immaculate as they were when they entered the room. It's just me that's a big old sex mess.

'Can I get dressed now?'

'No.'

'But ...'

'The night is young. And the fish is cooked. I'll go and sort it out while you do the wine, yeah?'

He leaves me, naked and streaked with sweat and come, to entertain our guests and set the table.

'Thanks,' I say to them. It seems polite.

'Pleasure,' they chorus, not inaccurately.

I don't spill any hot sauce on my naked flesh, but I am extremely careful to make sure each mouthful is securely pronged on my fork first. As we eat, we chatter about the club, about Mal and Dr Lassiter, about the hotel, about things I could discuss with perfect unselfconsciousness if only I was clothed.

Then Lloyd clears away the plates and orders me onto the table.

'What?'

'You heard. Get on the table.'

'Why?'

'Why do you think?'

He doesn't wait for my answer, elbowing his way into the kitchen, and I presume he doesn't hear my yell of 'I don't know!' because he is too busy clattering about with the dishwasher.

'I think you're dessert.' O enlightens me with a sly smile.

'But we bought fruit and cream ... oh ...'

'Fruity,' giggles Rachael. 'Very fruity. If you ever get bored with Lloyd, can I have him?'

Bored with Lloyd. Could that happen? I ponder this as I climb aboard the table with its snowy-for-now cloth. I move the candles in the centre to the end, blowing them out. I don't know if Lloyd was planning on a spot of wax play, but on the other hand, I've no plans to burn the hotel down.

'What do you think, girls? On my back?'

'I guess so,' says Rachael. O merely shrugs.

They sip their wine and watch me lay myself on the smooth linen, legs together, hands crossed over my breasts like a statue atop a medieval tomb.

'I did something a bit like this,' O remarks. 'At one of His Lordship's house parties. Were you there, Rachael? The Roman orgy?'

'Oh yes, I was. I was a slave girl. Not as much fun as I thought it would be, actually – I spent most of the evening refilling wine glasses.'

'At least you weren't the vomitorium attendant,' I remark.

While we are contemplating this fate, Lloyd returns to the room, bearing a vast platter of soft fruits and a pitcher of double cream.

Without stopping for any kind of explanation, he tips the fruit in a chilly avalanche all over my body then pours the cream on top.

I yelp and shiver and try to elude the thick stream, but all that happens is I crush a number of berries into the tablecloth, which will probably never recover.

'Dig in,' says Lloyd, discarding the jug with a flourish.

Giggling, Rachael kneels up on her chair and snags a strawberry from my stomach. I watch her eat, her nose dotted with cream. She looks luscious and sexy. O, ever decorous, uses her fingers to pick up a raspberry, which she then places delicately on one nipple and licks off with her tongue.

Lloyd joins in, looming over me, elbows on the table, burying his face deep into the delta of my thighs, forcing them apart. Fruits tumble in, cream drips down between my lips and coats my clit. Lloyd feeds avidly and greedily while the female diners are more delicate, hovering around my breasts and belly, careful not to smear cream on their lovely dresses.

He pushes fruits up inside me with his fingers then retrieves them with his tongue. Melon and mango combine with my own taste of honey, giving Lloyd the ultimate in dining experiences.

Daintier lips and teeth tackle my nipples, licking puréed passion fruit and cream off them. For a long time, I can hear nothing but laboured breathing, low 'mmm's of orgiastic delight, the smacking of lips while the three of them partake of me.

Lloyd drizzles my cunt with a raspberry coulis, licks it off but doesn't stop when it's all gone, his tongue continuing to work my clit with long, slow strokes.

O and Rachael stand back, all the fruit having gone now.

'If I come …' I manage to blurt.

'Hmm?' Lloyd speaks into my spread split lips.

'Would that be …?'

'Don't worry about that,' he mutters. 'We'll call tonight one fail.'

I let go of my tension, forget about incurring the third and final fail, and hook my ankles around his neck. In a welter of mess and cream and fruit stains, I allow a ragged orgasm to take hold of me.

It turns out to be only the second of many.

Over the course of the evening, O and Rachael fuck me with candles and vibrators while Lloyd watches, cock in hand, mixing his seed with the remnants of dessert that cover my breasts.

When they finally leave and we stagger to bed, leaving the clearing up until morning, I can barely keep my eyes open or my legs upright.

'So, Sophie,' he whispers, cradling me in the darkness while the kitchen staff haul barrels and crates about in the yard below. 'Two fails now.'

'That wasn't fair. Nobody could have succeeded with that one.'

'It was perfectly fair. And I was very kind to only count the first orgasm. If I'd decided to carry on, you'd be packing your bags tomorrow morning.'

'Why do you want that so much?'

'Oh, Sophie, why do you think?'

But I'm too tired to formulate thoughts and I slide into dreamland, sideways, away from the questions that won't stop asking themselves.

Chapter Nine

'So, let's talk about this,' says Lloyd over breakfast the next morning. 'Let's get some things straight.'

I don't like the sound of this. I gnaw on my croissant, suddenly finding its texture too bulky for actual mastication.

'That tablecloth is beyond hope,' I say, looking at the orgy of different purple shades. 'Unless you want to recycle it as a masterwork of abstract art.'

'Never mind the tablecloth. I'll take it down to the laundry later. I want you to tell me what's the worst that could happen.'

'Nuclear war,' I decide, swallowing my croissant crumb and returning the rest to the plate. 'I think that'd be worse than alien invasion, somehow. The knowledge that we'd done it to ourselves.'

'Shut up.' He looks quite rattled, not the laid-back Lloyd I'm used to. 'Sorry. Sorry, didn't mean to snap at you. But just stop it, OK? Just for once, take something seriously.'

'What do you mean, just for once? I take lots of things seriously. The hotel, for one.'

'I'm talking about us. If you move in here, if you commit to a future with me, what's the worst that could happen?'

193

I could lose you. That's why I haven't ever properly claimed you. Because if you're never mine to lose, then ... The logic is too faulty. I can't say it. And besides, I don't want him to know how much he means to me. Knowledge is power, and I want the power on my side.

'You might change.'

'So you like me as I am?'

'Of course.'

'I can't promise I'll never change. People do. But I'll be open with you, always. You'll always know what I'm thinking. If I'm going to change, you'll be the first to know.'

'I might change, and then you might not like me any more.'

'That would matter to you?'

'God, Lloyd, of course it would. You seem to think that there's no other expression of love or loyalty or commitment than the traditional sharing of worldly goods and finances. That's not the definition of it, you know.'

'I do know that, Sophie. I think you love me, though you've never said so. I think that scares you, and that's why you're so reluctant to do something that would be positive for us both, and fun, and practical and ... just the right thing to do. I want to know why it scares you. I want to know you.'

'That's the thing. I don't want you to know me. If you really knew me, you probably wouldn't like me.'

'You're so ... Oh God.' He rests his head on the table, pantomiming epic frustration. 'Sophie. Listen. I like you. I love you, in fact. I don't care if you have secret plans to assassinate the Cabinet. I don't care if you poisoned a guinea pig in nineteen ninety-four. I don't care if you have sex with other men. I love you. Do you understand that? Can you comprehend it?'

'I don't think I can.' I twist the tablecloth in my hand,

looking at a particularly gorgeous effusion of indigo. 'Sorry.'

He pauses to drink some coffee, watching me all the while. 'When your father left,' he says, 'how did that affect you?'

'I was gutted. I was only five. I didn't understand.'

'But you came to understand?'

'No, not really. I never did.'

'You've always said that life carried on as normal and it was fine and you were fine and you all coped really well.'

'We did! I went to school and did well and had friends and all that.'

'What friends?'

'School friends. Girl friends.'

'You aren't in touch with any of them.'

'Well, no. I moved away.'

'Email? Facebook? Phones?'

'What's your point, Lloyd?'

'You won't let anyone get beyond your inner wall, will you? They can get so close and no closer. I'm no psychiatrist but ...'

'You think it's because my dad left? Abandonment issues? How trite.'

'Well, it might be a cliché, but things become clichés for a reason. Usually there's some truth in them.'

'I don't think so.'

'And there was the whole Chase thing, before we got together. What *was* that about? A remote, unavailable man, twenty-odd years older than you ... hmmm ... let me think ...'

'Fuck off. You are way, way off beam.'

He curls his lip, rolls his eyes. 'Have it your way,' he says wearily, then he seems to disagree with his own words, leaning forwards to speak with intense urgency.

'Actually, no. Don't have it your way. Have it my way. Move in with me, Sophie. Just break through your fears and take a risk. I'll make it worth your while. I'll make you happy, I promise.'

His face seems to swim in front of me, only his eyes retaining pure sharpness. I feel a heat and a constriction. I'm on a tower, and everyone's shouting at me to jump.

I could do it. I could do it.

I break our gaze.

'I'm not ready.'

'Shit,' he says under his breath. He swigs from the coffee cup again. 'Look, I was hoping I wouldn't have to do this challenge. But I'm going to. I need to know how it ends. But you'll stick to the deal, won't you? No matter whether you pass or fail, you'll stick to the deal.'

'I always stick to a deal.'

'Good. Right. I know that. Just needed to hear it.'

'What's the challenge?'

'I'm not going to say yet. I need to make a few arrangements first.' He drains his cup. 'See ya.'

He leaves without the usual kiss, or slap to my thigh, or growly bear hug.

I feel like I'm losing him already.

* * *

'Dress for sex.

Take a taxi to Brace Street and go into the Peep Show at number 5. Tell whoever's behind the counter that you're here for Mr Bulgarov. He'll direct you up some stairs. We'll be waiting for you on the top floor.

You should be there for eleven.

L.'

Lloyd is out for the afternoon on a procurement job, so this message arrives by email with the heading, 'Challenge'.

I read it through three times before I realise that the Peep Show on Brace Street is the same one I once performed at, the one below the illegal gambling club where Lloyd used to run the bar.

This gives me an immediate and consuming sense of unease.

If I emailed him back, 'Yes, I'll move in with you' … no. I have the feeling this challenge will be about confronting something. Something I don't want to confront, but perhaps should.

Dressing for sex involves squeezing into a beribboned black satin basque straight out of the Moulin Rouge, together with G-string and matching teeny ruffled skirt. Lace-topped thigh-high stockings are next, then I pull on an expensive tuxedo-style jacket, which covers more than the skirt even bothers to attempt.

In the mirror, I look template-sexy, but I can see the vulnerability behind the lipstick and the false lashes. All the same, the basque and other fixings are like a uniform, pulling me out of self-doubt and into a professional frame of mind.

Lloyd sometimes accuses me of approaching sex as if it were a job, and I can see his point. I am my own harshest Performance Reviewer. My objective is always to provide an unforgettable fuck, the best of whoever's life. If I don't achieve this, then I mark myself down, consider myself unfit for promotion.

Eliciting an emotional response has never been on my

job description, but now it's happened, I don't know what to do about it.

Lloyd loves me. He's said so. He wants me in his life for the duration.

I'm sure he means it.

I'm sure he *thinks* he means it.

Don't we always think we mean stuff, at the time? And then …

The buzzer heralds the arrival of my taxi. I slip my feet into stiletto heels and leave my mirror reflection to introspect alone.

It's strange to stand outside the Peep Show frontage again. It's even seedier-looking than I remember, several of the neon letters having malfunctioned so instead of being called KittyKat, it looks like K tt K t. The shiny reflective fabric in the window is torn in a few places. I wonder if passers-by could look directly in at the figure of a naked dancer. I'm almost tempted to put my eye to a crack, but I don't want to attract negative attention, or spend too much time on this cigarette-butt-strewn pavement, so I enter the building with as much purpose as I can muster.

The guy behind the counter doesn't recognise me, but I remember him.

'No jobs going,' he says without looking up from his newspaper. 'We got more girls than we can handle and not enough punters. It's the recession, love. Sorry.'

'No, I'm here for Mr Bulgarov.'

He looks at me properly. Is that a flicker of recognition? I hope not and look away.

'Ah.' He lets the word hang portentously in the air, giving me an insolent up-and-down inspection. He doesn't say, 'the whore' but he's thinking it. 'In that case …' He opens a door to the side of the counter and waves me up. 'Top floor, love. Knock three times.'

I climb the rickety stairs, tripping over a couple of girls smoking on a landing, exchanging comfortless anecdotes about their last places of employment.

The top floor is a long way up. By the time I reach it, my ankles are about to give way and I have to take a moment so as not to make my entrance puffing like a steam train.

I can't hear anything behind the thick reinforced metal of the door. I put my hand against it and try to push but it's impenetrable, probably triple-locked, bolted and barred.

I put back my shoulders, lift my chin and knock three times.

There is silence, then rattles and clicks from the other side. A spyhole in the centre of the door is suddenly occupied by a big fish eye. I smooth my hands over the satin tux jacket and pout.

Eventually, the door is half opened. A kind of human cliff face stands in the space revealed, broad and vast and slablike.

'Your name?' he asks in a heavy accent of some kind.

'Sophie.'

'OK. Come in.'

The room is small and low lit. In one corner, there's a bar area. Lloyd stands there, wiping tumblers with a tea towel. I don't try to catch his eye. It's much more important just now to get my bearings.

In the centre of the room, four men sit around a table, playing cards. Three of them are middle-aged while one is younger. He has a mean, sleek look about him. All of them project an aura of serious wealth, their wrists weighed down with chunky watches, their suits perfectly cut, fat Cuban cigars wedged between the lips of two of them. None of them looks at me. They are all too busy surveying their hands of cards or pushing piles of tokens around the table. A bottle of Grey Goose stands at the centre of play, ready to refill any empty glasses.

Already uncomfortable, I start to feel awkward. It's embarrassing to just stand here, dressed for sex, while none of the men in the room display the slightest bit of interest in me.

Eventually, one of the older ones looks up. 'Ah, you're here,' he says.

Self-evidently.

'Uh, yeah,' I say. 'What do you want me to do?'

He sweeps his gaze around the other three players. 'We thought you could add a little incentive to our game. We're playing five hands. The winners of the first four get a sexual service of their choice. The winner of the fifth gets to take you home for the night. What do you say?'

Lloyd's silence deafens me from across the room.

He wants me to say yes? He wants me to say no?

No would be a fail. Of course he wants me to say it.

'Yes. That sounds fine.'

'Good. Well, take off your jacket and let's have you standing on that chair in the corner. Give us something nice to look at, and something to play for.'

The other gents smirk and chuckle, watching me take my display position. It's not easy to maintain in these shoes, but I strike a pose, hand on hip and watch them from my height.

They are not playing poker, or even whist, but pontoon, or blackjack as the American gentleman in the party calls it.

I take a good look at each of the four, trying to figure out which would be the best to spend the night with. Lloyd, behind me, is quiet and discreet, only making a sound when one of the players calls for more cigars or a drink. I want to forget that he is there, but I can't.

The young guy has the face of an assassin. I really hope I don't get him.

The American looks kinder, in a silver foxy kind of way. He has broad shoulders and looks a bit like a newscaster for CNN or something – avuncular but sharp.

A third man at the table appears to be Russian. He is thin, a little haggard, not wearing as well as the American, though just as expensively dressed. He has astonishingly blue eyes, though, that transform his face from tired to alert in the time it takes to blink.

The final man looks familiar, and it takes me about five minutes to realise, with a frisson of shock, that he is a Cabinet minister. One of those expansive Old Etonian types that our prime minister is so fond of, greying at the temples, heading into jowliness and gout.

Play is desultory, but eventually the Russian wins the first hand.

I expect him to ask for a blow job, and he does.

I step down from the chair, moving towards the lewd smiles of the gamblers until I am beside the Russian.

Without ceremony, he unbuttons his trousers and removes his semi-erect cock.

'Get on your knees,' he orders gutturally.

Maintaining perfect expressionlessness, I drop to my haunches in front of him, then kneel. I put out a hand to touch him, but he bats it away.

'Use your mouth only,' he instructs. 'Hands off.'

I shuffle closer and bend forwards, licking the curving underside of his shaft first in an effort to bring it to full erection. It isn't a huge organ and should be easy enough to take the full length if I keep my throat relaxed. I breathe gently on it, kissing it, feeling it harden under my attentions.

'Stop playing with it and suck it,' scolds the Russian, putting a hand under my chin and nudging my mouth over his cock tip. Those are the last words he addresses to me for some time.

While I gobble and suck, the men discuss great blow jobs of their life.

The Cabinet minister's took place at the Playboy mansion, apparently. The Russian got his mistress to suck him off in the royal box at a football cup final. The American enjoyed three episodes of fellatio in quick succession at an orgy in San Francisco, but he wasn't able to stretch to a fourth.

As for the younger man, his took place in an alleyway, the girl on her hands and knees in the dirt. He took his cock out of her mouth and came over her face, then made her go into the neighbouring pub for a drink with him.

'Shall I do that?' asks the Russian idly, while I bob up and down on his stiff cock. He must feel the tension that takes momentary hold of my body at the idea – I don't like it on my face, never have done, though sometimes it seems like the right end to a particular encounter. But not this one. There are still four hands to play, for heaven's sake. He laughs. 'I don't think she wants me to.'

'Make her,' says the younger one eagerly, but the American demurs.

'Hey, no, we want her in a good mood for the rest of us, right?'

'I suppose,' the Russian concedes. 'OK. Just because I'm a good guy, I'll make her swallow instead. Oh yes. That's good. Keep sucking. You've got a great mouth for it.'

'She's got a great everything,' remarks the Cabinet minister. 'Lovely arse. I can't wait to get it out of that skirt. If you can call it a skirt.'

'Is she deep-throating you?' the American wants to know.

But I have tipped my Russian oligarch just over that edge where speech becomes too difficult.

'I don't know what to ask for,' the American continues, canvassing his friends for their opinions. 'Such a lot of possibilities. Well, that's if I ever win a hand, of course.'

'Unlikely, with your record,' chips in the younger man.

'No need for snark, Egerton. You're only here as a substitute anyway, remember.'

I rub the Russian's balls with my chin and he comes, spurting richly into my mouth, grabbing my hair and mussing it, rather to my chagrin. I gulp it down, give his shaft a final circular lick then remove myself from the rich man's tool.

I keep my head bowed, not sure if I'm allowed to look him in the face.

He strokes the bit of my hair he's already tousled, a gesture of vague goodwill for a job well done.

'That was good. One of the best. You guys could do much worse than ask for a blow job from her.'

They take note and I rise to my feet, ready to take my position on the chair, but the Russian clicks his tongue and halts me with a hand around my lower arm.

'Hey, hey, one more thing. You lose some clothing every time.'

Oh, I see.

I kick off my stilettos and go to stand on the chair in my stockinged feet. I wonder what will happen if the Russian wins the next hand too. Will he ask for the same thing? Will he be able to get hard again so soon?

As it happens, the dilemma doesn't arise. The next winner is the American, despite the scoffing of Egerton.

'Awesome!' he exclaims, throwing down a perfect hand.

'And now, let me think. What wish can this sexy little genie grant me? Come over here, honey.'

I approach him with more confidence than I did the Russian. He seems a little more human than the others in the room, bar Lloyd of course.

He makes me stand between his knees while he explores my satin-covered body with big beringed hands.

'Can we actually fuck her?' he asks nobody in particular. He could ask me, but that doesn't seem to occur to him.

'I have condoms behind the bar if you want to,' says Lloyd.

'So we can? OK, honey, turn around and bend over the table for me.'

Lloyd tosses him a pack of three, which he catches with one hand. 'Years of baseball practice,' he says, chuckling.

I hear the cellophane wrapper crackling and I pivot my hips, avoiding the eyes of the other three men, who are leaning low over the table, looking at me.

They are going to watch me getting fucked. They've already seen me suck off another one of them. From the corner of my eyes I catch the feral gleam in their eyes and hear the subtle sound of salivation.

They lower their heads so that they are level with my breasts. My nipples are concealed by the cups of the basque, but the flesh above them spills over in abundance.

I wait for the American to touch me. For a moment, I have the strongest urge to look around at Lloyd, to see his face.

If he looks unhappy, I'll stop this. I'll fail.

I gather a hold of myself and keep my eyes to the front. I'm not going to look at Lloyd. I'm going to let this stranger fuck me in front of a group of other strangers, and my lover. And I'm going to enjoy it.

So I wiggle my hips a bit, letting the ruffle shift and shush across my bum, the frills tickling my upper thighs.

'Mmm, hot for it, eh?' says the American. 'I hope you're ready. I can't spend time getting you warmed up, doll, we've got business to see to. Hands to play. Tell you what, why don't you get your fingers down in that sweet little pussy, get it ready for me.'

The other men can't see me do this, because my lower half is under the table, but I slip one hand inside the G-string and touch my clit. It feels dry, so I give it a rub. I need to stop thinking about Lloyd. I need to let my consciousness defer to my sex drive, in the way it usually does. Why is it being such a stubborn bugger tonight?

I push my forefinger up into my tight passage, encountering resistance when I try to fit in another. I return to my clit and rotate my pelvis, pressing down on my insistent fingertips. Ah, yes, finally, my mind swoops away and I see myself from above, a girl who needs fucking, by all of the men in the room, until she can no longer stand.

'Mmm.' I start to feel it, the trembling high up in the hips, the slow outward spread of the warmth. My fingers are slicked in moisture and they fit easily into my cunt now. I can even get three up there.

The other men are too spellbound to speak, but the American still has mastery of his vocal cords. 'Are you getting good and wet for me, honey?'

'Uh-huh.'

'I've got a nice thick cock for you, gonna ride you good. You better have those legs spread wide.'

I part my trembling flanks for him. I know he can see my hand, bunched inside the tiny lacy knickers, working.

'You like to get fucked by strangers, honey?'

'I love it.'

I'm outside myself now, fully in my zone. I can't wait for him to mount and push his big fat American cock up inside me.

'This is one hot bitch,' says the younger man admiringly. 'I'm going to see I win the next hand.'

'You better make sure you're big enough to handle her, son, cos she's getting stretched.'

The American backs up his words as soon as the condom snaps on.

He pulls my hand roughly from the G-string and pushes the gusset to one side, sinking himself in my cunt with one rough stroke.

'Oh yeah,' he purrs. 'Good and tight. A real hot little pussy here. You like that, honey?'

'Mmm, so full.'

'Right. Now hold on tight, sweetheart, cos I'm gonna pound you. Real. Hard.'

His big hands settle on my hips, then he makes good his promise, pulling halfway out then slamming me against the table. Luckily, it's a gaming table with a smooth padded rim or there'd be bruises for sure.

He bangs me – there's no other way to put it – brutally and fast, lifting my feet from the floor with the force of each thrust.

'She's getting it,' says the Cabinet minister admiringly.

'She's loving it,' says the younger man. 'Look at her. She's in a trance.'

I want to shove my hand back down my knickers, but I need both hands to keep me anchored to the table while the American gives me one of the most punishing fucks of my life. I want to touch my clit, want to get myself off, but he's not interested in me, or my pleasure.

Lloyd would be angling his cock so that it swept over my G-spot, or stroked my clit on the way out.

This man has no such consideration.

He comes in ten hard thrusts, grunting and pinning me to the table until I can't breathe. When he releases me, my legs feel numb for a moment and I flop into a semi-crouch, hanging on to the padded edge.

The American falls back into his chair, puffing mightily. 'That's how a man fucks,' he claims. 'She can't even stand.'

I know it was all grandstanding for the benefit of the other men, and I ought to feel affronted, but I just feel relieved to have ticked another box on the challenge sheet. Two down. Two to go, then the spending-the-night thing. I hope it's not with him. Actually, if it's him, I might well concede.

I pick myself up. The G-string rubs a little painfully against my swollen pussy lips. I turn to stagger back to my chair, but the American clears his throat. 'Forgetting something?'

I shimmy off the tiny ruffled skirt, leaving me in underwear only. I risk the briefest of glances at Lloyd. He is getting something down off a shelf. Did he watch? Or did he turn his back for the duration?

The third winner is the Cabinet minister, who goes for a blow job. He is neither especially well endowed nor demanding and in a way it's quite peaceful to just bathe him with my tongue while he lies back and sighs and the others talk about investments and world banking.

Once he has come, I swallow it down and remove my basque, returning to the chair in just suspenders, stockings and G-string.

Only the evil-faced one has not had some part of me yet. I wonder if I'll get away without having to service him. Maybe the American will win again. The Cabinet minister might be OK to spend the night with. He seems pretty reasonable. The Russian seems more of an unknown quantity and the younger guy … just no. I just don't like him.

Standing on the chair in just the scantiest of wisps, I feel cold, my nipples standing painfully erect. I hear Lloyd clattering glasses and I can't stop myself from twisting my neck in his direction.

He looks as pale as death, his eyes hooded and watchful. I want to get down.

The Cabinet minister wins the fourth hand. He isn't up to much, so soon after I have drained him dry. He settles for a sexy lap dance and hand job, but he never gets fully erect, and lets me off after five minutes during which the others drum their fingers and roll their eyes.

'OK, the big one,' says the Russian grandly. 'Get naked, my beauty.'

I daren't look at them play the hand, so I kneel on the chair with my back to them, leaning over to present my bottom to their view. I let my hair hide my face so Lloyd won't be able to see what I'm thinking.

Which is: *Stop them.*

Or at least he could join in the game and give himself a chance of winning.

Doesn't he want to? Does he actually want to hand me over, give me away?

It occurs to me that this might be a test within a test – that, in order to pass, I have to fail. He might be waiting behind that bar, holding his breath for me to call time on it all and confess that I only want to leave this place with Lloyd.

If I did that …

There is a flurry of 'lucky bastard' type comments, and

I gather that the worst-case scenario has come to pass and the assassin-faced one has won.

Before I can hold up my hand and pull out of this thing, though, he says something that halts me in my tracks: 'Too bad it isn't me she'll be spending the night with.'

He sounds bad-tempered enough for it to be true. I turn and sit down on the chair, listening to the conversation. Of course, it excludes me. I'm just the prize.

'You're sure you aren't standing in for him in *every* respect?' chuckles the American, but the winner is already on the phone.

'Yeah. You won. OK. I'll bring her right over. Right.'

'So, I'm not going to your place?' I speak at last, looking between Evil Face and Lloyd.

'I'm delivering you,' says Evil Face flatly. 'I'm here representing my employer tonight. He's staying at the Hilton.'

What's wrong with the Luxe Noir?

'I see. So ... is that it? Do we go now?' I'm asking Lloyd.

He puts down a tea towel and nods. 'I'll see you tomorrow,' he says.

Just that. But it sounds wistful, hopeful, and a bit scared.

He wouldn't put me in danger. He'd never give me to somebody dangerous. He'd have vetted this guy thoroughly. It has to be somebody he's known a long time through this job. It's OK; it's fine.

I don't feel fine, though. Evil Face flaps a hand at me when I start getting dressed.

'That won't be necessary,' he says. 'Just put your shoes and jacket on.'

He hands me the satin tux. I slip it over my nude body and fasten the single button, just about covering my breasts, though my pussy will flash every time I take a step forwards.

'Good evening, gents.' I take a formal farewell of the other competitors.

They wave limply, already back to full absorption in the whisky and cigars.

'Cheers, doll, take care,' says the American, the only one to offer speech.

Evil Face puts his hand on my upper arm and steers me towards the immensely fortified door, which is opened by the huge goon, who has watched everything with a face suggestive of drugged stupor.

I totter in front of Evil Face. I'm still a bit sore and stiff from the American onslaught and it isn't easy to negotiate the steep, creaky staircase.

The smoking girls are long gone, but an empty condom packet lies on a landing, next to an empty tissue box. The closed doors around it must belong to a brothel. The atmosphere is oppressive and stale, misery compacted into every molecule of air. The opposite of sexy. Why would a person come here?

We walk out through the shop front of the peep show. A punter at the desk stops counting out banknotes in order to give me a good, long stare.

'She one of yours?' he asks the receptionist, but I don't hear the answer, because we are already outside on a dark, rainy pavement.

I look around for a car, but there isn't one.

'It's just around the corner,' says Evil Face. 'You can walk.'

'In this?' I gesture down at my barely concealed nudity.

'Sure. Look around you. You fit right in.'

It's true that the area around the park gates is home to little knots of working girls in tiny skirts and lots of leopard print, but I am still one step further on than them in the flesh-baring stakes and their eyes follow me along the alleyway that cuts through from the sleazy area to the district of fabulous wealth. Funny how all cities seem to have a similar geographical juxtaposition somewhere on the map, like a topographical joke.

I am grateful for the limited cover darkness affords me, but the light soon returns on the other side of the park. The hotel frontage is awash with golden light and I negotiate the steps and the lobby as quickly as I can, avoiding all eyes until we reach the lifts.

Upstairs on the top floor I can breathe again. My mystery man has the penthouse suite. Somehow this makes me uneasy. All the worst excesses at the Luxe Noir take place in the penthouse suite – some of the things the maids have had to clear up in there make even licentious little me shudder.

I could still walk away.

I pat my jacket pocket, looking for the rectangular reassurance of my mobile phone. Lloyd wouldn't put me in danger. Oh! Perhaps it's Lloyd in there! I know he's pretty friendly with the guys at this hotel. Though he'd have had to fly down the fire escape at the gambling den to get here before me.

This burgeoning hope is given extra weight when Evil Face taps me on the shoulder before I knock on the door. 'One more thing,' he says. 'He doesn't want you to see him.'

Chapter Ten

'What?'

My escort takes a length of black silk from his pocket. 'I have to blindfold you. OK?'

Now I really am confident that I am meeting Lloyd in there. I assent without protest, allowing the man to cover my eyes and tie a tight knot at the back of my head.

He knocks, but doesn't wait for an answer. The door is opened and I step carefully in, my heels sinking into plush, Evil-Face's hand on my elbow.

'Here she is,' he says. 'Special delivery. I'll leave her to you now.'

There is no reply, again. It's a person whose voice I'd recognise. I smile as a different hand takes my elbow, leading me onwards.

I try to repeat my triumphant guessing game hat-trick from the Soho stockroom, using my nose and my general awareness of Lloyd's mannerisms, but he has obviously learned from that day, because he is silent and scentless tonight.

I need to make him talk. 'So, how do you want me?' I ask, running a finger down the lapel of the tux.

His response is non-verbal – the removal of said item of

clothing. He undoes the button lazily, unhurriedly. A doubt makes itself known, way down in the pit of my stomach. *This isn't Lloyd.*

The way he slides his hand into the small of my back, holding me there while he, presumably, takes in my nakedness only magnifies this doubt.

There is something very different here. This is a man in absolute control of himself – he is scarcely even breathing. Lloyd would be at me, on me, all over me by now.

He spins me around, and the hands that land on my shoulders aren't Lloyd's. Longer fingers.

'Who are you?' I ask uncertainly.

I have this feeling ... but it just couldn't be. It really couldn't be.

It's some high roller we've had at the Luxe Noir, an elegant stranger.

We stop moving and his right hand sweeps its way down my side to my hip, patting it lightly, while he keeps a hold of my shoulder with the left. One of his fingers brushes my neck, a whisper of a caress.

His lips touch my nape. Oh God. I feel like swooning.

There is something incredibly powerful here. Suddenly, I realise that I am being Tempted. This man represents a different path for me and Lloyd has obviously chosen him very carefully.

I cry out as he pushes me abruptly onto the bed, which is directly in front of me. My upper torso lands flat in a valley of duvet and I bury my face along with it. Any further olfactory clues are going to be drowned out by the scented pillowcases, whose alarmingly musky aroma dominates the air.

I feel the expensive cloth of his suit jacket brush my wrist as he turns me over onto my back. Now he is breathing more heavily. I reach up, wanting to feel his skin, his height, his size, but he puts my hands over my head and presses them down briefly, indicating that that's where they should stay.

He sits on the side of the bed. I sense his hands, close to me, about to be laid on me. I tense up.

'I'm not sure about this,' I say.

Nothing happens for a moment. I think perhaps he is waiting for me to elaborate.

'It's not that I'm not used to scenarios like this. It's not that I'm scared of having sex with an anonymous stranger. If you knew anything about me, you'd know that. But there's something deeply ... wrong ... about this. And I can't even explain why. But I don't think I can do it.'

I hear him exhale, not quite a sigh, but almost. A cuff link, heavy and cold, makes momentary contact with my hip. My toes are curled tight.

Am I supposed to just leave? I sit up experimentally. He doesn't prevent me.

But I'm not going without knowing who he is. I can't. 'I need to know who you are.'

The duvet rustles – he has stood up. He walks away in the direction of the door.

'No, you can't just leave! I think I know who you are, anyway.'

The footsteps still. I feel I could reach up into the air and touch the tension, looping across the ceiling like washing lines.

Just speak, damn you!

'Chase.'

Terrible silence. I know I am right.

Then he speaks. 'Sophie.'

I rip off the blindfold and stare. 'Am I hallucinating?' I ask the vision in dove grey who stands before me.

'No.'

'I thought you'd left the country.'

'I did. This is a one-off, a favour to your beau.' He says 'your beau' with such vindictive force that I can't help feeling Lloyd must have blackmailed him into it. But why the hell …?

'That's the weirdest favour I ever heard of. What did he say? How did he ask you?'

Chase shrugs. 'Spend one night in a penthouse suite fucking Sophie or certain truths will be told. He must have worked hard to find my location, which impressed me, I suppose. And there was a quite considerable element of sweetener.'

He raises an eyebrow at me, taking my breath away.

All that time I spent in pursuit of him and he never gave me an inkling that he found me attractive. Why now? Why here?

'Do you really think so?' I hate myself for simpering and blushing when I should be asking difficult questions, but my body has never been much of a one for obeying my brain.

'You know so.'

There's a long beat of silence during which neither of us can move or look away from the other.

'I should leave,' I mutter. I don't convince myself, so I don't suppose he is taken in either.

'But you don't want to,' he says. He moves closer, just a couple of steps. 'Do you?'

'It's too dangerous.' I'm talking to myself, but Chase still answers.

'Lloyd wants this.'

I shake my head, utterly bemused. 'Why? Why would he?'

Chase sits on the edge of the bed, his eyes still locked with mine. 'Think about it.'

It's not easy to think with the man I lusted and yearned

after for years sitting so close to my naked body, but I try it anyway.

'Well, like everything we've done lately, it's a test,' I come up with eventually.

'Yes.'

You're the biggest temptation he could ever put in my way. I don't say this out loud though. I'm still angry with Chase over the way things ended before, and I don't want him getting ideas.

'But how do I pass the test? By walking out of here unshagged?'

'No,' says Chase. 'That's how you fail. Lloyd's idea was that we fuck with you blindfolded – you would find out afterwards that it was me. And then you could make your choice.'

'Choice? What choice? I can't choose you anyway – you're a fugitive living overseas. You have no place in my life.'

'Practically speaking, that's true. But what Lloyd wants to know is if an encounter with, well, this sounds a little arrogant, but the words he used were "your heart's desire" would change the way you felt about him. Make you dissatisfied, restless, determined to find someone who, if not me, made you feel the way I did.'

I pause to process this. It sounds madder than mad, but I can see a speck of rationale in there somewhere. 'He's insecure,' I say. 'I didn't realise that.'

'Well, I would say he had his reasons to be, wouldn't you?' He gestures at me, the prize in a gambling game. I don't feel like much of a prize now though.

'No. Everything we've done has been for the benefit of both of us. We've created our own sex life, and just because it isn't the hetero-monogamous norm, people feel sorry for

217

him and wonder when he's going to meet a nice girl. But to him, I am a nice girl. Maybe *only* to him. But it doesn't matter what anyone else thinks, does it?'

Chase sniffs. 'I wouldn't stand for it myself.'

'That's why you're wrong for me.'

'I suppose it is. So. Are you leaving now?'

I hug my knees to my chest and stare at the chandelier-heavy ceiling. 'If I do ... then I haven't done what Lloyd wants. I haven't put myself to the ultimate test. And if I don't, I guess he'll always wonder. And, perhaps, so will I. Though I'm almost sure I know what I want now. All the same ... come and sit next to me, Mr Chase.'

He allows himself a smirk, settling down to lean on the headboard at my side.

'I should tell you up front,' I say, 'that I want to hurt you.'

He draws back a fraction, his eyes wary.

'Are you surprised? Why? You hurt me. On an ongoing basis, knowing that you were doing it, enjoying it. You're cruel, and you're a cheat and a liar.'

'But you still wanted me.'

'Yeah, but why? Why do you think I wanted you?'

'Modesty forbids ...'

'I'll tell you why. Because I couldn't have you. And my theory is that, once I have had you, I'll forget all about you.'

'Theories are all very well. Practice is what counts.'

'I know that. Now that you're here on a plate, though, I have the strongest feeling that I could walk away without a second thought. I'm almost bored by the thought of fucking you.'

This fires him up. His eyes narrow and he grabs a wrist. 'Bored? Oh, you won't be bored. I can promise you that.'

The pressure of his hand on me lifts away the tension.

My fight or flight response has picked fight, and my blood pumps accordingly.

He leans down to my ear and speaks into it in that low, deadly voice that used to fill my dreams. 'When we worked together ... tell me the fantasies you had about me. What did I do to you?'

'They changed over time.'

'How did they start out?'

'I'll tell you if you're honest with me.'

The muscles in his cheek twitch. He's not keen on the concept of honesty.

'Honest with you about what?'

'About your time at the hotel. And about what you thought of me.'

'A truth game? You might wish you'd picked dare.'

'As I understand it, we're doing both.'

He considers this. 'I accept your terms. But you go first.'

'OK. You don't get to lie or cheat or squirm your way out of the deal, though. Or I'll rat on you to Lloyd, who clearly Knows Too Much.'

Chase humphs and shrugs. 'Do you want me to undress?' he says.

'No. Keep your suit on. It's kind of relevant. Cuff links and all. Are you sitting comfortably?'

'Almost.'

My eyes follow his down to the incipient erection straining against his suit trousers. 'Comfortably enough,' I amend. 'Then I'll begin. A long time ago in a galaxy pretty close to here, there lived a girl without a father. I hate to say it now, because I've always denied it to myself and to others, but that's why I wanted you. You're older than me, and you have an air of authority about you, and you were completely

219

untouchable and unwinnable. I must have thought that if I could get you, somehow, then I would have what I'd been missing in my life.'

'God, how depressing. I have no desire to be anyone's father.'

'No, just as well, because you'd be a shit one.'

'Thanks.' He smiles. 'Can we get to the fantasy now?'

'I fantasised about having your approval. Sounds so simple, doesn't it? Just a bit of positive attention. It wasn't as if that was lacking in my life – all those men, all the time. But they weren't special. Easy come, easy go, and I knew at bottom that they didn't approve of *me*, just the ready availability of my cunt. Our relationship was different.'

'Our relationship?'

'I know it was employer/employee, but there was respect and a rapport between us. Wasn't there?'

'I liked you. You were easy to work with, and eager to please.'

'I know.' I wince. So eager to please. It was pathetic. 'I think you knew that there wasn't much I wouldn't do, to impress you, to get a pat on the head and a few words of casual praise. My fantasy was about things going further than that. At first, it was about rewards.'

'So ... an outline?'

'Here's an example of something I used to masturbate to.'

He puts a hand down to his crotch, loosening his buttons, and settles in for the tale, laying his long arm along the headboard, behind me. 'Yes?'

'After I've performed some super feat of hospitality, you call me into your office. I stand there, in my reception gear, fitted jacket, tight skirt, blouse, stockings, heels, waiting for your words of praise.

'You sit behind your desk, fingers steepled, that stern look of yours on your face. I begin to be afraid you're going to tell me off instead. But no.

'"Come closer, Sophie," you say.

'I walk all the way up to the desk.

'"I've heard some good reports of you. Your service has been exceptional. I've decided that you deserve a little token of my appreciation. Take off your jacket."

'I don't know what to expect, but I take it off and put it on the desk.

'"You're a very good girl, aren't you?" you say. "Always doing as you're told. I want to see just how good you are. Take off your skirt."

'The fantasy was as much about hearing you say these things, your voice, as it was about the sex. I would hear it in my mind, telling me to do things, rude things. It turned me on without fail.

'So I take off the skirt, as demurely as I can, and put it on top of the jacket. You can see that I'm wearing suspenders with my stockings now, and you can see the little white lacy knickers peeping out from the hem of my silky blouse.

'"That's very good," you say. "The blouse now."

'I stand in front of you in my underwear and high heels, arms at my sides as if I'm on an army parade ground, head back, tits out. Not for the lads, though. For the man. For you.

'I know and you know that I will do anything you ask of me.

'You stand up and face me, turn me around with your hands on my shoulders, take it slowly, drinking me in. "This is your new uniform," you tell me. "This is what you'll wear whenever you're in my office."

'"Yes, sir."

'Other versions of this include me sitting on your lap taking dictation while you finger me, or you fucking me while you're taking a conference call, or me sucking you off under your desk while you're in a meeting. But I'll stick with this one for the time being.

'So there I stand, down to my underwear, and you have had a good look at me.

'"Good girl," you say and those words "Good girl" make me so happy, deliriously happy, so warm and so wanted and loved and cared for and appreciated ...'

I tail off and look at Chase. He looks troubled, but the erection hasn't gone anywhere. I turn my head away and continue. 'You pat me on the head, stroke my cheek, drop a little kiss on my brow. Then you sit back on your desk, perching on it, about a foot away from me.

'"Now the bra," you order.

'I don't know where this test will end, but I don't care either. I take off the bra without demur and hand it to you.

'"Touch your breasts." You make me cup them, squeeze them, stroke them, squash them together, then you make me pinch my nipples or circle them gently. You want them as stiff as can be, so I breathe on them and then poke out my tongue and lick them delicately until they are sore and throbbing. My crotch is damp now and my clit growing fat and wanton.

'As if you know this – and you probably do – you say, "Now the rest."

'I take off everything else, slowly, giving you plenty of time to appreciate the unveiling.

'When I am fully nude, you stand back up and move to the side of the desk.

"Now, lie on your back on this desk, Sophie."

'I place myself on the flat cold surface, shivering a little, but I'm feverish as well, ready for anything you want to give me.

'You make me spread my legs so my toes point to the corners of the desk and raise my arms above my head. For what seems like an age, you stand looking down at my open pussy lips. You bend your head to inspect them at closer range. I feel your breath on them, but you never touch them outright.

'"You'd like me to touch you here, wouldn't you?" you say.

'"Yes, sir."

'"Perhaps one day, if you're a very, very good girl, I will."

'I moan. You aren't going to touch me! I can hardly bear it. "Not today?"

'"No, not today, Sophie."

'You can see how wet I am and you comment on it, in detail, at length, then you speculate about how tight I would be, how hard I would grip your cock. You make sneery remarks about how many other men have had me, but I feel too wildly turned on to be hurt by it.

'You make me lift my hips so you can get a good look at my bum. You make me spread the cheeks and you home in close, checking my tight hole, asking me how often I've had anal sex and whether I enjoy it.

'I have to confess that I do, and you aren't surprised. You make me describe in detail all the things different men have done to my arse until I can barely get the words out any more because I'm so desperate for you to fuck me.

'But you don't have any pity and you make me tell you my favourite positions, my best sexual encounters, whether I like thick cocks or long ones, whether I like to be held down, whether I like it from behind, whether I've ever been

223

double-penetrated, what's my record for the number of men who've fucked me in one day.

'Question after question rains down on me in your unholy aphrodisiac of a voice until I'm squirming on the desk.

'Then you command me to touch myself, to make myself come, so you can see how I do it.

'I'm massively relieved, but at the same time disappointed, because I want your fingers all over me, so much, so very much. But I lick my fingertips and reach down, getting to it as quickly as I can, rubbing my clit, pushing the fingers of my other hand up inside my slick cunt.

'You keep up a running commentary all the time, telling me how wet I am, how fat my clit is, how much I need it, how you aren't surprised I need all those men because I have the hungriest cunt you've ever seen.

'When I come, you touch me, finally – putting your hands on my ankles to stop me kicking. I feel completely under your control and I say your name, over and over.

'You tell me I'm a good girl.'

Throughout this monologue I have deliberately avoided Chase's eye, going into a kind of trance to overcome the inherent difficulty of narrating a fantasy to its object.

I turn to him once I have finished speaking. He has one hand on his crotch and there is sweat on his upper lip.

'Strange, I suppose, that you never touched me in that one,' I say. 'But it was an early version.'

'I want to ask you those questions,' he says, in a low, intent rasp. 'I want you to answer them.'

'But it's your turn now. Your turn to tell me a story of what you would have liked to do to me, if you only you weren't so bloody self-controlled.'

He shuts his eyes and screws up his face for a moment,

regaining some of that aforementioned self-control, which seems to be on sabbatical tonight.

'I hired you because you brought men to the hotel. I knew what you were and, at first, I must admit, I feared for you. I thought you'd get into some dangerous predicament or other. Occasionally, I'd fantasise about rescuing you. Sometimes I'd fantasise about being the person who put you in the dangerous predicament. So you see, my feelings for you weren't straightforward. Sometimes I liked you for your fearless sexual adventuring, and sometimes I hated it. Sometimes I thought that somebody ought to stop you, and that somebody ought to be me. But it couldn't be me. I was in no position to offer you what you sought.'

'But you thought about it?'

'Often. You troubled me.'

'Troubled you?'

'Yes. I wanted to be impervious to your brazen charms, but I found I couldn't be. I considered it a personal failing. I try not to get emotionally involved with people.'

'Especially when you know you're going to rip them off and ruin their lives.'

'Especially then.'

'So, you had fantasies? What were they?'

'I'll give you an example. I catch you up to no good when you should be at work – though, to the best of my knowledge, you always kept your extracurricular activities out of working hours.'

'Yeah, uh, mostly,' I mumble, recalling a few incidents when that might not have been the case.

'You don't know I've seen you, so I call you into my office as soon as you've finished and tell you I want to do a spot check. You don't know what I mean, but once I've ordered you to pull down your knickers and bend over, you start to get the picture.

'Sure enough, the smell of recent sex is on you and your cunt is looking well used, as I mention to you.

'You beg me not to sack you, I think you even burst into tears, although you're not the tearful type, I know.

'I say I'll let you keep your job, but there's a condition.'

'Oh, I'll bet there is.' I try to sound scornful, but this scenario is making me giddy and my breath flutters in my lungs.

'The condition is that you stop having anything to do with other men and surrender yourself to me.'

'Surrender myself?'

'Completely. Place yourself under my absolute control. Oh, the plans I had for you – in this fantasy, I mean, not in real life.'

'What plans?'

'I think one particularly sleepless night I drew up a daily timetable. Blow jobs with the coffee, having you chained under the desk, that kind of thing. Tying you up, having you every which way, exhausting you, making you beg for mercy.'

'Hmm. I'm not a beggar, I'm a chooser.'

'I know you are. That's what maddens me about you. You seem to genuinely enjoy your promiscuity.'

'And women aren't supposed to, are they? They're supposed to sleep around because they're so terribly lonely, or so awfully damaged or whatever. It upset your little apple cart, didn't it? You wanted to either save me from it, or punish me for it.'

'Yes,' he admits. 'I did. But I knew I couldn't. It was frustrating.'

'I imagine so.' But I'm beginning to see that I had a

lucky escape, and this gives me so much strength that I feel surrounded with the glow of it. 'So, tonight,' I say, putting a hand on his thigh, 'you can live out your fantasy.'

'Some of them went a little further than you'd like, I should think,' he warns me.

'How far?'

'I don't want to say.'

'Chase, I know the difference between fantasy and reality. Just because you get off to the thought of something doesn't mean you'll do it.'

'The fantasies were sometimes violent. I suppose because my attraction to you was so unwanted and so problematic. I would, well, slap you around a bit. I was cruel.'

'You *are* cruel,' I point out. 'We all figured that out ages ago.'

'So, living out my fantasies then? Where do we stand on that now?'

'I'm not sure.' I think about the purpose of all this, the nature of the test. 'I think the idea is that I live out *my* fantasies. So, no slapping. And I don't trust you enough to give you control anyway. I don't trust you at all, in fact.'

'It's understandable.'

'And I still want to hurt you.'

'I'd rather you didn't.'

'You don't get to choose. OK. Stay there. I'm going to get this out of my system, and I think it'll only take a moment.'

I straddle his knees, facing him. He looks furious and confused, on the verge of pushing me away, but whatever hold Lloyd has over him is pretty strong, it seems.

'Take off your glasses.'

'You're going to hit me, aren't you?'

'I'm not a violent person. No fists, nothing like that.'

He removes the spectacles.

My open palm catches him square on the cheek. The slap reverberates around the room, sounding much harder than it actually was. A patch of red rises satisfyingly on his skin and I bunch my fists and hug myself, instantly ashamed.

'Well done,' he says dryly. 'I hope that did the trick.'

'Not really. This is what we're going to do.'

I hop off the bed and take myself to lean against a large, highly polished desk, big enough to hold a conference around.

'Here I am, Chase, naked and available. We're in your office and this is your desk. Come and do what you would have done, if it had ever been possible. Not what you did in your fantasies – what you actually would have done, in real life. I need to know.'

He spends some time just watching me from the bed, as if weighing up options. I lean back, flex my legs, perform a number of standard come-hither moves, but he responds to none of them.

Perhaps I should leave now. I don't even care about failure any more.

But then he is on his feet in a flash, bending me backwards over the table, more by the force of his presence than anything corporeal and I am looking up into eyes that gleam with determination.

'Have you any idea how long I've waited for this?'

I shake my head, holding my breath until it hurts.

He puts a hand on my cheek, cupping it, pressing his thumb into the soft skin beneath my chin. One finger strokes me beneath my ear lobe. It is almost too sensual to bear and the phrase 'I am undone' flits through my mind. If I had a bodice on, I think he would be about to rip it.

His lips hover about mine, as if undecided whether to kiss

me or bite me. Eventually, they find a third way, opening to emit speech.

'Years,' he whispers. 'So many years of having you within my reach, and never being able to touch you. Knowing that you wanted me to, knowing that I couldn't. Can you imagine what that does to a man?'

'Roughly the same as it does to a woman, maybe. I should know.'

The cloth of his jacket nudges my breasts, tormenting my nipples with little blasts of sensation. His crotch, hard and protuberant, fits snugly into the yielding delta between my thighs.

This is how it could have been.

His lips have done with talking. They fit themselves to mine, over mine, holding my mouth briefly shut before descending into frenzy. We devour each other, teeth, tongues, arms, hands, legs. He jolts me against the table until my back aches and then he lifts me on to it so I sit with my legs locked around his hips, pushing my hand down to his imprisoned cock, giving it a hard squeeze.

He kisses exactly the way I thought he would, passionate and yet controlled, with not a hint of vulnerability or uncertainty. He knows what he wants and he gets it. Everything I saw in him, everything that turned me on about him, is distilled into this huge Eve's apple of a kiss. Here he is, the tree of knowledge in human form, and I am no better than those poor saps in the Bible.

Does that make Lloyd the serpent?

The thought of Lloyd throws me off my stride. A wave of discomfort at the idea of him seeing this washes over me like cold water.

I make a weak attempt to pull away from Chase, but

he won't have it, putting a hand on my ribs and laying me flat on the table while he suffocates me with the intensity of his kiss.

You wanted this, Lloyd. I'm doing it. I hope it makes you happy.

He starts to bite and I try to protest, but without knowing why or how, I find myself enjoying it, the way I used to enjoy play fights with my cousins as a child. Adrenalin pumps and I find new reserves of spirit and strength, using them to bite back, to growl, to push and kick.

His force is superior, of course, and his hands are every-where, all over me, all at once, and they are none too gentle either.

When he breaks the kiss, I shout, 'I hate you, you fucker!' and he laughs loudly and sinks his teeth into my neck.

I use my pelvis as a weapon, jerking it upwards, trying to grind him to pieces, but he enjoys this, and enjoys subduing me and pinning me down even more.

By the time his hand reaches my pussy, ready to take it as his right, I am helpless.

'Tell me you want it,' he growls, his fingertips primed and poised. 'Go on. Tell me or I'll stop right here.'

I can barely breathe, the blood rushing in my ears.

'Do it.'

He gives my clit the lightest of feathery strokes then he stands up, releasing me from my pinions. Even now, I can't really move, the struggle having sapped all power from me.

I gaze up at him, little blue spots dancing in my peripheral vision, taking in his well-cut suit and his elegant neck, his perfect hairstyle and the look of naked ferocity in his eyes. The devil went down to Savile Row.

He takes off his jacket, with its lining of grey-green silk, and casts it away from him, on to the bed. I used to admire that fluidity of movement, that prowling grace of his.

My mouth feels bruised and my bones ache.

I am wetter than he deserves.

I watch his fingers move lazily over the knot of his tie, freeing his neck from its tyranny. The length of silk slides under his collar and out; he winds it around his hand as if contemplating using it for bondage purposes and I catch a breath.

No. He can't tie me up. I don't trust him.

He looks from me to it, regret shadowing his face, then lets it fall to the ground.

Next his top button is undone, then the one beneath.

I wait for him to remove the whole shirt, but he doesn't.

Instead, he pulls me up and spins me around and bends me over the desk the other way. I yelp at the sensation of the cold wood on my nipples, and yelp again when he takes my wrists and twists them behind my back. I kick out at him, finding his shins, but if he feels it, he doesn't let it show.

'Like this,' he says, pushing his still trousered thighs into mine. 'This is how I'd have done it.' With his free hand he smacks the inside of my legs until I have them open wide enough to please him. 'With so many competitors for your attention, I'd need to make sure I made an impression on you.'

'If you hurt me I'll kill you.'

'I'm not going to hurt you, Sophie. I'm going to make you want me, even though I can't have you. I'm going to make you see what you missed.'

'I didn't miss anything. You were never available.'

'Don't fight it. Give in to me. Let yourself go.'

His free hand starts to massage my pussy lips. I twitch and squirm, but he's too good. My muscles relax and my body yields to him. Just this once, he can have me. Just this once, these juices are for him.

'Oh, you do want it, don't you? Are you this wet for all your men?'

I don't reply. I don't want him to know anything about me.

'No wonder they always came back for more,' he continues, brushing my clit, left to right, right to left. 'You're soaked, absolutely saturated in sex, aren't you? I used to think of advertising your services, changing the name of the hotel bar to The Sure Thing. But we didn't need advertising. Everyone knew where to go to get a good, hot fuck when they were in town. Your number's in half the little black books of the business world.'

His pace increases; his pressure grows.

'I wondered what it would take to impress you, Sophie. I wondered what a man had to do to make you want more of him. You took all the sex you wanted, but you never needed anybody, and that bothered me. Then Lloyd seemed to capture your attention and I was so angry. So jealous. What did he have, that jumped-up cocktail waiter, that I didn't? I had to get rid of you all anyway. I was glad to get rid of you all. But I felt I'd missed my chance with you. If only I'd done *this*. Perhaps I'd have you chained to my bed on my Pacific isle right now.'

My breathing is fast and shallow. He lets go of my wrists, but I don't want to move them. He uses his other hand to stroke my bum cheeks, pinching and squeezing.

'You're close, aren't you?'

I nod.

'How close?'

'Very.'

'So close. So very, very close.'

I'm there, I'm there, I'm … not.

He takes his hand away and smacks my bottom, very lightly, but it's like a vicious swipe in my maddeningly over-sensitised state.

'You want me.' It's a statement, not a question. He wants my confession.

'Yes. Just do it. Get it over with.'

'Romantic as ever, Sophie.'

'Just sort yourself out and do it.'

'Ah.' I think he'd been hoping I wouldn't mention the need for condoms, but I certainly don't want this night to be unforgettable for the wrong reasons.

The noises he makes in unwrapping and snapping on the rubber are violent and impatient.

'You need protection, Sophie?' he says grumpily from behind me. 'You aren't so self-sufficient as you like to think.'

'We're all at the mercy of biology,' I point out, equally bad-tempered.

This is going to be one tetchy fuck.

'Some more than others,' says Chase from between gritted teeth, and then he is in me, quick as a blade, if a lot blunter.

Oh. He feels good.

I didn't want him to feel this good.

He reaches around for the fronts of my thighs, giving himself optimum leverage, and begins to thrust. There is no ceremony or finesse, and that makes it easier.

Every time his cock lodges its full length, I imagine a little portion of my infatuation with him getting knocked out of me.

One for the lonely nights.

One for the dreamy days.

One for the fruitless flirtation.

One for the imagined tenderness.

One for the betrayal, the anger, the confusion.

'I'm going to make you come,' he rasps, pounding away.

'No, you aren't.'

Good as he feels, thrillingly rough as he fucks, he isn't going to make me come. I just don't want him to.

He doesn't like my answer, but he thinks it's just playful goading and puts his fingers on my clit. I suppose he thinks that's how I come.

It can be.

Sometimes the stimulation of fingers on my nerve endings, sometimes the pressure of a warm, wet tongue. Sometimes the friction of a cock, or a dildo, rubbing against my G-spot does the trick. But none of it ever happens unless I've given myself to the transaction, and that's what Chase doesn't understand. He can finger and lick and fuck and suck as much as he likes, but I won't ever be properly there. Not for him.

I figure he's a man with a pretty overwhelming sense of pride, though, and he isn't going to finish this unless he thinks he's driven me to the starry-eyed orgasm of my life. So I fake it.

There's a first time for everything, after all. Well, maybe a second.

'Oh yes,' I hear him croon behind me. 'Oh yes, Sophie, that's it, you're taking it well, you've taken it so well.'

And then he drills me right into the table, so I swear at the sudden impact against my pelvis and I assume, from the trembling of his loins and the painful grip of his hands, that he isn't faking anything at all.

'Oh.'

His head falls on my shoulder. His face is hot and his mouth nuzzles my bitten skin.

'Sophie,' he whispers, clasping his arms around my breasts.

I try to wriggle forwards, to get his cock out of me. I don't do pillow talk.

'There we go then,' I say, trying not to yawn or sound at all tired. 'Fantasy fulfilled. What time's your flight tomorrow?'

He sighs, sounding pained. 'Never mind that. Come to bed.'

'Oh, I don't think I want to do that.'

He puts his lips to my ear. 'Shower first?'

'No, I mean, I should go.'

With a herculean effort, he detaches himself from me and rises to his feet, looking less impressive than usual with his trousers around his ankles and his shirt flapping around his haunches.

'Go?' he says, as if the word is in some ancient mystical tongue. 'You want to go?'

'Yeah. I do. Grab us that jacket and I'll call a cab. Actually, could I borrow your shirt?'

'Aren't you tired? Don't you want to stay?'

'Not really. We've done what we came for, haven't we?'

He looks genuinely devastated. I can't tell him I faked my orgasm. It would just be too cruel. I know it's no crueller than he was to me, but I don't ever want to think of myself as being on the same level as him.

'Didn't you ... wouldn't you like to ... do it again? In bed? In comfort?'

I give up waiting for him to lend the shirt and grab one from the wardrobe. Beautifully pressed and smelling of something leathery. I put it on, enjoying its smooth, cool feel against my bare skin.

'I don't think that's a good idea,' I tell him.

'You'd find it harder to leave?'

I look away and smile, mainly to myself. 'Yeah, yeah,

that's it, Chase. I'd find it harder to leave.'

God knows, he doesn't really deserve the sugar-coating, but perhaps I'm kinder than I realise.

I put on my jacket and shoes, check my pocket for my mobile phone.

'I understand,' he says, looking as if he doesn't.

'Good.' I tiptoe up to kiss him on the cheek.

He catches me in a tight hold for a moment. 'It was, wasn't it? Good, I mean.'

'Of course it was. Everything I dreamed it would be. But we don't live in a dream, Chase. Time to wake up and get on with the day.'

'You really are every bit as independent as you seem, aren't you?'

'Perhaps a little too much so,' I whisper.

He releases me. 'I wish you'd stay,' he says.

'Sorry. Thanks for this, anyway. Laid a ghost to rest. Cheers.'

I can't believe my last word to him is *cheers*, but I can't think of any others, so I wave awkwardly and dive for the door.

The vision of him, half-naked and oddly vulnerable, his hand reaching out uncertainly, imprints itself on my memory.

Why would I feel sorry for him? For such a long time, all he had to do was ask. It's his own stupid fault.

Anyway, pity is one thing. Love is another.

I lean against Chase's suite door and speed dial Lloyd.

His phone is switched off.

Chapter Eleven

Huffing, I stomp towards the lifts, resolving to call a cab from the lobby.

Will Lloyd be at home? What if he's still in the gambling den? With his phone switched off, that seems the likeliest possibility. I have no desire to re-enter that atmosphere of suppressed evil and dissipation. But I feel I have to see Lloyd, now, more urgently than I have ever needed to.

I have no idea, looking at my strangely-not-me reflection in the mirrored lift, what I'll do when I find him. Part of me wants to slap him for putting me in that position with Chase. Part of me wants to hold on to him for grim death.

I examine the dishevelled girl in the long shirt and tux jacket more closely. Those bite marks will take time to fade. All my lipstick is kissed off and my mascara has smudged below my left eye. I look like a really, really low-rent Sally Bowles.

I'm halfway through singing a drunk-sounding version of 'Mein Herr' when the lift door opens.

I strut across the marble singing 'You're better off without me, Mein Herr' until the night receptionist looks up at me and says, 'Sophie Martin?'

'That's me.'

She nods over towards the cocktail bar, which must surely be closed at this hour. I turn away from the desk and teeter towards the smoked glass dividing the darkened bar from the low-lit lobby. Damn these heels.

I peer around the doorway, into the gloom. In the corner, I can just make out the silhouette of a man. He has a drink on the table in front of him, a tumbler, and he's staring down at it, his shoulders low.

'Lloyd.'

He looks up and leaps to his feet. 'You ... you're here.'

'Why the fuck did you turn your phone off?'

'I didn't! I ...' He grabs it from his jacket pocket and stares at the screen. 'Oh. Sorry. Battery's flat.'

'Just as well Chase didn't try to kill me then, eh? Jesus, Lloyd! What were you thinking?'

'I really thought it was charged up.'

By now we are facing each other, inches away, in the centre of the deserted bar.

There's a weird quality to the air between us; it seems thick and swirly, like a fog. His eyes are brimming with something – not tears. Something else.

'I would never have put you in danger. Did he do anything to you? Are you OK?'

'I'm OK. Can we go?'

'Sure, I'll call a cab. Or rather, you can.'

'No, it's not that far. I want to walk.'

'You came down,' he said, wonderingly, as we leave the bar, still not touching. 'I thought I'd be there until morning.'

'Did you?'

'You're pissed off with me, aren't you?'

We nod our goodnights to the receptionist and pass out

of the sterile lobby and into the city, its night beat pulsating faintly under the never-quite-darkness. Sirens, street lamps, dreams, nightmares tangle together with the stars.

'Pissed off?' I stop at the foot of the steps.

'You think I went too far,' he says.

'You risked everything. You risked me.'

'But do you understand why?'

'Yeah. Yeah, I do.'

'So?'

'So. I think I'm going to take these shoes off.'

I slip my feet out of the tyrannous towers of heel and carry them instead, swinging the slingbacks from my finger. I set off along the pavement, which is cold but less dirty than those in the cheaper parts of town, at least. I wouldn't be walking barefoot outside that peep show, that's for sure.

We cross the road and walk along the perimeter of the park. Some paving slabs are canvases for chalk masterpieces, living to delight another day as long as it doesn't rain. I spot a near-perfect rendition of Toulouse-Lautrec's *The Kiss*, glowing red under the lamplight.

'It seems such a shame it has to fade,' I say, stopping to gaze down at it.

At last he touches me, the palm of his hand on my elbow. 'Sophie,' he says. It sounds urgent. 'Please talk to me.'

'I am talking to you.'

'No, come on.'

'Let's go into the park.'

'It's closed.'

'I know a way in. There's a broken railing. Come on.'

I lead him about a quarter of a mile up the street, then duck in through a warped rail, dragging myself through the hedge to the other side.

I start to run, ecstatically barefoot, through the wet grass, past the twisted dark shapes of the trees, towards the lake. I feel as if I might start to lift off the ground, bumping along and then rising into the air like a kite. I've never been more free.

At the lake's edge, I turn and watch Lloyd catch up with me.

He bends slightly, puts his hands on his thighs, waiting for his breath to settle.

'Sophie, please tell me you're OK.'

'I'm OK. Really, more than OK. Much more than OK.' I laugh and twirl around, dipping my toe into the silted waters.

'You sound a bit manic.'

'I'm not manic. I'm free. Something's shifted up here.' I tap my head. 'It's like I know what I'm doing.'

'I wish I did.'

'Everything that stood in my way, everything that scared me – it was all in my head. All those fears I had about you losing interest in me, leaving me, wanting to pin me down or imprison me, well, they've gone.'

His brow lifts and a brightness returns to him. 'Really?'

'Yeah. And the biggest thing is, even if you do leave me or lose interest in me, or whatever, I can't let fear stop me taking that risk. The risk is worth taking.'

His lip quirks up. He still looks disbelieving. 'So you're saying …?'

'I'm saying that I want to be with you. In our own way, the way we've been. With all the fun and … and more than that too.'

'More?'

I take his hands and laugh up into his face. 'I love you, you knob.'

'Well, I love you too, you bitch.'

I pretend to slap him and it turns into a kiss, the two of us clinging to each other, pressing into each other. The bite marks and the bruises are forgotten, his kiss the best analgesic ever. Somewhere in the fog of passion and tongues, our balance goes missing, we stagger drunkenly on the kerbstones and then topple sideways into the shallows of the lake with a huge splash and a scream.

An alarum of quacks and flapping wings surrounds us as we laugh like idiots, unable to get up for falling back down, trying to help each other up with no success at all, until we temporarily give up and huddle together against the chill water, teeth chattering, fingers slimy with pondweed.

From a distance I notice a gang of swans approaching at speed. 'We have to get out,' I say to Lloyd with a shiver. 'Those fuckers are vicious.'

He grabs my arm and manages to haul me to my feet and back onto land.

It's the very darkest part of the night and, though it's summer, I am aware of the need to get out of these wet clothes before we succumb to hypothermia.

'Let's go.'

I start the run across the grass but he is soon sprinting faster than me, pulling me along so I stumble and whoop with laughter all the way until we get to the hedgerow. It takes a while to locate the broken railing again and, when we do, we are so cold and wet and pleased to see it that we squeeze through without regard for what might be waiting for us in the street beyond.

A police officer is patrolling the pavement and we straighten up, two dripping apparitions, directly in front of her. She halts abruptly and stares, her hand on her extendable baton handle, then she relaxes when she sees we are just night-time revellers, probably a bit happy-drunk but no kind of threat.

'Evening, officer,' says Lloyd smoothly, 'nice night for it.'

She stares for a moment. 'You know that the park isn't open at night, don't you? It's trespass.'

'Is it?' we both say, looking at each other in mock surprise.

'You know it is. But you look like you have an urgent appointment with a shower, so I'm going to pretend I've seen two very bedraggled ghosts tonight and tell you to take care on the way home, OK? Goodnight.'

She walks on and we chorus thanks before running hand in hand across the road and back to the Luxe Noir.

We pause on the bottom step and look up at our dominions; floor after floor of guests paying us for the pleasure of our hospitality. It is our kingdom and we are its monarchs, working in harmony now, day and night.

'This place,' I whisper. 'It's ours.'

'Yes,' says Lloyd, his arm around my shoulder. 'For as long as we want it.'

We kiss again, a kiss like a baptism, a kiss like the start of a life, expressing infinite forgiveness and infinite hope.

'Let's go round the back,' suggests Lloyd. 'Don't want the night staff to see us like this.'

* * *

It's the best shower of my life, watching the grey-green muck disappear down the plughole along with the last traces of Chase. It's all the better for sharing it with Lloyd, who lathers up my hair, soaps my skin and makes extra-specially sure my most intimate parts are thoroughly cleansed.

'You did it, then?' he asks, once we are warm and clean

'S'OK.'

He unties my sash and opens the robe wide, kisses my nipples then installs himself between my thighs, spreading them for a closer inspection of the scene. 'Oh yes, you've been busy tonight,' he diagnoses.

'I think I knew that.'

He grins at me. 'This little pussy likes to stray, but she always comes back.'

'Maybe you have the best cream.'

'There's a thought.'

He crouches down, putting his hands underneath my thighs, holding them steady while his face moves in closer. The first stroke of his tongue is almost dangerously good, and I let out a little 'oh' of bliss.

The need that had been deadened by our sojourn in the lake was reawakened in the warmth of the shower, and my clit is pulsing with it, almost jumping forwards to offer itself for licking.

He obliges with deadly exactitude, a master of his art, knowing exactly how and where and how hard to use his tongue. At first he is all hot breath and artful teasing, then he deepens his technique and his strokes, covering my cunt in the dewy evidence of his possession. My pussy becomes his instrument and he plays it like a virtuoso. He leaves my sore spots alone, but he pulls apart my bottom cheeks all the better to consume and overwhelm me, his whole face working at me until, much quicker than I intend, I come hard, tossing my head from side to side on the pillow, wailing as if I mourn the loss of control. For a moment it always seems that way, as if I should be ashamed to feel such pleasure, ashamed to let it happen, then the rapturous flood of sensation mixes in with the shame and makes everything golden.

He gives me a long, firm lick for luck, then kisses the tops of my thighs all over before lying back down beside me.

'All better?' he whispers, stroking my hair.

'The best,' I sigh, my eyelids heavy, my body sinking into the mattress. 'The very best.'

When I wake up, he is still sleeping.

I've woken up in this bed many times, but never feeling like this, like something is different, something has changed.

I like to watch him sleep, like to see his pale eyelashes flicker and his face so flushed and far away, but this morning I am like some kind of adoring sap, wanting to gaze upon his unearthly beauty or something. And yet there is nothing unearthly about it. He has luscious full lips and some cute freckles and the beginnings of laughter lines at the corners of his eyes. He's a reasonably good-looking bloke but Adonis doesn't have to worry about the competition. Why am I so bowled over by the sight of him?

My body aches, reminding me of the night's excesses.

I have given my heart.

I lie back down, pulse racing. I've done it. I've taken the step I never thought I would. I told Lloyd that I love him. Now he knows exactly the extent of the power he has over me. But then again, I know exactly the extent of the power I have over him too. As long as neither of us turns evil, it could be fine. It could be good. Whatever the world wants to throw at us, we'll have each other. At least, that's the theory.

Nothing left to do but test it.

I reach down under the covers and peel them back, oh so gently, over Lloyd's naked body. Sleepy warm skin, just enough muscle definition without it being too much, the gentle rise and fall of his chest. And – yes – the semi-engorgement of his cock.

Very lightly, I place my fingertips beneath his scrotum, assessing its heaviness and tension. Pretty heavy, pretty tense. What is my darling Lloyd dreaming of? Something rude, no doubt.

He stirs a little, grunting sweetly. I move my hand to the hardening shaft, making light sweeping motions up the length of it, barely touching it, enjoying the way it fills out and grows under my touch.

I feel he has earned his favourite kind of alarm call.

I bend and lick it from root to tip, tracing a circle around the head when I reach it, then I seal my lips around it.

He jolts as if electrified and starts to wake up with a great deal of spluttering and chaotic breathing.

I keep my eyes on my work, taking the first few sucks, waiting for him to come to consciousness.

I sense him sitting up slightly to look down at me.

'Oh babe,' he says, then his head falls back on the pillow with a resounding flump.

I make noises of murmuring delight around his helpless cock and start to milk it for all it's worth, taking hold of the sac below and massaging it as I work.

Lloyd wants to say things but he can't. It's delicious to hear him shudder and struggle with speech, then give up.

He's fully erect, velvety steel in my mouth, and I stretch my jaw to accommodate him, work at loosening my throat to take him all the way in. But I don't have to work for long because the salty liquid bursts into my mouth before I'm ready, and I swallow it quickly, licking up all the traces from his cock before releasing it.

'Mm, what did I do to deserve that?' he asks with a yawn, after we've kissed our tastes into each other's mouths.

'Everything.'

'Does that mean I get woken up this way every morning?'

'Don't push your luck, Ellison.'

'Why change the habit of a lifetime?'

My laugh turns to a sneeze, then another. In my advanced state of mooniness, I haven't noticed that I've been burning up and shivering all over since I awoke. It takes Lloyd's hand on my forehead to realise it.

'Fuck's sake, Sophie, you need to break this habit of falling in lakes. Wait there, I'll get the thermometer.'

'I'm fine.'

'Shut up or I'll make it the rectal thermometer.'

'Promises,' I say with a cough.

He returns from the bathroom and sticks his digital thermometer under my tongue. 'Yep,' he says, examining the reading. 'You're staying right there today.'

'You don't get flu from falling into lakes,' I tell him. 'That's a myth. I bet one of your dodgy gambling mates was infectious.'

'Yeah, and you've been spreading your germs on my cock. I'm going to get cock flu now.'

I giggle deliriously. 'You're an idiot. Is that anything like bird flu?'

'I'm not sure I want to find out. OK: honey and lemon, paracetamol and a cold flannel. I think that's what it said in the Boy Scout handbook.'

'You were never a Boy Scout.'

'Ah, but I was.'

I lie juddering and aching while he sorts me out with various palliatives.

'Chase wouldn't do this for you,' he mentions.

True enough. Chase had hated it when anybody was ill, appearing to see it as a personal failing.

'Chase is a twat.'

'I thought that was me? I'm the twat around here. I don't want anyone stealing my twat thunder.'

'You aren't, though, not really. Only in a nice way. You're ace.'

'So are you.'

He kisses my forehead and I drift into fever, knowing that I am loved.

Lightning Source UK Ltd.
Milton Keynes UK
UKHW040712240920
370450UK00001B/80